The Most Beautiful Thing
Fiona Robyn

Also by Fiona Robyn

Non-fiction

A Year of Questions   2007
Small Stones: A Year of Moments   2008
A River of Stones (Ed. with Kaspalita)   2011

Fiction

The Letters   2008
Thaw   2009
The Blue Handbag   2009

The Most Beautiful Thing

Fiona Robyn

Woodsmoke Press

The Most Beautiful Thing
ISBN 978-0-9571584-0-5

Published by Woodsmoke Press 2012
Copyright © 2012 Fiona Robyn

Woodsmoke Press
111 Belmont Road
Malvern
WR14 1PN

kaspa@woodsmokepress.com
www.woodsmokepress.com

Dedicated to Kaspalita – I am protected by his light.

"This is how we begin – in the morning with small birds near and echoing train yards in the distance – afraid. Exactly like one another."

~ Terrance Keenan

"I have often felt, and I still feel, like a ship with a precious cargo; the moorings have been slipped and now the ship is free to take its load to any place on earth. We must be our own country."

~ Etty Hillesum

As the plane shuddered down the runway and then pushed, screaming, into the air, Joe Salt felt his eardrums burst. Or, at least, this was what he imagined had happened. Nobody had warned him about popping ears. He pressed his palms protectively against the sides of his head, knowing it was too late – the damage was already done. He hooked the tip of his forefinger into the whorl of his right ear and then inspected the tip of it – no blood. Only the ridges of his fingerprints. He studied the swirling concentric lines and thought of isobars on a weather chart. Cold fronts, warm fronts, occluded fronts... troposphere, stratosphere, mesosphere, thermosphere...

Joe craned his neck to circumnavigate the bulk of the middle-aged woman sitting between him and the window. She smiled at him; a quick, forced smile. Hopeful. He ignored her, as he'd ignored the first few smiles she'd aimed at him whilst he was being shown to his seat by the air hostess, who'd lifted his bag into the overhead luggage compartment for him as if he was seven years old and not fourteen. Instead he watched the ground drop away. He could see a reservoir – a neat oblong stippled with waves, glinting in the sun. The trees became bits of sponge like in a model railway, and the roads were pieces of thin rope, thrown down to criss-cross the patchwork of fields. Across it all floated great swathes of cloud-shadows.

And here were the clouds themselves. The windows filled with them as they continued to rise, and the plane shifted and bucked like a sulky horse. All at once they were above them.

1

The tops of the clouds were all at the same height, a layer of whipped cream floating on hot chocolate, or island suds of bubble bath. *Cumulus*, thought Joe. Behind the humming of conversation in the plane there was a roaring sound – it reminded Joe of his mum's hairdryer. The air was cold and dry, as if all the goodness had been extracted from it. The pilot came onto the intercom and started saying something in Dutch. The language was rapid, tangled and guttural. When he repeated it in English he pronounced 'congestion' with a hard 'g', and Joe sniggered.

So here he was – being hurled through the troposphere at twenty three thousand feet for the first time in his life.

He was still gazing at the clouds and thinking about the air hostess's breasts, small and solid underneath her uniform, when something snagged his attention. It was the smiling woman – she was looking at him and her mouth was moving. Joe's mum was always infuriated when he missed what she'd said – she was convinced he was ignoring her on purpose. He'd given up trying to explain to her that his ears just didn't work properly when he was thinking hard about something else. His dad seemed to understand. He spent entire days in his study with the door shut, the outside world rushing on without him.

When the smiling woman spoke again her voice was louder, and she enunciated her words as if Joe was an idiot.

"Um, hello, excuse me?"

Joe turned to the woman and focussed on the patch of skin at the top of her nose while he waited for her to continue. This was a trick he'd taught himself at school, after the fiftieth time Mr. Jamieson had shouted, "Look at me when I'm speaking to you, Salt!" He didn't think he'd get away with it, but people didn't notice the lack of genuine eye contact. The smiling woman didn't speak for a few seconds and Joe wondered if he ought to say something. What was the convention for making conversation in these situations? He wished someone would just tell him the rules. He raised his eyebrows and that seemed to do the trick.

"I just wondered if you wanted to swap seats with me, love. You could see better out the window then."

He nodded his assent.

She was still smiling at him. Joe had a sudden urge to be anywhere but here. He felt furious at his dad for sending him away. The woman started fiddling with her earlobe, pulling at it as if she were milking a cow.

"Are you travelling alone?"

He nodded.

"Oh, you lucky thing. Done this before, have you?"

Joe shook his head and looked down at his fingertip again. If he concentrated hard on the tiny ridges maybe she'd see he was busy and shut up.

"And who are you going to see in Holland?"

"My Aunt Nel. She lives in Amsterdam."

His voice was husky, and he cleared his throat. He realised that he hadn't spoken to anyone yet that day. He'd said goodbye to his dad wordlessly – most of their communication was silent. His mum was still asleep, and Dad said it was best they didn't disturb her. She'd been sleeping more and more recently. His dad had checked him in at the airport, and he'd negotiated the Departure Lounge with nods and gestures.

"Ah, you can speak. Well, you are a brave thing to be doing this on your own. If there's anything I can help you with, you just ask me, okay? Shall we then?"

She released her seatbelt and hovered over her chair, motioning for him to slide underneath her to the window seat. It was a tight squeeze, but he mostly managed it without touching her. When she settled down she gave him one last smile before, mercifully, pulling a magazine from her handbag. He looked at the sky. When he swallowed, something happened to his ears. He turned back to the smiling woman. His mum was always telling him he should talk to people more.

"I think my eardrums burst, but they seem to be all right again now."

The woman lowered her magazine and looked at him curiously.

"Do you mean they popped?"

"What does that mean?"

"They feel a bit funny and everything sounds muffled for a while. It's to do with the air pressure or something."

Now he was interested. Maybe this woman was a potential holder of useful information.

"Could you tell me how that works?"

"Oh, I haven't got a clue, love. Have you got something to do for the trip? I think I've got a piece of paper in here somewhere if you wanted to do some drawing..." She rummaged in her bag.

"No thank you, I'm fine." He didn't manage to sound quite so polite this time.

"Okay, love."

She looked down at her magazine again, and Joe turned away. His Walkman (with a new Cocteau Twins tape) was in the overhead storage. How annoying – that would have protected him from having to speak to her again. He'd just have to avoid her gaze for the rest of the flight. He slid the metal tongue of his seat belt into the buckle with a satisfying click and settled back. A child was whining, and someone in the seat behind Joe sneezed – a throaty, wet noise like pigs truffling in mud. Here he was – up in the sky, where the weather happened.

Joe's thoughts drifted to his fourteenth birthday, the day before yesterday. A strange kind of birthday. It was the last day of term before the summer holidays. He'd got a few presents over breakfast, but they all stank of bought-by-Dad. He was so hopeless at choosing. His new Cocteau Twins tape didn't count – he'd asked for that. What was he meant to do with a childish book about snakes, and a pack of 'magic' playing cards? As he unwrapped the cards he'd noticed his dad's eyes on them. Joe suspected they'd be spirited off to his office at some point. His black hole of an office – once something went in there, it never came out. Joe wondered how his dad ever pulled himself free of the gravitational pull.

When his mum was in charge of presents, she'd at least ask him what he wanted, in a way she thought was sneaky. ('What kind of music are young boys listening to these days?' or 'I'm not sure how much fun those roller skates would be, Joe, what do you think of them?') He could usually rely on his Aunt Nel to send him something cool, but she'd be giving him his presents in person this year.

Their teacher, Mr. Jamieson, usually announced their birthdays – he must have kept a list somewhere – but his mind must have been on his own holidays as no mention was made of it all day. His friend Podge (known as Oliver to his mother, Pocock to the teachers, and Ollie when Joe wanted to butter him up) had slapped him on the back and said, "Happy birthday, mate," and that was the most attention he'd got all day.

5

Not that he cared about his bloody birthday anyway. Birthdays were for little children, for mummy's boys. But it might have been nice if his mum had made him his usual cake. A yellow sponge with glacé cherries. No icing, just candles poked in through the crunchy surface – the crusts of cakes are always the nicest bits, sweeter than the insides. She'd made him the same cake ever since he was... well, ever since he could remember. When he'd said at dinner, "Where's my cake?" his mum had got up and left the room. His dad had given him a stern look. How was he to know she'd get upset over a stupid cake? He was the one who should have been upset. He knew something was going on. Nobody told him anything.

It had been a pretty rubbish birthday, and then Saturday had been pretty rubbish too. His parents had gone out somewhere all day, his last day before he flew out to Amsterdam for the whole summer. He sat in on his own, sulking.

When he thought about it, the whole year had been pretty rubbish. He'd had that throat infection for weeks on end. He'd taken an instant dislike to Mr. Jamieson at the start of the year, and the feeling had proved mutual. Then there was his mum's weird behaviour. And to top it all off, his best friend Podge (it would be more accurate to say his only friend) had been a complete pain.

Podge had always got on Joe's nerves, but recently it was like he'd spent ages practising how to drive Joe completely mad. Podge never had an opinion of his own, and always asked Joe what he'd like to do. If they ended up doing something that bored Podge, he didn't say anything, he just started fidgeting with his shoelaces or staring off into space. During the past month Joe had lost his temper with him three times. Podge couldn't even have an argument properly – instead of shouting back he'd turn bright red (especially his ears) and run back to his own house. The next morning they'd act as if nothing had happened, but Joe hated Podge for not fighting back.

Podge had been the one person in the Universe who Joe could talk to properly. He told him everything. It had been getting to the point where he couldn't be in the same room as Podge without wanting to put his hands around his neck and squeezing hard. Who would he talk to now? Even Joe's rabbit, Albedo, had died in May. Albedo was a fine rabbit. Joe loved the way the rabbit would sit on his lap and lick his hands and wrists. That rough tickle. He loved the silky softness of the fur around his ears, and how he'd come to Joe whenever he called (unless he was in the middle of eating the marigolds). That rabbit was the best friend he'd ever had.

Joe felt a prickling in his throat. Bloody ridiculous. He was as bad as Podge, getting upset over a stupid bloody rabbit. He wondered if he'd been spotted, but the smiling woman was engrossed in her magazine. He cleared his throat and squeezed his eyes shut to blink away the tears. He thought about the air hostess (with her lovely breasts) to distract himself. Bobbing breasts... plump bottoms... parted lips...

Sometimes Joe wished he had someone sensible to talk to about all that sex stuff. There was plenty of talk in the playground. A boy called Matthew Payne was the self-appointed playground oracle of all things sexual. But Joe still had certain (embarrassing) questions. When he masturbated too often and his spunk started running out, was he doing himself any physical damage? When he was doing it, was it wrong to imagine Miss Janes, his art teacher? And what about the girl next door? You could already see her boobs under her school shirt, but she was only twelve. If he carried on like this, would he end up preferring his own hand to proper sex?

He was lost in reverie until a 'ping' brought his attention back to the plane. The ping was followed by a chorus of seat belts being clicked together, like a giant metallic insect with lots of legs. There was a faint unpleasant smell – like sweaty socks or old farts under the duvet. He wrinkled up his nose. When they started to descend he noticed his ears pop again. He made a mental note to look it up. He was thirsty. Stupid plane. Bloody smiling woman, bloody parents. The wheels touched down and the reverse thrusters engaged with a violent whoosh. Bloody Amsterdam. He crossed his arms and scowled.

Joe refused the hostess's offer to carry his suitcase as they headed towards the Arrivals Gate. As they walked along the fluorescently lit corridors, his suitcase got heavier and heavier. He rested it on the ground momentarily and then jerked it along for a few paces, skimming the polished floor. The air hostess offered to take it again – he shook his head at her gruffly. They passed through 'Nothing to Declare' and walked into a babble of noise and colour. A group of friends and relatives stood behind a barrier, waiting patiently for their loved ones. Taxi drivers held up signs – 'Smith' scrawled in blue felt tip, 'Mr. H. van Stee' neatly printed in black.

Joe put his free hand into his pocket and took hold of his luck pebble. It was just an ordinary stone – he wasn't superstitious like Podge's mum and her silly horoscopes. His parents took him to the beach once and he'd spotted it at the tide-line – it was smooth and blue with a white splodge on one side. He'd spent a long time looking at that splodge, and feeling the stone texture under his fingertips. The day he found it had been a happy one – his parents had actually been getting on with each other for a change – and so the pebble had good memories attached to it like a veil.

"Can you see her?" asked the hostess.

Joe continued to scan the waiting crowd. What did Nel look like again? Mum had shown him a photo before he left, but he couldn't remember it now. It could be that woman with the pink hat, but she didn't seem to be returning his gaze… Behind her another woman was approaching at a run. She was wearing paint-splattered navy overalls and a long, striped cardigan. There was a smear of blue on one of her cheeks. She looked directly at Joe and he looked away, embarrassed. He was starting to feel panicky, and tried to concentrate on the feel of the pebble in his palm. He was breathing like Miss Stevenson had taught him. In… one, two, three. Out… one, two, three, four, five. In… one, two, when he was interrupted by a hand on his shoulder.

"Joey!"

It was the woman in the overalls. She looked far too young to be Nel – Nel was more than double his age, twenty nine. Although she was a whole decade younger than his ancient mum. Colour came to his cheeks. Stupid face. His mum said he'd grow out of blushing, but these days it was happening more than ever. He held out his hand. She looked amused, but then turned serious and took his hand politely, squeezing it hard, before enveloping him in a hug which almost took the wind out of him. She smelt nice – sweet and musty. His arms hung loosely by his sides. Before he'd decided whether or not to hug her back she'd released him. The hostess smiled and disappeared. Nel stood there, appraising him.

"I won't say 'haven't you grown' or you might want to hit me. I like your t-shirt, very trendy."

Her Dutch accent was much stronger than his mum's. Her vowels were off, and some of the words sounded more American than English.

"Thanks, Tante."

Nel picked up Joe's case, making a show about how heavy it was, and jerked her head to indicate he should follow her. As they walked he could feel her eyes on him, looking him up and down. He felt painfully self-conscious. He hated his gangly limbs, his fluffy hair, and his hollowed-out eyes. His Grandma Pearl was always pinching his cheek and lamenting the lack of meat on him. Nel walked fast and Joe struggled to keep up. She led him to the taxi rank, and after the driver had put Joe's suitcase in the boot they both climbed into the back seat.

Joe watched the scenery swish by. First there were boring grey motorways, and then they started passing shops. Joe read the names as they passed: Gerben Kuyt Fotografie, Café Hoopman, Albert Heijn. He saw a young couple greeting each other with three kisses on the cheek – mwah, mwah, mwah. And there were bicycles everywhere. Businessmen in suits on bicycles, girls dressed up for a night out on bicycles, mothers with their children in a basket on bicycles. They travelled in packs, and turned without warning. How did they manage not to crash into each other?

When Nel started speaking, she made Joe jump.

"So – what's news in the world of Joe?"

"Oh, I'm fine thank you, Tante." Joe heard his own voice – overly polite, fake, like he was talking to a teacher. He hated it. But his parents always complained when he used his normal voice. They'd invariably say, 'Speak up', and when he did they'd say, 'Don't be rude, Joseph'. He couldn't understand it.

"Come on, what have I missed? What has happened to you since the last time I saw you? It's been ages."

Nel looked at him and let the silence drag on. It occurred to him that she might actually be interested in his answer. Adults never usually were. They might say, 'How are you?' or, 'What happened at school today?' but what they really meant was, 'Reassure me that you've got over that silly crying incident at breakfast,' or, 'I know something happened and I'm giving you a chance to confess before I start telling you off'. What could he tell her that would keep her happy?

"Oh, mostly normal stuff, you know, reading, and school, and seeing my friend…"

"Oh yes, your little friend – what was he called… Oliver?"

Joe winced at the word 'little'.

"Ollie, yeah. But I call him Podge."

"How does he like that?"

"What, Podge? Oh, I think he hates it. He doesn't mind really, though."

"Oh."

She let the silence hang again. He tried again.

"Dad let me subscribe to the Weather magazine. It's under my name and everything. I want to join the Royal Meteorology Society but I can't until I'm sixteen, Dad says I can when I'm old enough. I can't wait for my first magazine, it should be there when I get back."

"Of course, the weather! How could I forget about that? And how are your studies going?"

Joe perked up at the word 'studies'. People usually used different words like 'special interest' (his dad's), 'obsession', or worst of all 'hobby'. He wasn't even allowed to mention the weather to his mum anymore – she said it drove her potty.

"Well, I'm running out of books, really – I need to go to the Royal Society's library but Dad hasn't had time to take me yet. He's said we can probably go when I'm a bit older."

"And have you brought your Shipping Forecast tape with you?"

Joe nodded.

"Of course, of course!" she said, brushing a hand across his cheek.

Nel was smiling at him as if they were sharing a joke, but he wasn't sure what was funny. What was it his mum had said? If the conversation runs dry, then ask a question. Not an 'information question' as she called them, designed to gather facts, but a 'curious question'. He didn't really understand the difference, but his mum said it was very important. What was he curious about?

"Why is your hair all different colours?" He suspected this might be an information question after all, but his aunt smiled even more broadly. He was pleased.

"Oh, I dye it, Joe – I can't stand my natural colour."

"Why not?"

"Oh, it's boring, I think."

"How does it work?"

Nel went on to explain henna – where she bought it from, how her friend Marleen puts it on for her once every few months, and how she slept with her hair wrapped up in cling film and with an old towel draped over her pillow. She promised she'd show Joe how it was done before he went back to England. Maybe they could even put an orange streak in his fringe, she joked, to remind him of his days in the Netherlands.

They drove alongside the canal for a while, and turned right and then left to get to Nel's street. There was a jumble of older buildings and ugly modern flats. A few tired shrubs in pots lined the pavements, and on a bench with chipped navy paint an old man was smoking a pipe. A thin ginger cat darted across the street in front of them as they pulled over. It looked like an ordinary street to Joe – he'd been expecting things to look different in Amsterdam. For some reason he'd pictured tall black street lamps with swirls of iron, and the houses all painted red and orange. Maybe he'd seen something on TV.

At the creak of the handbrake, Nel looked at Joe with wide eyes and started biting her thumbnail. Podge bit his nails when he was feeling jittery – it drove Joe mad. Did Nel feel jittery? Joe didn't know what she had to be nervous about. He was the one in a strange country with a woman he hardly remembered.

Nel paid the taxi driver and spoke to him in Dutch. The sounds were harsh and alien. It was like listening to his mum speaking to her Dutch friend on the phone – she became a different person. Apparently Joe had spoken Dutch when he was very little, but had forgotten it all. He could just remember his parents arguing about it when he was young – his dad wanted him to keep it up, but his mum was against the idea. It didn't make sense to Joe when he thought about it now.

Nel jerked his suitcase violently out of the boot and onto the pavement. Joe was pleased he hadn't brought anything breakable. She unlocked the green front door and ushered him up the stairs ahead of her. The stairs were narrow and dark – Joe could hardly see where to put his feet. After two flights of steps she leaned across him and unlocked another door. He smelt her breath – a mixture of peppermint and cigarettes. She let him in and then brushed past, disappearing through another door.

Joe was left alone in the living room. What a lot of stuff! The room was a riot of colour, like the big roundabout on his way to school – crammed with gaudy petunias. By the front door were three towering piles of magazines pushed up against the wall, and jumbles of shoes piled on top. He counted thirteen coats – fur, tweed, a fuchsia pink raincoat. Did they all belong to Nel? Who would need so many coats? Thick variously-patterned rugs were laid out edge to edge across the floor, and the sofas were draped with layers of throws, as if they were tethering them to the ground. Joe took in a few of the strange objects around the room – a row of white ceramic rabbits, a large wooden owl covered in hieroglyphics, a double bass case, a dressmaker's dummy with a sinister smile. He had an urge to start picking things up, but stopped himself just in case Nel might think him rude. Nel reappeared and studied him again, as she had at the airport.

"So here you are."

Her voice cracked. Joe was alarmed. He hadn't thought Nel was the sentimental type. He'd had enough of crying recently. He walked over to her coats and took the fur fabric of one between his finger and thumb, hoping she might gather herself together before he turned back to her. After a few moments of silence, she spoke.

"Come on, trouble, let me show you to your tiny room."

The next morning Joe was woken by a loud bang. This was followed by scraping noises, and he recognised the sound of furniture being moved around. A spike of annoyance speared him like metal. Everything had conspired to annoy him lately. Mr. Jamieson, Podge, his parents… Now the whole of Holland was against him too. His birthday present from Nel – a book he'd already read. That nasty-tasting margarine on his toast last night. This tiny box room with its weird petrol smell and no proper bed – just a thin single mattress on the floor. And what was his aunt doing moving things around at nine o'clock in the morning?

He turned over and pressed the pillow to his ear, but gave up after a few minutes. Wasn't 'early mornings' one of the things Nel had warned him about in her letter? His suitcase was lying open on the floor, clothes strewn around it like an exploded bomb. He reached over and slid his hand inside the flap where he found the edge of the envelope and pincered it out. He re-read her letter as if he was swotting up for an exam.

Dear Joe,

You'll know by now that your mum has arranged for you to come and stay with me in my little flat for the summer holidays. I haven't seen you for such a long time. I thought I should warn you about what you're letting yourself in for, staying with me.

Not like he had a choice. When he suggested staying with Podge's family instead his mum just made that tutting noise and rolled her eyes.

> Well, I'm sure we'll have a lot of fun together. Your mum is sending me a list of the food you like to eat, and I'll make sure I've got the right things. I know how choosy you are. You'll be sleeping in my studio, so hopefully it won't smell too much of paint (!!) – it's not very big, but it looks out onto the street – the best view in the flat – so you can sit at the desk and draw a little if you like.

Joe glanced up at the desk. He did concede that it looked like a good place to read. It wasn't a very big window but the sun was streaming in.

> I've got a spare cassette player you can have in there too, so you can listen to your tapes.
>
> Make sure you bring your swimming shorts, and a few books to keep you busy – there is an English bookshop near here and some English books in the library, but they might not have the things you want to read. We can go and have a look together.

Joe couldn't wait to see inside the libraries in Amsterdam. All those books in a different language! He wished he hadn't forgotten how to speak Dutch.

Your mum tells me that you're getting up later and later at the weekends now, and I must warn you that I get up at 7 a.m. every day, except Sundays when I have a nice long lie in until 10 or 11. I like to have breakfast and then start my painting, as other things get in the way soon enough and before I know it, it's time for bed again. So if you don't sleep through things very well you might want to bring a woolly hat so you can pull it down over your ears in the mornings!

Your mum's probably already told you about how disorganised I can be, not like her at all. We'll just have to struggle through the rest of it, all the things I've forgotten. I hope you won't miss your parents too much. Your dad said he'll give you a ring once a week.

Looking forward to meeting you at the airport – I'll wear my green hat so you can tell it's me.

Lots of love,

Tante Nel.

The letter annoyed him. It didn't contain any important information, like what he was expected to do during the day, or whether she had any pets. She hadn't even worn a green hat to the airport – useless! Dad was always going on about how 'dippy' she was – now Joe could see what he meant. He wished his mum were here. He imagined her now, knocking and opening his door a crack to ask him if he wanted a cup of tea. He always answered with a grunt, a kind of 'grhgmppph' noise, and his mum would say, 'Coming right up!' It was their morning ritual. She hadn't done it for a while now. Maybe she thought he was getting too old for it.

He would have killed for a cup of tea. But he didn't want to venture out of bed. It was chilly in the room, and he was warm and cosy under his duvet. He had an erection too, and he couldn't wander around his aunt's flat like that. Stupid little man. That's what his Dad always called it, his 'little man'. Better than what Podge's parents call his – his 'wee willie winkie'. Joe had pissed himself laughing when Podge told him by mistake one day. Podge was annoyed at first, but saw the funny side and even confessed to Joe what they called his sister's – her 'floo floo'. Joe had laughed until water streamed from his eyes.

He squeezed one hand between his thighs, where it felt comfortable, and thought about touching himself. Masturbation was one of the first things he'd considered when he arrived at his aunt's. Where was his room? How far away was it from hers? How thick were the walls? At home he'd worked out the perfect routine. Once when he went up to bed (and his parents were safely downstairs in front of the television), and again in the morning after his mum had brought him his tea (she always went back downstairs to the kitchen). Lately he'd added a third occasion, at school in a toilet cubicle. This felt riskier, even though he used the toilets no one went to because they smelt of stale piss. He kept telling himself he'd stop, but the idea that he might be discovered seemed to add to his excitement. Last Tuesday he'd made two visits. Later Podge had asked him if he had the squits.

What if Miss Janes came into the toilets one day and surprised him? His thoughts drifted to Miss Janes, which made him even harder. What would happen if he didn't do it here in Amsterdam as often as he was used to? Would he end up with an erection all the time? A stiffy, as Podge called it. Or, even worse, a boner. As if there were a bone running all the way through his cock. Imagine cutting it off, barbequing it and nibbling at it like a chicken leg! He allowed himself a wry smile. The graphic image also had the effect of softening his chicken leg, especially when he imagined biting into it. He could worry about his wanking schedule later. Tea was more of a priority right now.

He sighed heavily, realising he was going to have to get out of bed and sort it out himself. Why hadn't his mum asked Tante Nel to bring him tea in the mornings? Hadn't they talked about these kinds of things in all those late night phone calls?

He screwed up his courage and threw back the duvet. The air was cool against his naked torso. He dug around in his suitcase for his grey hooded top, discarded clothes flying as he searched. It was his favourite. He hadn't worn it on the plane just in case someone was sick on it – his dad had told him some people got air sickness like sea sickness. He'd been quite concerned when he'd discovered the paper bag in the pocket of the seat in front – were they expecting it to happen to everyone? The top was packed right at the bottom. His bloody mother must have put it there. He'd told her he wanted to pack his case himself.

The floor was now entirely covered in his clothes. He glanced at his luck pebble on the window–sill where he'd put it last night, and his pile of books. At least the room was starting to look like his own. Maybe he could put up a poster. He'd got a gorgeous one of Liz Fraser from the Cocteau Twins. He should have rolled it up and brought it with him. He'd even got a picture of her in his wallet – one he'd cut from a magazine, the size of a passport photo. He'd glued it onto a square of thick card for durability. It had got soggy where he'd kissed her too sloppily, and the paper was all rucked up like the skin on school custard. He struggled into his jeans. The metal of the zip was freezing against his skin. There. He felt better now he was dressed. Less like a little boy. Now, where was that cup of tea?

Joe found Nel drinking coffee and reading a paper in the kitchen. She looked like she'd been up for hours. He smiled politely and said good morning. He guessed his mum had complained to Nel about how grumpy he was in the mornings, so he'd planned to make a special effort to be pleasant. Things were going okay until he tasted the cornflakes. They were thinner than proper English ones, and they weren't sweet enough either. Nel suggested sprinkling some sugar on top. Ridiculous – it would just dissolve into the milk and it was the flakes that weren't sweet enough!

Nel opened up all of her cupboards so Joe could inspect the available food. She raised her eyebrows, but at least she didn't comment as he refused her suggestions one by one. He was fed up of people having a go at him about not eating enough, or eating the wrong things. Another example of how grown-ups wanted to control his life. Eventually he settled on chewing on a piece of bread without any butter as he drank his tea.

Once his pathetic breakfast was over, he had a shower in Nel's tiny bathroom. He'd been able to smell his own armpits whilst he ate his bread. Secretly, he quite liked his own stink – it made him feel like a man – but he didn't want Nel to think he was dirty. Nel's bathroom smelt of damp, and there was something black growing on the shower curtain. He tried to arch his body away from the plastic when he turned the water on – it was cold and slimy against his skin.

He soaped his back, running his fingertips over all his old spot scabs and the smooth lumps of the ones still germinating. His thoughts wandered to the weeks stretching ahead of him. He'd rather be anywhere but here. Maybe he could go on strike. He'd refuse to go anywhere, just sit in his tiny bedroom and read books all day. That would show Nel. That would show his mum and his dad how unhappy they'd made him. After getting dressed again he got back into bed with his book. He waited for Nel's knock, ready to say no to whatever she had planned.

She popped her head around the door and smiled hopefully.

"I thought we could go on a trip to the zoo to celebrate your birthday."

She waited, and when Joe didn't look up she added, "There are lots of birds."

Joe had first become fascinated by birds at the age of eight, when a new neighbour scattered bread and peanuts on her patio. Joe could see the birds swooping in from his bedroom window, and he watched them squabble and eat. Whenever this next door neighbour hung out her washing or watered her pots, Joe ran out to ask her what their names were.

Eventually he persuaded his mum to get a bird table of their own, and a bird identification book. He couldn't believe how many different species there were – before he'd started looking properly he'd thought (with the exception of blackbirds and robins) that all birds were slight variations on the theme of small and brown. Greenfinches, siskins, chaffinches… Once he saw a tiny goldcrest in their apple tree, and they were even visited by a great spotted woodpecker once, resplendent in his red, white and black. Joe had joined the RSPB, and gone on day trips with his dad to the local wildlife reserve. He couldn't get enough of birds. Nel was still waiting for his response, and so he sighed and put his book down.

"Okay then."

Even to him, his voice sounded flat and grumpy. But Nel looked pleased, as if they'd reversed roles and he was the parent reluctantly agreeing to a trip out. He felt a grin tickle the edges of his mouth but kept a straight face. He didn't want her to think he was happy about any of this.

On the walk to the tram stop they passed the old man on his blue bench (Joe wondered if he ever left it) and those funny bollards that reminded Joe of penises. Joe was almost run over by a bicycle – Nel grabbed him by the shoulder and dragged him backwards. They reached the canal and followed it towards the centre of Amsterdam. Joe looked at the tall houses on the other side of the sparkling water and wondered who lived inside them. Some of them had balconies, or open blue shutters. Others were leaning precariously – at the intersection between roofs there was a triangle of blue sky, or the gap was filled with planks or bricks.

Joe had been excited about getting on a tram, but when it finally arrived it looked like an ordinary bus. Nel let Joe sit near the window. She then asked him a single question about British birds. This unleashed a stream of ornithological information. He told her that cuckoos lay between twelve and twenty four eggs in a season, and that the goldcrest was the smallest bird in the UK, even though everyone always thought it was the wren, and that the smallest walking bird was the pied wagtail. He told her that bird eggs had to be incubated because birds were warm-blooded, and that a woodpecker's tongue wraps around its brain so that it doesn't get brain damage when hammering its beak against a tree. He was telling her about the mating habits of blackbirds when Nel had a coughing fit. He wondered if he ought to bang her on the back, but eventually she recovered herself.

"Are you all right, Tante?"

"Something shot down the wrong hole...what do you say in English again?"

"I've just remembered that I might be boring you. How long have I been talking?"

"Oh, half an hour or so?"

"Oh dear. Mum said that if it's more than ten minutes you can guarantee the other person is half asleep. Were you bored, Tante?"

"Well, Joe, I did drift off a bit when you did the list of all the birds you've seen, but mostly... I happen to be interested in birds. And I also happen to be interested in the things you're interested in."

He nodded in reply, and went back to looking out the tram window. It had started to drizzle, and the spray was making patterns on the glass. He thought about cloud droplets and coalescence.

"Did you know that drops of drizzle have diameters of between 0.2 and 0.5 millimetres? And that sometimes rain evaporates before it reaches the ground? You can see it, it's called a fallstreak."

Nel looked amused. "No, I certainly didn't."

He thought she might be patronising him, and furrowed his brow, but her smile held such warmth that it dissolved his annoyance. Just like evaporating rain, he thought. He found his mouth turning up at the corners, and surrendered to a grin.

It was only a short walk to the gates of the zoo, but Nel still managed to cram in a cigarette. A golden eagle statue was perched on the top of each gate post, and Joe almost told Nel that they maintain territories as large as sixty square miles, but he thought he might have overdone the bird facts for one day. They queued for their tickets and walked through to the entrance. There was a faint whiff of manure on the air. Nel looked around excitedly, and Joe glanced at her – with her great floppy sleeves and her multi-coloured ruffled skirt she looked a bit like an exotic bird. All those shades of pink and brown. Joe could see a camel and some sort of bison ahead, but he couldn't concentrate – his throat was too dry.

Joe tugged on one of her sleeves.

"I'm thirsty." The words came out in a whine.

"Come on then, let's have a cup of coffee before we start looking around. We might even find something acceptable for you to eat." She ruffled his hair, and he ducked away from her.

They filed into the café, and joined the queue. Joe scanned the counter for something edible. There were brightly coloured fruit drinks nestled in chipped ice, unrecognisable chocolate bars, and sandwiches with strange pink meats. He wrinkled his nose and settled on a coke and an ice lolly. It was frozen in the shape of a rocket and it reminded him of the ones he liked at home. He couldn't go wrong with that.

Nel found them a table next to the window. They sat in silence for a while, busy at work – Nel stirring three cartons of milk and four sugars into her coffee, and Joe licking his lolly. Nel took a sip and leaned back in her chair, blowing air slowly through her mouth as if it were smoke.

"Okay, is it?"

Joe nodded and shrugged simultaneously.

"So how's my sister, then, Joe?"

He looked up at her sharply, then picked up his coke and took a mouthful. His voice was muffled when he spoke.

"She's all right, I suppose."

"Hmm. I know she hasn't been coping very well, especially since, you know."

"Since what?"

"Since she didn't get onto that course."

"Oh, that course. Yeah, the course." He tried to sound nonchalant.

She narrowed her eyes. "You don't know what I'm talking about, do you Joe?"

He coloured and took another gulp to avoid her stare. How did people always guess when he was lying? Podge was rubbish at lying too, his voice went strange. One of the boys in their class, Richard, was fantastic. He'd taught them a game where they took turns telling each other two true facts and one false fact, and the other two had to guess which one was the lie. Richard was a genius at it – he won every time.

"Look, if I tell you anything that you don't already know, can you keep it a secret? I don't want to get into any trouble with your mum. You know what she's like…"

She winked conspiratorially, but Joe wasn't looking at her. He wasn't too sure about his lolly – one of the layers seemed to be banana flavour.

"Yeah, course."

"And you definitely want to know?"

He nodded and shrugged again, as if he didn't really care much.

Nel wafted her coffee underneath her nose before she took another sip, half-closing her eyes like a cat. He'd noticed her doing that at breakfast. It was reassuring to recognise one of her gestures, it made her more familiar to him.

She put down her cup. "Your mum always wanted to do something creative, like me. She was into clothes, fashion. She used to get books out from the library when we were children, pore over them in the front room. Fashion in history, books on designers, dah dah dah. She had a little sketch book with her all the time, perfecting these little mannequins. She'd draw them and then she'd dress them in her own designs. She was always sucking on the end of her pencil and looking up to the ceiling, thinking of new skirts or new patterns for the material."

Nel mimed this action while she was talking and Joe snorted. He kept forgetting that she was talking about his mum. It didn't sound like her at all. Nel continued.

"I was more interested in playing with my dolls, and then boys. I was much younger, Ineke didn't really have much time for me. Mum was disapproving, of course, she thought it was silly, and Dad just told her she wouldn't make any money and they weren't going to support her forever. She had decided to go to the UK to learn English properly, and then try to get into a design school in London. And then..."

Nel felt around for her cigarettes, took one from the packet and put in on the table.

"I think Ineke was relieved to get away from our parents, but it was more difficult... Her English wasn't brilliant when she first met your dad, you know. You wouldn't know it now. I was always the one who was obsessed with London – the

26

galleries, the music, the language. I was the one who wanted to live in England. And now she's over there, and I'm here, trying to make enough money to keep myself alive. It should have been the other way round."

She paused to study him more closely. He was absorbed by trying to coax individual grains of sugar out of the corners of the empty sachet and then crushing them into powder with his spoon. After a few moments he flicked up his eyes.

"So it was me who persuaded her to apply for this design course last year. Maybe I should have kept out of it. But she just seems so miserable in that job of hers. Working with that idiot of a boss, putting her down all the time, making her feel useless. Nasty man."

Joe's mum had never mentioned her boss at home.

"I said she should go back to her dreams – that she'd be letting herself down if she didn't. Maybe I underestimated how hard it would be, with responsibilities, with a husband who doesn't really…" She glanced at Joe. "So anyway, she found this course, but they needed to see a portfolio at interview. You know what a portfolio is?"

Joe nodded.

"She hadn't done any drawing for so long. It took her months and months to get anything done. She's such a perfectionist. She threw everything away except her best three drawings. They said they wanted more than that, in the interview. They said they needed someone who 'eats, breathes and sleeps design'. The idiots. I think they took one look at her and wrote her off. She still dresses well, doesn't she Joe? But the fire has gone from her eyes, I suppose."

Nel sighed. "It was a big deal for her. She was angry at me, for encouraging her in the first place – putting 'silly ideas in her head', she said. Then she changed her mind, and she doesn't blame me anymore, but she blames herself, which is worse. Maybe she had a dream in her head, before. Maybe it was better to leave it there, where it was safe, where it could keep her going through long days at the office with that horrible man. I blew out her dream, Joe – she's in a worse state now than she was before. I feel terrible. And I don't know how to make it better."

Nel sat and looked at Joe, who was still playing with the sugar. Eventually he looked up at her.

"Where are the toilets, Tante?"

"Here, I've got to go too. Let me get my stuff together. Okay, lieverd?"

She bumped him on the cheek with the back of her hand. He turned his head away.

As Nel had predicted, the birds were the star of the show. Joe did like the giraffes, who nibbled at their food with elegant neck manoeuvres. He was impressed by the monkeys washing pieces of fruit in their moat, and they both laughed at the baby monkey who kept trying to jump up a too-steep slope and sliding back down. But they spent most of their time with the birds.

Joe got a kick from reading the Dutch names and trying to memorise them – the easy Pelikaan and Kraan, the impossible Purperglansspreeuw (Purple Glossy Starling) and the Snowy Owl, Sneeuwuil, which sounded to Joe like a sneeze. Joe and Nel agreed that the Crimson Horned Pheasants (Rood Saterhoen) were the most beautiful, with improbable polka dots scattered across their lipstick-red bodies.

They stood for a long time in front of the Quail's cage. These modest brown birds were small and plump – Joe tried not to think about them on a plate. Some of them had made depressions in the dirt floor so they could settle in like cats on a cushion. The best thing about them was their call – a kind of throaty, bubbly trill which exploded from them and set their whole body quivering. They tried to predict which one would go off next, and Joe got it right twice.

The only low point for Joe was when Nel went off to the toilet and left him alone to watch a gibbon performing acrobatics. As Joe watched it swinging from one cross beam to another, an old man in a battered hat started speaking to him in Dutch. When the man sounded like he was asking for Joe's agreement, Joe nodded without thinking, and this released a further torrent of Dutch. Every so often the man would pause, and Joe had to pretend he understood by nodding and smiling. He wished the man would go away, but eventually he must have asked a direct question, as he stopped talking and waited for Joe to say something. Joe mumbled "Sorry" and the man stepped backwards and said, "Ah, English! I speak many languages, but I can't guess, you have to say!" When Nel returned a few moments later he walked away from the man without apologising or even catching the man's eye. He felt bad about it all the way home on the tram.

On the way back they stopped off at a library, and Nel took Joe through to the English section which she knew well herself. She told Joe she'd become fluent in English through reading as much as through studying it at school (and watching television, like everyone else in Amsterdam). She liked the classics – Hardy, Austen – but admitted to being particularly fond of Agatha Christie.

Joe scanned the tall shelves. There was too much fiction for his liking. He pulled out a fat book, 'The Golden Notebook', and opened it at random.

"The point is," said Anna, as her friend came back from the telephone on the landing, "the point is, that as far as I can see, everything's cracking up."

Joe sneered. There was no such person as Anna, or her friend. Even the telephone and the landing were completely imaginary. How pointless, to read about made-up people and their pointless made-up lives. He flicked through the pages and read:

Do you know what people really want? Everyone, I mean. Everybody in the world is thinking: I wish there was just one other person I could really talk to, who could really understand me, who'd be kind to me. That's what people really want, if they're telling the truth.

He couldn't easily sneer at that, and when he thought about it he felt unsettled, so he put the book back and looked for the reference section.

This was where he belonged. He found a couple of books on birds, one on the weather, and one about the history of the radio. He thought they might mention the Shipping Forecast in it. It was a heavy pile, and Nel insisted they divide them for the rest of the journey home.

When they turned the corner into Nel's street, Joe could see something like a large package on the pavement in front of her apartment building. The blue bench was empty – maybe the old man had popped inside his flat to use his toilet. Joe was in the middle of telling Nel about orographic uplift when he saw the bag move. He stopped walking and stood there with his mouth open. Nel followed his gaze. After a few seconds, the bag moved again. She turned towards Joe and held her finger up against her pursed lips, gripping his arm as they tiptoed towards her front door. It had started to drizzle – Joe felt the fine mist dampen his face. His heart was beating fast.

The bag was a man in a sleeping bag, curled up on his side and apparently fast asleep. Nel whispered to Joe.

"It's okay, I know him. Do you want to let yourself in and go upstairs? You remember the way, yes?"

"Can I stay here with you?"

"Why's that?"

"Oh, no reason, I just don't want to..."

He trailed off.

"Okay Joey, no problem, just sit on the bench over there and I'll see if I can wake this schavuit up. You've got your books to read, haven't you?"

He nodded and went to sit down. He opened a bird book and pretended to read, keeping his eyes on Nel the whole time. He watched her put a hand on the man's shoulder and shake him gently, crooning something that sounded like 'yu-ROON' with a rolled 'rrr'.

Nel's voice got louder and louder until the body suddenly jerked out straight. The man's eyes opened wide and he exclaimed in Dutch. Joe wished he could understand the words. They had a hushed conversation – the man looking around him, his movements jerky. Nel seemed to be trying to reassure him. At one point Joe heard his own name, and they both looked over at him. He looked back down at his open book. The man's eyes were strange. Nel was trying to persuade him to do something and the man kept saying 'nee'. Their voices rose. Then the man opened up his sleeping bag and Nel looked inside. Her eyes widened and she stepped backwards. When she recovered her balance she hissed at him under her breath and threw her keys on the ground for him. When he'd shut the door behind him, she went over to Joe.

"I'll explain all of this later, darling. Can you go straight to you room when we get upstairs? It's complicated… Are you hungry?" Joe shook his head. "Right – let's go up – straight to your room, okay?"

Joe slumped on his bed with his book open on his lap. He'd tried reading the same page five times now and had given up. Maybe this book was just boring. It's difficult for him to tell the difference between fascinating and boring books until he gets them home. The very worst ones had nuggets of gold in amongst all the rubbish. The books about his favourite subjects were usually best – ornithology, of course, and meteorology, and horology… "All the 'ologies", as his dad liked to say, impersonating Maureen Lipman on that stupid advert. He thought he might have a new passion blossoming, too. He'd seen clips on TV about World War One recently and had felt a familiar fizzing in his stomach. He'd started scanning the Radio Times for similar programmes, and he took a book about fighter planes out of the library in Milton Keynes. All the usual signs were there.

He guessed it might be like falling in love. In those first heady weeks and months everything was unknown – so much was new. After he'd read the first thirty books or so it got more difficult to find out new information, but then the comfort of familiarity kicked in – he'd rediscover a fact like an old friend, or relish the pleasure of spotting mistakes on TV programmes.

He made a fresh attempt to read the paragraph he'd started. 'Although a common and widespread species, it has a somewhat more restricted distribution than its compatriot, the Turkey Vulture, which breeds well into Canada and south to Tierra del Fuego.' His eyes started to droop.

His head woke him when it jolted back up. At first he thought he might be on a train. Joe lived in constant fear of falling asleep on a train and waking to find himself resting on the shoulder of a strange man. That, or missing his stop and ending up in Brighton. It felt like only a few moments had passed but it was dark outside, and he was starving. Where was Nel? What had happened to dinner? Even his mother didn't forget to feed him.

There was a loud bang from the living room. It was more of a clang, like a cartoon mouse hitting a cat around the head with a saucepan. After a few seconds of silence there was a moaning noise. Was it a woman's voice? It sounded panicky, like a trapped animal. What had that bastard done to Nel? His heart banged – kaboom, kaboom. He wished he had gun on him, like in the movies. He could just slip his hand underneath his pillow and hold the semi-automatic down close to his thigh as he stealthily crept outside to save Tante's life. Should he stay in his room? Hide in the cupboard? What if she was lying out there right now, bleeding to death? What would his mother say if he let her sister die?

Now there was another noise. 'Shhushh, shhushh', material against material, something heavy being dragged. Right – he had to go out and save her. That man was getting ready to bury her – he was taking her into the bathroom so he could cut her up into little pieces in the bath. The murderer might have to suffocate her first, if she wasn't dead yet. He looked around the room for something he could arm himself with. He reached for one of Nel's paintbrushes and noticed that his hand was shaking. He held it with the brush end towards him, ready to stab it into the man's eyes, his balls. That's what they'd taught them in self defence at school. Go for the bollocks. What else did they say, what else? The only defensive manoeuvre he could remember was hooking his fingers inside the eye sockets and pulling hard. He can't imagine wanting to get that close to the murderer's face. He took a deep gulping breath and threw open the door.

The curtains were drawn, and the room was lit by flickering candles. Joe's eyes slowly adjusted to the darkness. Someone was dragging a body towards the bathroom, bent forward with their long hair falling down over their face. It was Tante. She had her hands hooked underneath the body's underarms and was struggling with the bulk of it. The man had stopped moaning – he was limp and lifeless. And there was blood. There was a dark smear on Nel's cheek, and thick drops of it on the man's pale blue jeans. There were spatters on her cream rug. And the room was a mess. A book had been torn into shreds, and covered the whole scene like giant confetti. A full ashtray had been tipped onto the middle of the coffee table. On the rug was a brass dish with pot pourri scattered around it.

Nel turned her head and looked at Joe in shock. She lost her grip and the man's torso slumped to the floor. His head dropped onto the carpet with a thud, and they both winced. They stood staring at each other. The only sound was the ticking of the clock. Eventually Nel found her voice.

"Joe! You should go back into your room!"

"What are you going to do with him?"

"Back into your room!"

She sounded furious, but he couldn't move. Where had all the blood come from? He looked more closely at the body and noticed a piece of material bound tightly around one of his wrists.

"Why did you cut his wrist?"

"He cut his own wrist, the idiot. That's why I had to knock him out. I couldn't get him to be sensible."

Nel noticed something on the sofa and leapt towards it. Something glinted as she shoved it into a drawer.

"It's all right, everything is under control, lieverd. You can leave me to tidy up if you like. Are you hungry? Shall I make you a nice cheese sandwich?"

The question put him off balance. He'd been starving five minutes ago, but now his stomach was as hard as a drum.

"What are you going to do with the body?"

"Oh, I'll put him in the bedroom. He's not dead, Joey. He's called Jeroen. It wasn't a very deep cut really, I've seen worse. I didn't mean to knock him out, I just... I ran out of options. I thought a little bang on the head might help him to see sense."

She lifted an empty glass from the table and held it over Jeroen's nose and mouth. Condensation bloomed and faded and she turned to Joe triumphantly.

"See?"

Joe walked over to him and crouched on the carpet, examining him at close quarters. They both looked at him quietly for a while. One of his arms was twisted awkwardly, and Nel moved it gently so it lay beside him. His plump lips were parted and they could hear his breath whistling softly in and out. He had such long eye lashes. They looked like a girl's. Nel brushed a dark lock of Jeroen's hair from his forehead. He did look peaceful, lying there. What would Nel do now? Joe didn't feel afraid anymore. His belly growled.

"I am pretty hungry, actually."

"Mmm, me too. We haven't eaten anything since lunch, have we? Is omelettes on your list of approved foods?"

"As long as they don't have tomatoes or mushrooms in them."

"How about cheese? Onion? Or ham?"

"Urgh, onions are disgusting. Ham and cheese, please."

"Okay – ham and cheese it is. Let's get this lump out of the way first, though, shall we? Now you're here you might as well help me. We'll put him in my bedroom. What's that expression you have… death weight?"

"Dead weight."

"Yes, dead weight. He's a dead weight!"

She laughed crazily, and Joe snorted. He was already planning a letter to Podge telling him all about this. Although he ought to wait until they definitely knew that Jeroen hadn't died. Head injuries could be unpredictable like that, his dad had told him. His dad knew someone at work who fell off a ladder and was fine all evening, having dinner with his family, watching television, and then that night he died in his sleep.

Nel steered Joe to the left side of Jeroen. She showed him how to put one hand under his armpit and grab onto his wrist with his other hand – had she done this before? Maybe she often had unconscious men in her flat. Nel said, "One, two, three", and then they both lifted and pulled. Joe was astounded at how heavy he was. They dragged him across the living room, pausing at the door of the bedroom so Nel could tidy a path to her bed. There were canvasses everywhere. The glasses half full of dark grey water were the same design as the ones in the kitchen. He hoped she cleaned them properly. There were photos of trees strewn all over the bed.

They swung Jeroen onto the mattress and Nel untied the laces of his trainers. She then lifted him upright and gestured for Joe to lift his hooded top and then his t-shirt over his head. His chest was perfectly smooth – not like Joe's dad. He'd caught a glimpse of his dad's a few years ago when he walked into his parent's bedroom without knocking, and was shocked by the thick carpet of curly hair, with strange bald bits around his nipples. He'd never seen a naked woman, unless you count the magazine Podge got hold of. He can't remember ever seeing his mum naked, although he supposes he must have once.

He hoped they weren't going to take Jeroen's jeans off, and was relieved when Nel removed his socks and seemed satisfied. They each took a corner of the duvet and covered him up. He was resting awkwardly on the pillow and so Nel adjusted it. When she put his head back down onto the pillow he let out a groan and grimaced. They waited but he didn't make any more noise. Nel kissed two fingers and pressed them onto his forehead before looking up at Joe.

"Right. Ham and cheese!"

Joe didn't wake up until lunchtime. After their late night omelette Nel had made them some milky decaffeinated coffee, and they'd stayed up into the early hours watching a Dutch horror film. It was cheaply made, with unconvincing zombies and cardboard acting, and it had them in hysterics. They finally yawned their way to bed, and Joe left his bedside lamp on when he went to sleep. He pretended that he couldn't be bothered to reach over and switch it off, but really the zombies had affected him more than he cared to admit.

He pulled on some jeans and a t-shirt and emerged from his box-room. Tinkly piano music floated through the flat. He found Nel in her bedroom with the door wide open, absorbed in her painting. All traces of Jeroen had disappeared. Nel didn't mention it, and so neither did Joe. He did find a smear of red on the shower curtain, and did wonder briefly if Nel might have cut him into pieces after Joe had fallen asleep.

After a lunch of bread and ham, Nel announced they were going on a canal trip. The trip started a short walk from Nel's flat, near Anne Frank's house. They climbed down onto the boat early, and Joe observed the gaggles of flabby tourists milling about on the side of the canal. They wore a touristy uniform – slacks, too-bright shirts, sun visors. Something about them disgusted him. He shifted his gaze to the railing along the edge of the water. There were layers of old paint – dark green, yellow, and the silver of the metal showing through. It reminded Joe of a weather map with tightly packed contours. Debris was scattered along the path – scrunched up tissues, cigarette butts, blobs of grey chewing gum squidged between bricks. The smell of diesel wafted through the air.

The driver of the boat appeared from a canal-side café, putting out his cigarette before descending into the boat and introducing himself loudly as 'Bram'. He looked like a man's man, not like his father, and Joe had a brief fantasy of playing football with him in the park. When everyone was aboard Bram climbed onto the sides of the boat to cast off, and took his place at the steering wheel.

As the boat chugged into the right hand lane of the canal, Bram started his patter. He repeated everything he said in Dutch, French and English, sounding as if he'd said these things three million times before. It was difficult to understand his English, but Joe did hear him say that the houseboats weren't connected to the sewage system, and that the waste went directly into the canal. He turned to Nel and made a face, and wondered why he couldn't see any turds floating around in the water. He was too embarrassed to ask her.

Nel opened their window, and Joe enjoyed the breeze on his face. He wished Nel lived on a houseboat and not in a boring flat. One of them had a hammock on the roof, and one had three sleeping ducks on the wooden porch. He could see inside some of them, to a huge candelabra, or sofas and bookshelves, or a family sitting at a dining table. There was a washing line on one boat roof, complete with lacy knickers. Soon afterwards he spotted a woman leaning over a bridge, her plump breasts falling forwards.

Some of the bridges were very narrow inside, and Joe watched Bram as he steered. He looked so nonchalant. There were posts at some of the entrances, covered in scrapes of different coloured paint – not all drivers were as skilful as Bram. Joe wondered how you became a canal-boat driver, and whether he'd ever be able to negotiate the narrow canals with such casual aplomb, turning the wheel one way and then the other. Bram greeted the other drivers as they passed, and Joe imagined them meeting in a bar after work and swapping stories of swan attacks and near misses.

He loved going under the bridges. The bricks at the base were covered in a skin of black-green algae, and the water smacked and slurped against them. They passed a barge with a towering pile of black, tangled bicycles – Nel told him they fished them out from the canals, hundreds of them. Joe wondered how many of them had also deposited their riders into the water, and how many of them had been drunk. They passed a boat full of new bikes too – rows and rows of them, all different colours.

The hour passed quickly. The boat pulled in back to where it had started, and Bram shook everyone's hands as they exited the boat, telling them to enjoy the rest of their trip. He winked at Joe, and Joe blushed. If only he had a cool Dad. On the walk home Nel asked him which had been his favourite part, and he thought about the woman on the bridge with her boobs spilling out of her top.

Over the next few days, Joe and Nel did ordinary things together. It was a relief after the drama of the Jeroen incident. In the mornings Nel painted while Joe read or watched TV, and in the afternoons they went on domestic errands. Nel usually worked in a café, but she'd taken the week off to help Joe 'settle in'. They visited the supermarket, and Joe found some cereal he liked – Choco Chippies – which dealt with the breakfast dilemma. They walked up and down the canals, and Joe started to get his bearings. He liked the way they sliced parts of the city into nice neat oblongs, and enjoyed recognising shops and houses as they covered the same ground.

One afternoon they were served in a café by a waitress with a sixties quiff and a cobweb tattoo on her elbow. Another afternoon they stopped for ten minutes to fuss an old ginger cat, who purred and purred. Joe got the hang of walking single file when bicycles approached, and Nel taught him how to say 'hello' and 'thank you' and 'huge slice of chocolate cake' in Dutch. He helped Nel carry her washing to the local launderette, and even got involved with the hoovering (making Nel promise she wouldn't tell his mum, as he'd never touched their hoover in Milton Keynes). By the end of the fifth day, when out with one of Nel's friend, Joe was surprised to catch himself thinking about Nel's flat as 'home'.

That Saturday evening Joe was engrossed in a paragraph about rime frosts when the doorbell rang. Nel was in the kitchen and called through for Joe to get the door. He sighed heavily and put his book down. He had to use a tissue for a bookmark – why were there never enough bookmarks? When he opened the door, Jeroen was standing there, grinning. He was holding a bottle of wine, a bunch of flowers and a plastic carrier bag. His grin faded when he saw Joe.

"All right," mumbled Joe, not looking at him. He opened the door and let him come past. 'Not dead, then' he thought to himself, with a hint of disappointment.

"Hallo," said Jeroen.

They stood awkwardly in the living room until Joe shouted out, "Tante!" and abandoned Jeroen to go back to the sofa and his rime frosts. Nel came through with her hands out in front of her, still covered in suds from the washing up. She looked shocked to see Jeroen, and Joe noticed her blushing as she took the flowers and wine. Jeroen handed the plastic bag to Joe, saying, "A present for you." Nel gave Joe a meaningful look and he said, "Thank you," which he was about to say anyway. He opened the bag and pulled out an orange kite. He hated kites. Bloody stupid things – he couldn't see the point of them.

To Joe's relief, Jeroen followed Nel back into the kitchen, leaving him to read his book in peace. He could hear the adults murmuring – it sounded like Jeroen was doing most of the talking. Nel sounded apologetic. Nel had filled Joe in about her boyfriends a couple of nights ago. There were two. This one, Jeroen, was an art student who had lots of 'cool friends'. His work was 'amazing', Nel said. Then there was her older boyfriend, Henk, who was 'very generous' and who liked her art a lot. He was the one who'd arranged her first ever art exhibition. He was married, and his wife didn't know about Nel. She said he was a real gentleman, which made it sound as if he was ancient. Joe didn't like the sound of Henk, but he didn't like Jeroen much either. There was something weird about him. Jeroen knew about Henk, but Henk didn't know about Jeroen. It all sounded very complicated.

Nel called him into the kitchen. The table pushed against the back wall was hardly big enough for three people. When Joe asked if he could eat his dinner in the living room Nel said, "No." He thought she would, but it was worth a try. He was surprised she didn't tell him off for his moody look. He could hear his mum: "You've a face like a thundercloud." There didn't seem much point in keeping his face grumpy if it wasn't going to be noticed, and so he let his forehead relax. He pulled out his seat and sat down, all limbs, like a daddy-long-legs. His legs never used to get in the way like that.

He wasn't looking forward to dinner. Nel still didn't understand what he liked to eat. All week she'd been asking him how many carrots he wanted, or whether he liked courgettes. It said quite clearly on the list his mum wrote that the only vegetables he ate were frozen peas. Definitely not the ones from tins, which were completely disgusting – they had a texture like rotten brains, and were the same grey-green colour. Tonight she'd made some kind of a stew. She said he'd have to pick out the bits he didn't want. That was easy for her to say, but some ingredients completely contaminated everything else on the plate. Garlic, for example. At least she hadn't used slimy mushrooms in it.

Jeroen kept muttering things in Dutch. Joe imagined what he might be saying.

'This boy looks like a right idiot.'

'I am planning on taking over the world.'

'I'm wearing ladies knickers underneath my jeans.'

This last thought made him snigger, and Nel gave him a pointed look. Joe sighed. Jeroen didn't make any attempt to speak to him during the meal. Nel asked Joe a couple of questions in English, but he was unresponsive. He was pleased when they switched to Dutch so he could concentrate on identifying his food in peace.

Joe was taking a second helping of boiled potatoes when the phone rang. Nel left the room and Joe looked down at his food and carried on eating. He kept telling himself it was the same as his mum's casserole, and he was starving, but he could feel the edges of nausea – it was something about the squelchiness of the dumplings, and he was sure there was onion in it.

He started counting in sevens to distract himself. He often manipulated numbers in his head when he was bored, or when he wanted to take his mind off something. He'd start at a random number to make it more difficult – 39, 46, 53… After a while Nel returned, picking up her cutlery abruptly and ignoring Jeroen who was staring at her. Joe caught a whiff of onion so went back to counting sevens. He was interrupted by Jeroen.

"So, Joe, what you think of Amsterdam?"

His accent was fascinating – like Nel's, but magnified a hundred times. Joe soundlessly mouthed the same words to himself until Nel cleared her throat and he remembered he ought to answer.

"Oh, it's kind of funky, I suppose."

Jeroen looked quizzical, and Nel said something in Dutch. He laughed.

"Ah, funky!" He pronounced it wrong: 'fone-kee'. Joe snorted.

"What is your favourite place so far?"

"Well, I liked the falcons at the zoo. You know, falcon?" He could see that Jeroen was drawing a blank. He flapped his arms and said the word again, more slowly and loudly. Jeroen laughed again, and flapped his own arms.

"Fall-kon? Like a bird?"

"It *is* a bird. A bird of prey, he eats mice, and other small rodents, you know, mice?" He wrinkled his nose and swept his fingers outwards to indicate whiskers. Nel was already giggling, but when Jeroen copied him again and said, "Small rodents?" she burst into laughter. The tension in the room dissipated, and Joe thought maybe Jeroen wasn't so bad after all.

After dinner Jeroen went into the living room to smoke a thin, disgusting smelling cigar while Nel and Joe stacked the dishes and washed up. Nel asked him if he'd rather wash or dry, and he chose drying.

"Mum says I can't wash up properly," he explained.

"Me neither, so you have to wash," said Nel, tweaking his earlobe with her finger and thumb. Joe frowned and pulled away.

Joe couldn't see the washing up gloves, and asked Nel where they were. She raised an eyebrow and dug around under the sink where she found a pair, still in their plastic packaging. They were bright pink, and Joe felt embarrassed as he pulled them on. They should have been yellow. Everything was upside-down in Amsterdam.

He plunged his hands into the hot soapy water. He picked up the sponge and started to rub at the plates in looping circles. Nel took the clean plates from him silently, and he thought about the past week. Music drifted in from the living room, accompanied by the faint blue smell of cigar smoke. Joe thought the smoke had made his eyes water until he realised he was actually crying. He rubbed at them furiously, getting soap into them, which made them stream even more.

"Woah. What's happened here?" Nel asked. She took hold of his hand with hers to stop him from rubbing. She pressed a fingertip on each of his lower eyelids in turn and peered in.

"Nothing there."

"It was just soap," he said, blinking hard and putting his hands back in the water. He was mystified. Why was he crying? He sniffed at the cigar smoke again. It reminded him of his dad, who always had a cigar after Sunday lunch. Maybe he missed him? It seemed a ridiculous idea, but as he mulled it over he felt his eyes pricking again. He quickly started counting sevens. 124, 131, 138… He was grateful when Nel spoke.

"So how have we done with our first week? Except for knocking someone out, of course." She leaned in close to him and whispered this last bit into his ear.

He shrugged. "All right."

"You don't say much, do you? Your mum was right – anything could be going on in there." She tapped on his forehead. "Give me more, Joe."

He didn't know what she wanted, and so he shrugged again. His mum usually gave up when he shrugged. Nel muttered something to herself in Dutch, and then handed him back a plate.

"You missed a bit. Okay, let's try again. I'm a beginner at this too, you know. I can't guess what you're thinking, you need to help me out. Let's go through what we've done this week, and you can just tell me what you think."

"Well, there is one thing." He said it quietly, and without looking at her.

"Shit!"

He snorted. He liked it when she swore, but it was embarrassing. It reminded him of when they were in a café a couple of days ago, and she laughed so loud that everyone looked round at them.

"I would like to know what we're going to do for the rest of the summer. I like to have a plan. If I don't know, it makes me… well, things feel all weird. It makes my stomach ache."

"Okay, I see."

She turned back to the pan she was drying and didn't say anything for a few minutes. Joe waited for her to tell him off for being 'impertinent' (one of his dad's favourite words) but when she turned back she looked pleased.

"Okay. We can write down a plan for the rest of the holidays if you like? And we can have another plan too, for what you do every day. Like a timetable. We could use different coloured pens, make it pretty. See, I can tell you like that idea. Your whole face has cleared."

Joe was trying to understand why she was making such an effort. Especially after he'd thought such horrible thoughts about Jeroen. Why would she care so much? His eyes pricked again, and so he nodded his head and concentrated on the washing up.

Jeroen was flicking through a magazine when they went back into the living room, and Nel said they could 'leave him to it'. She fetched a felt tip and paper from her bedroom. First they drew up Nel and Joe's daily schedule.

- Nel awake at 7, drink coffee, start work at 7.30.
- Joe awake (just) at 10.
- Joe eats Choco Chippies for breakfast and makes Nel coffee to drink during her break (unless she's in the middle of something and then Joe can have the television on).
- Joe has free time until 12.

Nel wrote 'free time' on another piece of paper and put it aside.

- Lunch at café Van Dalen or lunch at home, soup (not tomato) or bread and ham (no tomatoes) or a burger or beans on toast. Etc. (all food to be approved in advance)
- Tuesday until Friday Nel at work in the café De Eland in the afternoon and Joe can choose whether he comes to the café, goes to the library or stays at home. Etc.
- Dinner 7pm – stew, pasta, macaroni cheese, burgers, meatballs, peas. NO mushrooms or tomatoes and any new vegetables to be okayed with Joe beforehand and not smuggled into the sauce.

Nel didn't know the word 'smuggle'. When Joe explained it for her he told her a long and fact-filled story about the popularity of wool smuggling in the 16th Century due to high excise taxes.

- On Nel's days off, Joe and Nel go somewhere exciting or Nel abandons Joe at Emmie's house and goes somewhere on her own.
- 9.30pm bedtime, or a bit later at the weekend if you're lucky.

Nel had used different colours for different parts of the plan – blue for mealtimes, red for her work at the café. The colour of these regular events looked like anchors. Next Nel drew a calendar of their remaining days together, with a box for each date. Tomorrow was Sunday, and then there were five full weeks before Joe flew home just before summer term started. He didn't like the look of all those white squares, and felt relieved when Nel started writing things in.

Tomorrow they were going to meet her other boyfriend Henk for lunch, and in the afternoon Nel was going to introduce Joe to her friend Maartje and her daughter Emmie in the next street. Nel then wrote in some other dates, some of which he knew about, and some of which he didn't.

Tomorrow Meet Henk for lunch, meet Emmie
August 1st Visit grandfather and grandmother

This was on a Monday morning, and Nel wrote it in four more times on all the Mondays in August.

August 6th bowling with Emmie
August 7th swimming
August 9th trip to theatre with my friend Jan
August 19th Nel's exhibition!!!
Saturday 3rd August Say goodbye to Joe ☹

Nel also told Joe he'd be staying with her friend Maartje and her daughter Emmie every Tuesday night. He guessed it might have something to do with Henk or Jeroen. Joe wasn't looking forward to meeting her. She was probably awful. Nel said Emmie was only thirteen – a whole year younger than him. *And* a girl.

By the time Nel had finished there were at least two certainties every week, and again Joe saw them like anchors. He wasn't sure how he felt about the trips to see his grandparents, and when he asked Nel why they were going every Monday she was evasive.

They finished by writing a 'free time' list, of all the things Joe could do when Nel was painting in the mornings, or whenever he was bored. It started with reading, drawing, watching TV, reading, writing letters, reading, reading or reading, and then it got even sillier. Nel added cooking dinner and practising backwards somersaults. But he had to admit that a couple of her ideas had promise. He especially liked the thought of drawing his own map of the weather in the local area, and keeping records as it changed. It was like having a new assignment at school. When they'd finished Nel put all the lists up on the fridge where he could look at them any time he wanted. Then she went to sit with Jeroen on the sofa. When Jeroen slipped his hand around Nel's waist, Joe thought it might be a good time to make his exit.

Before he picked up his book he sat up in bed and wrote his first letter to Podge.

Dear Podge,

(He'd started the first one 'Dear Ollie' but it had sounded silly and so he crumpled it up and started on a fresh sheet.)

Well, I've been here for almost a whole week now, and you won't believe what's happened. It's not as boring as I thought. The best thing ever is that my aunt nearly killed someone already. It was one of her boyfriends, because she's got two – an old one and a young one, I won't tell you their names because they're Dutch and I don't know how to spell them properly. Anyway, he was trying to cut his wrists so he'd got blood everywhere – it was a bloody mess, ha ha, you should have seen it. Tante said he didn't really want to kill himself but was trying to get some attention, but if that was true then I don't know why she had to hit him over the head to stop him doing it. I had to help her drag him into her bedroom and everything, he weighed a ton!!!

He's still alive, because he came to dinner tonight. I didn't get to see his scars because he wouldn't give me a good look at his wrists, he had really long sleeves on. What an idiot. Anyway, everything else is okay, the food here is pretty gross, the cornflakes are rank and I can't eat them. There's a really cool kind of chocolate called 'koetjesreep' (I just copied that from one of the wrappers on the floor), I'll bring one back for you if you're lucky. We went to the zoo and saw some new birds, I won't bore you with the names because I know you'll be rolling your eyes already. Let's just say they were pretty cool. I've been listening to the Cocteau Twins pretty much non-stop, and have already finished a book about the weather from the library. It was all right but the last one I read was better.

I'm completely dreading going to see my grandparents. I can hardly remember them. Tante says that her dad is an alcoholic, and she isn't speaking to her mum. Mum never tells me about stuff like that, Tante has told me about her love life and everything. I keep forgetting I'm meant to call her Nel. With only one 'l', but you just say it like 'Nell'.

Anyway, what's the news from Milton Keynes? Have I missed anything exciting? I bet not. I'm putting a tram ticket into the envelope so you can see what they look like, weird aren't they?

From Joe.

(He almost slipped here and put a kiss.)

He folded the letter and slipped it under his pillow. He didn't want Nel sneaking in and reading it before he woke up. He thought about the lists on the fridge. Knowing they were there did seem to calm down the butterflies in his stomach. He hadn't even realised how nervous he'd been until now. That night there was no tossing or turning, and no fractured dreams. The next morning, he felt like he'd slept for a whole day and two whole nights.

Joe had assumed his usual position in bed, his knees drawn up to his chest under the duvet, a book balanced on his knee caps, and his headphones on. He was swaying to the music, and one of his hands was moving almost imperceptibly – first his thumb and first two fingers, then a new wave of three starting from his index finger. One two three, two three four. Most of this album had a 3/4 time signature. These finger movements and a slight sway was the closest he'd ever come to dancing. His forehead was furrowed, as it usually was. His mum had told him it lost its creases when he was asleep – his muscles relaxed like calmed water – but he'd never seen it. Sometimes he tried to catch himself out in the mirror, but those dark lines were always there.

The door swung wide open and Nel peered in, taking him by surprise.

"What are you listening to?"

He frowned and lifted one of the headphones away from his ear.

"I said WHAT ARE YOU LISTENING TO? Don't tell me. Umm… could it be… oh, don't tell me…the Cocteau Triplets? The Cockatoo Twins?"

She pantomimed searching desperately for an answer, clutching at her forehead, shaking her hands. Joe snorted. She was always messing around with him, trying to make him laugh. Joe's part mostly involved snorting or rolling his eyes. It was like at mealtimes, when Nel would ask him what he fancied today, lobster in cinnamon cream? Lambs livers minced up with hazelnuts? Creamed snails? Midway through her pantomime, she had an idea.

"Shall we put your tape on the stereo? I thought we could have some coffee before we leave to meet Henk. You're not wearing that, are you?"

She didn't wait for his permission, and dived towards his Walkman. Joe wasn't sure about sharing Liz Fraser with Nel, but once she'd made her mind up about something it was pointless to argue. Nel disappeared with the tape and the music started. It was in the middle of Pandora. She turned it up louder. Joe listened to the song floating into his bedroom. It was odd to hear it come from outside, rather than being piped directly into his ears. Liz Fraser's voice skipped and glided through the rooms like a bird. It made him sad and happy at the same time.

"Are you cold?"

Nel had reappeared at his doorway. He continued staring at the wall and shook his head slowly. He felt like he was in a trance. Out of the corner of his eye, he saw her picking through the pile of clothes he'd left in the corner of the room.

"What clothes have you brought with you? Have you got anything smart? It's a posh café we're going to, you know. I don't want you to show me up…"

"Do I have to go? Can't I just stay here?" he whined.

Nel sighed. "No, you can't just stay here. We're meeting Maartje and Emmie afterwards, remember. You'll want Emmie to see you in your best clothes. Oh well, at least your hair is looking perfect today."

She had a glint in her eye, so he patted his hair with his hands to see what she meant. It was all over the place. A smirk twitched at the corners of his mouth. He focussed his eyes and looked up at her.

"I don't really like girls, you know. They're never interested in anything sensible. Just shoes and gossiping. They're pretty boring, really. It's scientifically proven that they have smaller brains, and that they can't..." He realised mid-sentence that Nel was a girl, or she had been once. He flushed and waited for her to be furious at him.

"Well, come on then, lazy, let's have a look at your shirts."

He sighed heavily and got out of bed. He went over to his suitcase and pulled out the only two items left inside – his 'smart shirts'. He'd chosen them from the shop himself, and thought the dark red one was pretty snazzy. It had a sheen to it, when you tilted the material the colours shifted. He'd never worn it – someone from school might've seen him and then he'd never hear the end of it. As he yanked them out, a pair of boxer shorts (lurking under the shirts) flew across the room and landed on one of Nel's bare feet. He flushed and snatched them back, screwing them up and throwing them under the desk.

An image popped into his mind uninvited – of Nel in her underwear. He replaced it immediately with his favourite fantasy – a girl in the sixth form called Callie. She wasn't the prettiest girl, or the most popular, but Joe felt she was the most beautiful by far. She had bright orange hair and ivory cheeks, and her freckles were almost paler than the rest of her, as if she were a photo in negative. She always wore her hair in two low pigtails, the black hair bands tangled with stray hairs. Joe wished he could get his hands on one of those pigtails, although he wasn't quite sure what he'd do with it. He pushed this image away too, and shook out his dark red shirt. He held it up by the sleeves.

"What about this one?"

"Oh, perfect. Although it might need a bit of an iron. Has Ineke trained you how to iron yet?"

Joe shook his head vigorously, demonstrating to Nel what a ridiculous idea this was.

"Oh well, not enough time to show you now. We'll save that exciting lesson for another day, eh? How about you pour your Tante a coffee while she slaves away for you."

The café wasn't far – they walked along the canals. Joe spotted a battered sofa on top of one huge boat, and a small black and grey dog lying on the prow of another. There was a navy blue boat called 'Sparling' – Joe liked the word and repeated it to himself as they walked. Later they passed a house with the windows wide open. There was a man with a big hairy belly lying on his back on his red sofa, fast asleep. Nobody would do that in Milton Keynes. He pointed the man out to Nel, and they both giggled.

They turned the corner into Spieglegracht, where the café was. Nel was telling Joe (again) how important it was that he behaved, when she squealed loudly. A man had slipped his hand round her and was squeezing her waist, a stern expression on his face. Joe looked around to see if there was anyone to help them, but Nel's face changed from shock to pleasure and Joe realised it wasn't a mugger, but Henk. Joe had thought he'd been well dressed for a mugger.

He wasn't what Joe had expected. Nel talked about him like he was some kind of movie star – rich, important, good looking... Joe had even described him as 'Henk the hunk' in a letter to Podge yesterday. He might have been rich and important but he certainly wasn't a hunk. His nose was too big and hooked. He was short too, with thinning hair. He did have creases around his eyes but he didn't look as old as Nel had made out. He greeted Nel in Dutch and kissed her on the cheeks three times – mwah, mwah, mwah – before turning to Joe.

"So, young man, I have heard lots of things about you. I hope you're hungry?"

His English wasn't as fluent as Nel's, despite his smart suit. Joe tried to think of something polite to say back – he could see Nel watching him anxiously.

"Yes, thank you sir. I could eat a horse."

At this, Henk pulled back from Joe and let out an alarming noise. It was a kind of roar – was it a sneeze? Joe waited to say, 'Gezondheid' (pronounced the Dutch way as his mother had taught him) but the noise continued and he realised that Henk was laughing.

"Well, I don't think they sell horses here, but they have lots of steaks. Maybe we could buy a whole cow instead for you?"

He exchanged a look with Nel and Nel smiled back, complicitly. Joe hated it when adults exchanged looks about you over your head, as if you wouldn't notice. He glowered and looked at his feet.

"Well, Henk, I'd like to eat a horse too, please. If there aren't any horses here then we'll just have to eat somewhere else, won't we Joe?"

Nel put her arm around Joe and squeezed him. He didn't respond, but he did feel less annoyed. Henk held out his arm and Nel took it so they could walk into the restaurant as a pair, and Joe trailed behind them.

The café did look posh – it had a black tiled floor and everything else was white. There were chocolates behind glass at the counter, and all the waitresses wore black uniforms with white pinafores. As they walked in, he noticed a couple looking at them – the woman whispered something to her husband and he nodded. Joe asked Nel why they were staring and she said, "Henk is in the newspapers sometimes".

Joe was bored by the conversation during the meal. Nel and Henk made an effort to talk in English, but Joe didn't understand much of what they said anyway. They kept mentioning names that meant nothing to him, and these people's 'work'. Their work was either 'interesting' or 'derivative'. His attention drifted. There was no music playing, just the buzz of the fridge at the back of the café and other customer's cutlery, quietly clinking. He tried to pretend he was listening to them, but he felt relieved when they switched to Dutch. The words sounded ugly coming from Henk, but Joe liked listening to Nel whether she was speaking English or Dutch. He'd tried to reproduce some of the throaty consonants in the bathroom last night, and Nel had called in, 'Is everything okay in there?'

Nel got agitated at one point during the meal. She raised her voice until an elderly lady at the next table looked over and tutted, causing Henk to put out his hand, as if he could turn her volume down by pressing on her shoulder. Joe amused himself by making up games. He ordered a burger, and he tried to pick up the thin fries in bunches of five, without counting them out beforehand. He got it right about 70% of the time. The fries were tasty – crispy and salty, and the burger was good too. It had a stupid pickle in it, which he removed, but luckily it didn't leave behind much of a taste stain. 'Taste stain' was a phrase he'd invented with Podge. Fried onions left a terrible stain once you'd pulled the slimy things out of a hot-dog, and he couldn't imagine eating pizza stained by pineapple chunks even after he'd picked every last one off.

He wished Podge were here. They could play their special version of I Spy. "I spy with my little eye, something with the third letter 'P'". In truth, Podge wasn't the best person to play this game with, as he regularly got his spellings wrong – with 'I' as the second letter of ceiling, and most amusingly 'M' as the last letter of comb, but Joe didn't have anyone else to play it with. After he'd finished his fries, he counted the pieces of cutlery in the room, the table legs, the toes, and finally as a special challenge the number of teeth. During this final calculation he stopped chewing, and Nel interrupted him right at the difficult part to ask him if his burger was okay. He grunted but had to start the calculation all over again.

Afterwards the waitress brought them yellow cakes moulded into seashell shapes and Nel had a glass of leaves and stalks in hot water. Joe turned down the offer of a sip as it smelt of toothpaste, and bit into his cake. It was soft, sweet and buttery. Nel said they were called 'financiers', a French word. As he munched, Henk started asking him questions. How did he like Amsterdam? He liked reading, did he? Was Nel treating him okay? Was he missing his family? Joe was able to answer most of these questions with an 'All right' or a nod or a shake of the head, and eventually Henk looked at Nel and laughed.

"You are a man of few words, yes Joe?"

Joe shrugged. It was an effort to concentrate on what Henk was saying. Sometimes he just didn't hear people properly. Was it because he wasn't interested? That's what his mum would say. He had to look at Henk's lips and imagine the words emerging one by one like bubbles. Counting the bubbles one by one, and then stringing them into a sentence. He'd rather drift off.

Where did he drift off to? To somewhere more private than this noisy room full of strange people and brash colours and interrupting smells. To somewhere tidier, to a place that asked nothing of him. Hank was still looking at him, and he felt a tightness in his chest. He asked Nel if he could go to the toilet. This was a trick he'd use when things got too much. If he wasn't careful, his body started to stiffen up and it got more difficult to breathe.

He couldn't remember when it had happened the first time. He did remember being in a supermarket with his mum – he can't have been more than five. It was really busy – maybe it was Christmas. The people and things around him had got brighter and noisier. He thought he was going to faint, and he started moaning to himself. His stomach hurt – everything hurt. He banged his forehead with the palm of one hand – it helped the pain, and for some reason the sound of skin hitting skin was comforting. His mum seemed just as disturbed by his behaviour as he was, and she left a whole trolley full of shopping in the aisle and carried him outside. He started feeling better as soon as the cold air hit his cheeks. He remembered that there was a big bunch of balloons outside, and he'd started to count them.

Joe found the café toilets and shut himself into a stall. The room smelt lemony, with a whiff of bleach. Podge's cat Brutus went mad around bleach, purring and winding between their legs excitedly. Joe put the toilet seat down and sat. Maybe he'd talk to his mum tonight. His dad had called him a few times, but he'd only spoken to her once. She'd sounded as if there was something wrong with her throat, and didn't say very much. After their short conversation his dad came back onto the phone and told Joe what he'd been doing during the day, what he'd had for lunch, what the weather was like. His droning voice was so familiar. If Joe pressed the phone to his ear and shut his eyes, he could almost imagine he was at home.

Joe counted the perforations along the edge of the square of toilet paper. Maybe he could be a mathematician when he grew up. He couldn't imagine being old enough to have a job. Most jobs sounded pretty boring to him. But maybe if he had a wife too, it wouldn't be so bad. A wife he could kiss when he left for work, like his dad kissed his mum. If his mum was in a good mood, that was.

Would a woman ever want to live with him? Would a girl ever want to kiss him? There were no signs of him getting a girlfriend at school. Even Podge had kissed a girl, when they'd played kiss or dare at Tom's house. It was Suzie Streeter, a girl with fine blonde hair the texture of candyfloss. Podge said her lips were really soft but her breath smelt of sour milk. He couldn't decide if he'd liked it or not. Joe was just starting to settle into a fantasy about Callie when he heard a man saying his name.

"Joe? Joseph?"

He thought of his dad first, and then remembered where he was. In a completely different country. It must have been Henk. He got up, flushed the toilet for appearance's sake and unlocked the door.

"We were worried you might have fallen into the toilet, Joe."

Henk smiled as if this was a joke, and so Joe snorted to be polite.

"I just need to wash my hands."

"Okay, as long as you are all right. We are going to get the bill."

They said their goodbyes, and headed towards Maartje's house. Nel linked arms with her nephew.

"So what did you think of Henk, then?"

Joe shrugged.

After a while, Nel tried again.

"Do you think he's a good man, Joe?"

She looked him in the eye pointedly. It was as if she was genuinely interested in what he had to say. He felt completely unqualified to answer. He'd only just met Henk. Hadn't Nel known him for years? Why would she need his opinion? Joe shrugged again and searched for something safe he could say.

"He asked me lots of questions which was good."

This seemed to satisfy her. So many of the questions that adults asked you were like a test. You got the answer right, and they left you alone, or you got it wrong and they asked more questions or got annoyed. Podge's mum was easy. She always wanted to hear good things – even if they were lies – her steak and kidney pudding was lovely, his cough was much better, he and Podge were going upstairs to do their homework. His mum was more complicated – sometimes she got annoyed when he gave her the 'right' answers. "I never know if I can believe you," she'd say, or, "Tell me what you really think for a change". It drove him mad when she said that. He wanted to say to her, "I did that last week, and you shouted at me!" He just couldn't win.

Maartje's building was dull red brick, tall and narrow, and had one of those massive hooks coming out of the wall at the top. Joe had devised various uses for it (a place to hang dead animals in the olden days to keep the meat fresh, or to catch suicidal people when they jump off the roof) before he'd asked

Nel what they really were. She'd said they were for moving big pieces of furniture into the house through the windows on a rope. Pretty boring. A few of them must have had a body hanging from them at some point.

They rang the bell and there was a buzzing noise and a click. The stairs were so narrow he could hardly fit his feet on them. Why didn't they make their stairs any wider in this country? Did Dutch people have smaller feet? When they reached the second floor landing, a girl opened the door to them. They were also hit by a sweet-smelling warm fog. Joe took a deep draught of it. Biscuits? Joe couldn't remember the last time his mum had baked anything. She used to, when he was younger. The girl's dark hair was pulled back into a tight ponytail. She wasn't smiling. Nel greeted her in Dutch and pulled her into a hug. Joe saw the girl stiffen and roll her eyes. He sniggered. Joe had developed various strategies for avoiding grown-up hugs – ducking away at the last minute, or coughing and pretending he was infectious, but the best was holding out his hand in an authoritative manner and accepting a handshake. He could tell Emmie about it later, although maybe it only worked for boys.

Emmie turned to him and said, "Hello Joe, I hope you like Gameboys." She had a distinct American accent. Before he could say anything back, Maartje appeared at the doorway beside Emmie. She had bleached white hair, pulled back into rows of tight braids. Joe thought she looked like a hippy. She also greeted Nel in Dutch, and Nel said in English, "Here he is!"

"So I see," said Maartje, and she held out her hand to him. "Pleased to meet you," she said. Her grip was firm, and she didn't smile either. Nel said something to Maartje in Dutch, and then she took him by surprise by kissing him on the forehead, a big smacker. She handed him his plastic bag of books and disappeared down the stairs. Joe watched her until she was out of sight. His cheeks burned. A kiss on the forehead – why couldn't she just shake his hand like Maartje? And right in front of Emmie as well.

Spending time at Maartje's turned out to be less painful than Joe had imagined. Emmie got straight back onto her Gameboy. She showed no signs of wanting to interact with Joe, which was a relief. Instead he got out one of his books and settled onto the far end of their big shapeless sofa. As he sat down he noticed that the grey jumper between them was actually a cat.

"What's his name?"

"It's a girl, stupid. She's called Miep. Don't tickle her on her belly, she'll bite you."

They'd never had any pets in Joe's family. Podge's moggie Brutus was the first cat he'd ever become acquainted with. Brutus was a great ginger brute, and Joe was terrified of him at first, but he watched Podge's mum stroke him and Podge's little sister poke him and he seemed to be pretty harmless. One day he worked up the courage to touch him along his back. He liked the softness of his fur under his fingertips, and was also encouraged by Brutus who arched up towards him. The cat seemed to be saying, "More please." In those days, everything else Joe did was wrong. He didn't listen to his teachers properly, he didn't care about his mum's feelings… He tried stroking Brutus under his chin (like Podge's mum did), and when the cat started purring Joe was hooked. From then on it became his mission to make Brutus happy.

It took Joe a while to work out that doing the same things to the cat every time didn't work. Once he scratched him just behind his ears and he went into ecstasies. It worked the second time too, but at his next visit the cat kept turning away from him. It completely stumped him. Was he applying a different amount of pressure? Did he smell of something different? He felt spurned and ignored Brutus until he went home. But then the very next day, Brutus sought him out and rubbed his cheeks up against Joe's hand until he started to stroke him. He loved the ear rubbing again. He wished cats were more predictable. But then human beings were *much* worse.

Emmie's cat Miep responded straight away to Joe's ear-rubbing, flipping her head upside-down and stretching out her claws. She even licked Joe's fingers with her delicate pink tongue. After five minutes of stroking, the tip of her tail started twitching, and Joe recognised this as something Brutus did when he meant, "Enough now". He went back to his book, feeling pleased with himself for understanding Miep's language. He could even communicate with Dutch cats.

Emmie flicked her eyes over in his direction a couple of times and then back to her game, expressionless. It was only ten minutes later, after a furious burst of clicking Gameboy buttons which culminated in her flinging the controls down, that she came to sit closer to him. Joe kept reading, hoping she might go away if he ignored her, but she started fiddling with a hole in the knee of her jeans. The grey parallel threads were showing, and he could see her pale skin. He felt the need to say something.

"Peregrine falcons keep their toes curled when they're in their nest so they don't crack their eggs with their talons."

"What's a penguin falcon?"

"Peregrine. A big bird of prey, like a kite or a buzzard, you know…"

"Buzzed?"

He sighed. Maybe this was what it was like to have a little sister. Podge was always complaining about his. Apparently she was infuriating – it was the only time Joe ever saw his friend properly angry. She'd come into his bedroom and ask if she could play with them, and Podge wouldn't say anything but his face would get more and more red until he'd storm from his room. He often ended up in the garden, where he'd pace up and down the gravel path, scuffing it with his shoes. He knew that if he didn't play with her, she'd run and tell on him, and then his mum would have a go at him.

How could he explain a peregrine falcon to Emmie? He looked in his bag, but he hadn't brought a bird book with him.

"Have you got a pen and paper? I'll draw you one."

Emmie shouted to her mum in Dutch. Maartje appeared a few minutes later with some paper and a beaker full of felt tips and pencils. She put them on the low glass table in front of the sofa, and Joe knelt on the carpet. He chose a dark grey pencil that was sharper than the others – most of them had snapped tips. Emmie watched as he drew an accurate outline of a peregrine, and then started to fill in the details.

He'd had a lot of practice at this. If you'd asked him to draw a horse he wouldn't have had a clue, but birds he could do. Birds, and clouds, but there didn't seem to be as much call for drawings of clouds. His mother had put the first one he'd done up on the fridge, but after that she'd just say, "That's nice, dear, what's this one called?" She didn't even listen properly when he told her the names – cumulus, cirrostratus, layers of altocumulus.

He glanced over at Emmie. She had a lock of her dark hair between her finger and thumb and was sucking on the ends. "Disgusting habit", his mother would have said. He wondered what her hair tasted like. He guessed it would be clean and appley. When he'd finished the drawing (not bad!) he wrote the words underneath, in neat capitals. He made a mistake halfway through and had to scribble a letter out, which made him cross. He had to pause and resist the urge to scrumple the whole thing up into a tiny ball and throw it across the room.

He couldn't get a purchase on the piece of paper to lift it from the table, and finally managed to slide a fingernail between it and the glass. He handed it to Emmie, saying the words again slowly. She nodded and said something in Dutch, something that sounded like "slichvk". She didn't smile, but Joe thought she seemed pleased.

"Is that the word in Dutch? Say it again, slower."

"Slecht – valk."

"Slichvk?"

"SLECH-VALK!"

Emmie threw her head back and started gasping rhythmically as if she was having a heart attack. Joe tried to think back to what he'd learnt in First Aid classes at school, but all he could remember was the look on Tom's face when the teacher asked him to give the (male) dummy the kiss of life. He was trying to remember what ABC stood for when he realised that Emmie was actually laughing. At his pronunciation, and at him. Bloody girls. Podge's dad was right – they're all the same. They seize every opportunity to put you down, to make you feel stupid.

He turned away from her and picked up his book again, trying to concentrate on the words. Emmie stopped making the odd noise as suddenly as she'd begun, and Joe watched her from the corner of his eye. She picked up the drawing again and held it close to her eyes.

"What were the other ones you said? Kite? Buzzed?"

He ignored her.

"Oi, Joe."

She scraped his face with the edge of the paper, infuriating him further. He frowned. When would Nel be back to pick him up? Maybe he could just leave and find his own way back to her house, and wait for her on the doorstep like Jeroen.

Emmie tried a new tactic. "If you draw me those birds, I'll show you my collection. It's up to you, though." She feigned disinterest, turning back to her Gameboy.

"What collection?"

"Ah, you'll have to wait and see. It might be scarves from around the world, it might be tiny dogs, it could be anything!" She flung her hands out.

Joe didn't look at her, but he raised his eyebrows and then snorted. He put down his book and chose a dark red pencil.

By the time they arrived at his grandparents' house, Joe felt like a shaken-up can of coke. Nel had borrowed Maartje's car for the journey and didn't seem to be familiar with the concept of gears – every time she changed up or down there was a violent jerk. That was bad enough, but then there were the obstacles she noticed at the very last minute – a waddling line of ducks, an old man inching his way across the road with a stick – or the times she braked suddenly for no reason. He thought he could use the forty minute drive to read his book, but he started feeling sick and had to look at the horizon to settle his stomach. His dad had taught him that trick. Nel didn't seem to be in a talkative mood, so when his nausea had passed Joe let his eyes rest on the moving scenery and let his mind wander. Long car journeys were always a good time to think.

He could hardly believe it was already day sixteen of his trip to Amsterdam. His visit was going to last forty two days altogether, so he was eight twenty–firsts of the way through. He had visited Emmie twice more, and Nel took them out bowling (Joe was terrible and Emmie was brilliant). They'd invented a few drawing games between them, and Emmie had started to teach Joe Dutch. He wasn't making progress as quickly as he would have liked, but he'd already switched all his reading to Dutch (from the children's section in the library) and spent his evenings watching Dutch television or asking Nel the Dutch word for various objects around the house. Joe hadn't mentioned Emmie in his letters to Podge yet. He wasn't really sure how to bring the subject up – "I've got a mate now, but it's not a boy…", "I've found a cool girl to hang out with here, but it's not what you think…" He could hear Podge sniggering behind his hand, whatever words he chose. Better to leave her out of the letters for now.

Joe had also spent more time with Jeroen, and at the café where Nel worked, where he'd made friends with a bedraggled dog that half-belonged to the owner. Joe would sit at the canal-side and the dog wouldn't leave his side, even when Joe didn't slip him any tasty tidbits under the table. He hadn't seen Henk again, except when he picked Nel up at the flat, but heard Nel talking to him on the phone. They talked for ages, much longer than he heard her talking to Jeroen. He wasn't sure who he liked best – Jeroen was definitely cooler, but Nel seemed happier when she was talking to Henk. When Jeroen was there she acted like she was looking after two teenagers. Joe also couldn't help worrying that Nel would need to hit him over the head again, and this time she might really kill him.

Joe had been getting on okay with Nel. It was easier than living at home, anyway. Nel didn't hassle him about how he was doing things or what he was saying. At home, every time he grunted his mum would say, "Is there a caveman in the room?" and every time he put his satchel or a book down in the living room, even if it was just for a moment, his dad would tell him to put it away. Nel let him say whatever he wanted to. She'd told him stories about her alcoholic father (his grandfather) although she didn't say much about her mum, except that she 'hated her guts'.

Nel was all right, really, as adults went. At least he was allowed to be himself. He was realising how many things he stopped himself from saying or doing at home and at school to stay out of trouble. It was most of his personality! When he went back to Milton Keynes, he was determined not to change back again. His parents would just have to get used to it.

Nel announced they were nearly there. Joe realised how quiet she'd been during the journey. He felt a stab of guilt about his selfishness – his mum was always telling him he never thought about anyone other than himself. She thought he was the kind of person who didn't care, and it just wasn't true. He just never knew the right thing to say. What could he say to Nel now? "I've observed that you're very quiet?" That didn't sound right. "What are you thinking about?" Too nosey. At least he'd had the thought – maybe that meant he wasn't such a terrible person.

Nel let out a huge sigh and glanced at her watch. Joe looked at his too. It was just before eleven a.m. Nel had told Joe that she always arranged to meet her father mid–morning – this gave him a chance to get over the worst of his hangover, but it was also before he got too drunk again. Nel had said they were probably safe to stay for lunch, but by the late afternoon her father became 'less predictable'. Joe had never met a real live alcoholic before. Unless you counted the men at the bus station in Milton Keynes, swigging from cans of strong lager at eight o'clock in the morning.

Nel pulled into a cul-de-sac and parked the car (jerkily) on the curb. The row of houses looked ordinary – similar to the row of terraces round the corner from Joe's house at home. Before Nel had even switched off the engine a woman emerged from a blue door, smiling and waving madly. Joe thought she looked nice enough – could this be the woman who Nel wanted to strangle? Nel smiled curtly and turned to Joe, asking him to remember all his stuff. He'd brought a couple of books in case of emergencies, which his mum would never have allowed him to do. Nel had brought a huge bunch of flowers, which confused Joe too – if she hated her mum so much, then why not get a smaller bunch? They got out of the car and Nel linked her arm through his. Usually he would have pulled his arm away, but today he let her hold on to him.

His Grandma did a strange curtsey in front of him.

"Goedemorgen, Joe."

"Goedemorgen, Oma."

He was proud of his pronunciation – 'goo-dah-morg-eh oh-ma'. He'd practised it with Emmie. Nel raised an impressed eyebrow at him, which pleased him. His grandmother then turned to Nel.

"Nelika."

"Moeder."

His grandmother leaned in to embrace Nel, and Joe watched her stiffen. She received her mother's tight kiss on her cheek as if it was an injection.

An old man came to the door, and Nel looked past her mother and smiled warmly. The man's eyes were glittering in the light. Maybe this was what people meant when they said, 'His eyes were twinkling'? Joe had read the phrase in a book a couple of times and it had mystified him. When he caught sight of Joe, he let out a strangled noise.

"Waaaarrrrrrrrghh!"

He pushed past his wife and grasped the tops of Joe's arms, squeezing hard, and inspected his face. As he came closer, Joe could smell something sweet. He was surprised at how short his grandfather was – he must have been a good inch shorter than Joe, the same height as his wife. When Nel had talked about him, he'd imagined a much bigger man – not this barrel-chested, shrunken old person with a face full of wrinkles. His grandfather was still searching his face, and Joe didn't know where to look. All the time he was saying, "Mow-ye kline-sown, mow-ye kline-sown". Joe was starting to wonder if he would ever let go of him when his grandmother announced, "Let us drink some coffee," in halting English. His grandfather finished his appraisal with a serious nod (Joe felt he'd been approved), and he moved on to greet his daughter. Joe watched their tight hug, and Nel's eyes got shiny. She linked her arm through her father's and they walked towards the house, where Joe was hoping there might be cake.

There was certainly cake. On their way through Joe caught sight of the kitchen, which was gleaming. 'Not a thing out of place' as his dad would boast about his office after he'd tidied it up, even though it had been pretty tidy before, as far as Joe could see. In the living room the light struggled to penetrate the thick net curtains. The velvety three piece suite was a deep sage green, and there were fringed mustard cushions. Podge called this colour 'cat sick yellow', which always made Joe feel slightly queasy. The room was littered with lamps – standard ones, wall-mounted ones, and a bright orange one next to the television.

A low table in the middle of the room was sagging under the weight of food. Joe wondered if they were expecting anyone else. He counted three types of cake (one of them looked like lemon drizzle – his favourite), open sandwiches with cheese and ham, something that looked like meatballs, tiny pancakes covered in sugar… Joe found himself salivating. He wished he could take the whole lot home to Nel's house – he could survive on this for the rest of his stay. Nel couldn't even make him baked beans on toast without sprinkling 'a little cheese' on top, just to see if he liked it. It had tasted all right, but that wasn't the point.

His grandfather caught Joe eying the food and winked at him. Once Joe had loaded his plate and they'd all sat down, his grandmother started asking him questions in awkward English. Did he like school? Who were his friends? What were his hobbies? It got in the way of eating which was annoying, but she did seem interested in his answers. It was funny when she didn't understand his words and repeated them back in her strong accent. He glanced over at Nel every so often – she was talking rapidly in Dutch to her father and gulping her coffee. His grandfather was drinking coffee too, and Joe watched as he added an amber coloured liquid from a pewter flask. He poured the last of it into his coffee and then went to refill it from a cut-glass decanter. When he saw Joe watching him he winked again, and Joe looked quickly away. Weren't alcoholics meant to hide their drinking?

He told his grandmother about Podge and about how much he hated P.E. as he munched on his cake. The coffee cake was a bit dry, but the lemon one was beautiful. Would it be rude to put half of his coffee piece back and take a second slice of the lemon instead? He imagined his mum rolling her eyes at him, and so decided against it.

After Joe's grandmother exhausted her English, she left the room and returned hefting two photo albums. She sat next to Joe on the sofa and he could smell her – a clean flowery scent, like soap or talcum powder. She laid the first heavy book flat on his lap. The photos fascinated him, despite being mostly of people he didn't know wearing weird clothes. His mum's aunts and uncles, his grandparent's friends... There were a lot of

74

wedding photos – family groups with the women in big floppy hats and the men in old-fashioned suits.

His grandmother talked him through every photo, "This is Neelie, your mother's aunt, and this is my friend from work." She asked Nel for an English word every so often – the word for 'cousin' or 'purple'. The ones of his mum were the most interesting. In his favourite she was in a sunny garden, and had her head thrown back and her mouth open. She was laughing. He couldn't remember seeing her like that. Once she'd laughed over a board game they played at Christmas (after she'd drunk most of a bottle of wine), and once they'd gone to see a play at the local theatre which she thought was hilarious. Should he have tried to make her laugh more?

In the other photos, his mum had a big smile on her face, but it was the same smile she used when they had guests over. She wasn't smiling because she was happy, but because she'd been told to smile. Every photo was the same. But Nel, much younger, and much darker, didn't smile in any of the photographs. In earlier photos she sometimes wore a mischievous grin. But as Joe turned the pages she got sullen, grumpy. After a while she disappeared from the photos altogether, except a rare glimpse of her looking uncomfortable in a pretty dress at weddings and parties.

His grandmother found some of the photos funny, and once or twice she lifted the heavy book from Joe's knees and turned it around to show her daughter. Nel hardly looked up, and she put on the same face Joe had seen in the photographs. Joe started to feel sorry for his grandmother. Could she really have been such a terrible mother? He didn't want to disagree with Nel, it made him uneasy. They were nearly at the end of the second album when his grandfather got up, steadied himself on the chair arm and beckoned to Joe.

"He'd like to show you something, Joe. Are you okay to go upstairs with him on your own?" Nel asked.

He found himself full of a sudden dislike for his grandmother. He nodded and got up without thanking her.

His grandfather put a hand on his shoulder and steered him up the stairs. They stopped in front of a landing door. Joe could smell something sweet emanating from his grandfather again, as if he was surrounded by a force field. Was it the booze? He wished he was allowed to ask him the questions he wanted to ask. Do you keep a bottle in the toilet cistern? How expensive is it? Do you want to stop? How do you feel in the mornings? Does it make you sad? When he was younger he would have just asked them, but now he was fourteen and knew better.

Joe had asked Nel a few of these 'inappropriate questions', and so far she hadn't been annoyed at him. "Why have you got two boyfriends?" was last night's example. She explained that Henk paid for her apartment, and helped her out with her art, and had a wife. It was a helpful arrangement, but it also made her feel bad about herself, as if she was using Henk. She told him it was like when you knew someone was letting you win at a board game. Jeroen could be so needy sometimes, and being with him made her feel better – as if she was doing him a favour. And she did love them both in different ways, and she knew they both loved her. Joe also asked her why Henk didn't know about Jeroen. Henk hadn't said she *couldn't* see anyone else, he was married after all. It was just something they didn't really discuss. It all seemed very complicated to Joe. He didn't understand why she couldn't just choose one boyfriend – two was greedy.

Before opening the door, Joe's grandfather held his hand up and paused, building up the tension. Joe felt like making the noise of a drumroll but decided against it as he wasn't sure they had drumrolls in Holland. His grandfather might have thought he was mad. All of a sudden (making Joe jump) he flung the door open and motioned for Joe to go inside.

The door opened onto a different universe. A huge waist-high table filled the room, leaving narrow corridors. Every inch of the table was covered. Joe supposed you would call it a model railway, but it was more like this swathe of miniature town and countryside only happened to contain a few lengths of track. At one side of the room, over by the window, was Joe's grandfather's work desk, and floor-to-ceiling cabinets with hundreds of tiny drawers.

Joe moved into the room to get a closer look. Here was a miniature row of shops – the butcher with his striped apron and cuts of meat in the window, and the fruit and veg shop with piles of lemons and oranges out the front. Here was a circus, with tigers and an elephant in the big top, and here on the other side was a farm, with sheep and cows and tiny orchards. Joe was drawn to the graveyard, where amongst other macabre miniatures he found a skeleton hiding behind a tree. He pointed at it and his grandfather looked delighted.

When he had looked at everything, his grandfather shouted, "Joe!" before turning off the lights and flicking some switches underneath the table. After a moment of darkness, the miniature landscape came to life. The streetlights had tiny bulbs inside them, and the houses' windows became warm yellow squares. The football stadium was floodlit, and the fairground was a riot of colour. Even the Ferris wheel was moving round, the individual seats swinging gently and giving their tiny riders an amazing view. And there was the train! As it travelled around its kingdom, Joe imagined himself inside one of the tiny carriages. He wanted to share this with his grandfather and wished he could speak more Dutch than his current handful of words. If only Emmie had taught him some more useful phrases than, "The giraffe has a pain in its knees" or "You have a smelly bum". He wasn't sure he'd be able to work either of these phrases into conversation.

Joe's grandfather pointed to a streetlamp that had gone out, and invited Joe over to his work table. Joe watched him while he fitted a new bulb – using a funny pair of glasses which magnified everything. Then he slid open the drawers one by one to show Joe what was inside – the green spongy material to make trees from, skin-coloured plastic people, sheep, wheels... Joe felt like he could stay in that room forever. There was so much to explore and so many things he could make – he would never get tired of it.

His grandfather was showing Joe how to paint a person when there was a scream from downstairs. Joe looked at his grandfather with wide eyes. His grandfather looked back down and calmly put a few final touches to the little man. It was only after he'd blown on the man, put him in a tiny envelope and given it to Joe that he sighed and rolled his eyes. He put his hand on Joe's shoulder again and guided him back down the stairs.

As they descended there was a loud crash. Joe's grandfather gestured that Joe should wait behind him as he opened the door to the living room. Joe could see past him into the room. His grandmother was sitting on the sofa, her knees pressed tightly together and her shoulders hunched up. On the floor beside her feet was a pile of white china shards, underneath squashed lumps of cake. Nel was across the room, holding a second plate as if it were a custard pie. When her dad came in she looked at him in shock, and put it back onto the table. She looked back at her mother and opened her mouth, as if she was about to try and explain something for the twentieth time, but instead she paused and took a deep breath. She let out a long whistling sigh, and turned to her dad. Joe recognised the Dutch word for 'sorry'. Then she looked at Joe.

"We're going home now, Joe. Do you have your things?"

Her voice sounded normal but her face looked weird. Joe said goodbye to his grandparents. His grandmother pecked him sharply on the cheek, hardly looking at him, and his grandfather's eyes filled with tears. He squeezed Joe into a hug so tight that his arm ached afterwards. When they'd started on their journey home, Nel started to cry. Joe looked over and saw tears streaming down her face. She fumbled about one-handed in the glove compartment for a tissue. Joe wondered how much liquid there would be if he caught every tear in a cup. How salty would tears taste if you gulped a mouthful of them down? Would they taste sad?

Her crying reminded him of the way his mum cried, but his mum was even quieter. Years ago he'd gone downstairs for a glass of water in the middle of the night, and he'd found her sitting alone in the living room, in front of the TV with the sound turned down. She was in floods of tears. She'd caught him gaping at her and had got angry, accusing him of spying on her.

After that first time he'd got into the habit of checking on her. He couldn't help it – he'd wake from fractious dreams at one a.m. and lie there with his eyes wide open. He couldn't get back to sleep until after he'd been downstairs. He'd tiptoe down the stairs, avoiding the creaky steps, and carefully peer around the door. She didn't catch him again. He'd found her crying a few times every month for a while, but over time he caught her less and less often. Gradually he started to sleep through the night again.

Once in a while he'd still wake in the night and need to creep downstairs before he could settle back to sleep. The living room had been empty for years, but then he'd found her there twice in the past few months. The second time, she had her head in her hands and the TV wasn't even on.

Nel was still crying. What could he do to make it better? What would adults say in a situation like this? Podge was always crying, especially when they were round his house – he wasn't stupid enough to do it at school. Joe had found that the best strategy was to completely ignore him until the worst of it was over, and then try and distract him by talking to him about something completely unrelated. Would that work now? Maybe Nel would feel better if she knew he was on her side?

"I liked grandfather best."

To Joe's horror, the crying intensified. Although she did glance over at him and rubbed him briskly on his knee, so maybe he had said the right thing after all. Still, he didn't want to make her cry any harder, so he kept quiet for the rest of the journey. She cried all the way home, and then all the way through unlocking the door, walking up the stairs, taking off her coat and putting the kettle on.

"Do you want anything to eat or drink, darling?"

Her voice was thick.

"No thank you."

He thought wistfully of the table groaning with cake back at his grandparent's house. If only he'd thought to smuggle some away in his pockets!

Nel stroked Joe's cheek with her thumb as if she were rubbing away a smudge.

"I'm going to my room now to be miserable. I'm all right, so don't worry about me, okay?"

Joe nodded and she disappeared. He was worried. When would she stop crying? Would she get dehydrated? Was it his fault for going upstairs with his grandfather and leaving the two of them alone? He sat on the sofa and wished that Nel had a cat. He was all alone. All alone in a country he didn't belong in. He felt a surge of anger towards his mum. Why did she send him here in the first place? Why wouldn't she talk to him on the phone? He was getting sick of the excuses his dad kept giving him. 'She's just popped out to get some milk', or 'Your mother's got a bit of a headache today, son. She passes on her love'. A fat lot of good that was to him. Her second hand love. She should be here cooking his tea for him, washing his clothes, like a proper mum.

He felt really sorry for himself then and made a mental list of the horrible things she'd done to him. There was that time she didn't turn up for his school play, and that awful time he caught her reading his diary. She really was the worst mum in the world. Eventually tears of his own start plopping onto his open book.

This made him even more angry. She was never there, she never wanted to know what kind of a day he'd had, or how he was feeling. Now she was in a different bloody country. Maybe that was what she'd wanted all along. Maybe she never even wanted him in the first place. She never had any more children. Maybe she regretted having him from the day he was born. He didn't care about her, anyway. He'd leave home as soon as he could, then she'd be sorry. Maybe he'd live in Holland. She'd miss him then.

After a disturbed night and an extra hour in bed (despite the bright sun streaming in at the window) Joe knocked before walking into Nel's room as usual. He was used to finding her at work on her canvasses, and he'd go over to check on the painting's progress before making her a cup of coffee. It had become their morning ritual, and it pleased Joe that he was able to do something useful for her. This morning, she wasn't there. He assumed she was in the bathroom, and only caught sight of the lump in the duvet as he was walking out. She didn't make a noise and he wondered if she was pretending to be asleep until he left the room and left her in peace. He made himself a milky coffee instead, and drank it alone in his bedroom.

With Nel cocooned in her room, at first Joe felt a giddy sense of freedom. He could still remember the first time his parents had trusted him to stay at home on his own for half an hour while they popped out to the shops. It felt so luxurious – to know that the whole house was his domain. Reading in an empty house was a real treat. The words tasted better, somehow. When there were other people in the house he could hear their activity, and it snagged his attention.

But after a few hours, after he'd finished 'Meteorology for Scientists and Engineers' and started 'Tornados', made himself a cheese sandwich, and written a letter to his parents, he realised something. He wanted Nel to get up! He wasn't sure why. They never talked to each other much in the mornings anyway – she'd get on with her work and he'd get on with his reading – but it just didn't feel the same somehow, knowing she was in there under her duvet rather than working at her painting.

When she did get up, mid-afternoon, she shuffled into the living room in her dressing gown and ruffled him on the head.

"Are you bored, Joey? Would you like to go and see Emmie early today? You could play computer games?"

Joe shrugged.

"I'll take that as a yes. Do you want me to walk you there?"

He shook his head. He wanted to ask her how she was, but it was too embarrassing. He focussed on something practical instead.

"Are you going to lose your job?"

"Oh, no, no, no. I know I should have called. I'll give them a ring tomorrow, okay? Pack your bag and I'll see you down the stairs."

He went to Emmie's, and they went to the supermarket with her mum and then stopped off to eat ice-cream. Joe had two scoops of caramel, the best he'd ever tasted.

The next day he went over to Emmie's as well, and the next. Nel was meant to go into work, and meet Henk, and she didn't do either. Jeroen visited, but instead of drinking coffee in the living room they disappeared into her room and Nel only came out to send Joe to the library for a couple of hours. Joe thought they were probably going to have sex, and so he got out of the flat as quickly as he could and stayed out for three hours just in case. It was only after Jeroen had gone home that Nel started to perk up. She stayed in her dressing gown, but she had a shower, and then made French toast. She managed to get tomato sauce on her forehead, and Joe sniggered at her until she smeared some on his cheek.

That evening Nel cooked Joe his favourite meal – sausages and mash – following Joe's strict specifications as closely as she could. Ordinary sausages with none of that 'herby rubbish' in them, mashed potato made with lots of butter and no milk, and gravy made with gravy granules. If they *had* to have vegetables, then thinly sliced carrots were acceptable. There was even ice-cream and strawberry sauce for afters.

When they'd finished the washing up (Nel left a blob of soap foam on her nose for the duration to keep Joe amused), Nel put the Cocteau Twins on the stereo and suggested they play Scrabble. She didn't say so, but Joe guessed she felt guilty about her days in bed. Joe thrashed her twice, but the third game was more evenly matched. Nel had been sipping from a big glass of white wine, and after the Scrabble she started talking to him about her love life.

Usually Joe got bored when grown-ups talked to him for more than a few minutes. They'd either talk about subjects he had no interest in (like politics or gardening), or they'd asked him questions he didn't want to answer (what did you do at school today? or, when are you going to tidy your room?) His mum had a habit of cornering him when she wanted to complain about something, and she talked at him rather than to him. He told Podge that one of these days he was going to make a cardboard cut-out of himself and stick a tape recorder to the back of it, one that had a recording of him saying, 'Uh huh', and, 'Yes, Mum', at random intervals. Or, 'I know what you mean.' This is what his mum would say to her friends on the phone every thirty seconds, for what sometimes felt like hours.

Nel was different. She talked to him as if he was really there and kept checking that he understood what she meant, as if it was important to her. Usually when people talked about relationships it went completely over his head, like listening to the car mechanic tell his dad what was wrong with his Volvo. The other difference in listening to Nel was he wanted to help her. Maybe if he could understand enough about what was going on he could help her solve her dilemma, like a maths problem.

First Nel gave him a potted history of her love life. She said she'd always found it easy to get boyfriends. She made Joe blush violently by saying it was because she had 'good tits and good hair'. She also said it helped that she was a daddy's girl. Joe found it difficult to understand, but apparently she'd become an expert in getting her dad to approve of her while she was growing up, especially as she didn't like her mum very much. These skills made it easy for her to get men to like her when she was older. She said it helped if you pretended to be a teensy bit stupid (Joe definitely didn't understand why men would want women to be stupid, even when Nel tried to explain.)

When she was a teenager, she was desperate to get out of the house and away from her mum. She was younger than Joe when she got her first serious boyfriend, Geert. Before long she was spending most of her time at his house, learning how to be the perfect girlfriend. She showed an interest in Geert's boring comic collection, and complimented him on his boring drawings. She asked him for help with her homework, even though she already knew the answers. She wooed Geert's parents too. Geert's mum would bake her special biscuits and cakes, and his dad gave them money to go to the cinema or roller skating. After a couple of years Geert moved to a different city. Nel was surprised to find that she hardly missed him at all, and she found a replacement within a week. Then she set about learning how to keep the new boyfriend (and his parents) happy.

After a few years, she was thoroughly sick and tired of keeping everyone happy. She told Joe all the pretending 'made her head hurt', and she was starting to forget who she was. She needed to find a solution before she went mad, so she begun seeing other boys behind her regular boyfriend's back. These boys were different. She didn't want to spend time with their families – most of them were even more dysfunctional than hers. These boys had mothers who smoked dope all day long, or five younger brothers and sisters crammed into a three bedroom flat. Their homes felt like empty shells, with nobody there (or nobody who cared). Nel would arrange to meet these boys in a derelict house and they'd have sex and smoke and drink – just enough to 'take the edge off things'. She'd spend whole afternoons shoplifting or snogging these boys at the back of a cinema, and then she'd go home to her boyfriend's and play Monopoly with the whole family in front of an open fire.

This pattern continued until she was seventeen, when she moved in with one of the 'nice boyfriends'. She carried on seeing the 'bad ones' on the side. Sometimes things got muddled – one of her nice boyfriends hit her, and then one of her bad boyfriends got his life together and asked her to marry him (she said no), but mostly they stayed in their boxes. The good boyfriends never knew about the bad ones, and the bad ones usually knew about the good ones. Nel said the bad ones never cared very much, unless they were jealous types, in which case she'd just find someone else.

This arrangement worked pretty well for a long time. In her early twenties she was living with a nice man called Jurgen, who'd helped support her as she worked her way through Art

College. She'd do her painting in the morning, and work in the afternoon – or see one of her boyfriends. Then Jurgen started working from home, and Nel realised it was impossible to paint with him in the house. She just couldn't concentrate with him in another room, even if he didn't make a sound. And then he asked her to marry him as well.

She moved out, and a few weeks later met Henk at a local art gallery. They got talking over a piece they both admired, and Henk showed interest in Nel's own paintings. They were just round the corner from her tiny bedsit, and she took him back there after the show. He showed a genuine admiration for her work, and then, as Nel put it, for her good tits and good hair.

Henk told Nel about his wife right away. He didn't seem to fit into the bad boyfriend category, because he already had a very good job and a nice house and children and a dog. He wasn't nice boyfriend material either, because he was clear that he never wanted to leave his wife. He came up with a proposal – he'd find Nel a (bigger) place of her own, and pay the rent on it, so she could focus on her painting. He had always secretly wanted to be an art dealer, but had made his fortune by being a financial advisor to rich and famous people instead. He wanted to see her grow as an artist, to be her patron. This was the story they told each other, but Nel said he also wanted a little depravity in his life – someone he could fuck in secret while his wife, blissfully unaware, organised birthday parties for his children. (Joe was shocked when she used the f-word.) But the best thing, she said, was that she had her own space. She became a proper artist on the day that she moved into this flat.

And here she was, seven years later, with the same set up. Henk had paid for this place for all that time, and Nel covered her food and bills with her job in the café, waitressing.

There had been several Jeroens. Jeroen himself had been around for almost a year now, and there'd been some overlap – Nel counted them off on her fingers – Rikke, Nicolaas, another Nicolaas... They'd all been unsuitable in a variety of ways, except Pieter. Nel said she really liked him, but he couldn't take the situation with Henk. He'd said he loved her, and she thought she might have loved him too, but he was too poor – they would've had to move into a single bedroom flat, and where would her canvasses go? So he left, and was replaced by a methadone addict. Jeroen was working out okay so far, except for his outbursts, but then all relationships had problems, didn't they?

By this point in the story, Nel had refilled her glass and there was only a dribble of wine left in the bottom. Nel had allowed Joe half a glass, but he'd only managed a few gulps before the acrid taste made him gag. Nel put down her glass and concluded that things had worked out okay, but then she sighed. A deep sigh – it made Joe sad. In a smaller voice, she admitted that she wasn't happy at all. She had her freedom, but it wasn't a true freedom, she was paying for it by fucking Henk. Not that she minded fucking Henk, but she didn't have a *choice* in the matter. What if one day his wife found out? Or what if Henk started treating her badly? She would have to choose between forgiving him and becoming homeless – becoming an artist with nowhere to make her art. And that would mean she wasn't an artist at all, and if she wasn't an artist then who was she?

She looked directly at Joe, as if this last question was the whole point of everything she'd said. He felt her eyes burn into him and he tried to concentrate. What was the question again? If she wasn't an artist then who was she?

"Just Nel?" he tried.

She smiled, took his hand and kissed it.

"Just Nel. Yes, maybe that wouldn't be so bad. Just Nel."

She picked up her empty glass of wine and brandished it at him.

"Here's to Just Nel. And Just Joe. Now if I don't go to bed immediately I shall fall asleep right now and right here."

She put her glass on the table, and they retired to their separate rooms.

Joe tried to read his new tornadoes book in bed, but he couldn't concentrate. He turned off the light and lay there in the dark, thinking about Nel's relationships as if they were a scientific problem. He wanted to solve it for her, to remove her unhappiness, but whenever he started to make progress he came up against a question that he didn't know the answer to.

Maybe she could get a job that paid lots of money, work for a few years and then buy herself a house? He didn't know how much houses cost in Amsterdam. Could she find a man who'd give her the money to make her art and not expect anything in return? Would the government give her any money? He concentrated for ages on her finances, because when he started thinking about why Nel was in any of her relationships (especially with the 'bad boys') he got confused. If Nel could live on her own, without any Henks or Jeroens around, would she be happy? Or would she be lonely? Was she better off in these jumbled relationships or out of them?

Joe was dismayed by his lack of knowledge. What qualified him to tackle her relationship problems? He'd liked a girl called Julie at school for a whole term, and he hadn't even been able to look at her when she passed him in the hall. Once she was at her locker and asked loudly if anyone had got a pen. He fumbled about in his bag, his hand shaking, but by the time he managed to produce one she'd already got one from someone else and had disappeared off down the corridor. That was the sum total of his experience with relationships. Pathetic. What did he know about anything? A load of clouds, and birds, and the inner workings of the combustion engine. How was any of that any good to Nel? Or anyone?

He felt so bad about himself that he wanted to cry. Instead he wrote a letter to his mum, one he knew he'd never post. "I miss your cups of tea, Mum," he wrote. "Nel doesn't make them like you. I miss the stupid scratchy blanket on the back of the sofa that I put around my legs when it's cold in the evening. I miss being able to watch proper television, and the smell of my shampoo, and my own bed. And I miss you, Mum." And then he ripped the paper up into tiny pieces and sprinkled them into his wastepaper bin. He lay back on his pillow with his eyes wide open and ghost bits of paper floated in front of his eyes – they looked like dandruff. He forced his eyes shut and waves of sleepiness washed over him. He decided to think about Nel's problem tomorrow – maybe he could draw a diagram, or write some lists.

That night he found himself back in his old nightmare. He hadn't had it for years – not since his bad patch at school, before he met Podge. In the dream, he was lost in a huge, grand hotel, wandering down endless corridors lined with doors. The whole dream was infused with a sense of unease, as if things were going to go terribly wrong at any minute. At one point he could see down over a balcony to a massive ballroom with a chandelier, full of dancers. He was lost and alone. He wandered the corridors, wondering if he should try one of the hundreds of doors. Would anyone help him? He knew that there must be kind, friendly people inside some of the rooms, but how would he know which door to open? They all looked the same from the outside…

After what seemed like hours of getting more lost and more panicky, he chose a door. He flung it wide, and inside was a seething mass of naked bodies. He didn't want to look closer, but he couldn't stop himself. When he did, he saw that the bodies were joined together into a terrible monster – limbs joined to limbs, heads joined to heads. There were eyes, all looking at him, and lots of teeth. And then the mouths all opened and a noise came out, a kind of howl, and the thing started scuttling towards him, fast. This was where the dream ended, and he woke up – sweating, his heart beating hard.

The next morning he woke up feeling terrible. He hadn't got much sleep after his nightmare, and he was afraid he might have ended up back in the hotel. This had happened to him once when he was much younger. He'd woken up terrified, run to his parent's bedroom, and his dad had taken him back to bed and even read him a story to calm him down. The second time the dream had been even more petrifying. When he'd run back into his parent's room again his mum had got angry and shouted at him. He went back to his bedroom in tears, and sat upright until it got light so he wouldn't have to go back to the dream.

He hated the idea of not being in control of his dreams. Why did they even exist? They seemed pretty pointless, like a lot of other things in human beings – appendixes, crying, spots. But it wasn't just human beings that had superfluities. Adverts, mental arithmetic at school (why couldn't they just give us a calculator?) – in fact he couldn't really see the point of any of school. Gardens. Lipstick. Gerbils… Podge always had one of these in his room, and Joe couldn't understand it. It didn't *do* anything, and they kept dying. He'd already been through three or four.

The world was full of extraneous rubbish. If he was God, he could eliminate it all – like sweeping dirty plates from a table. He'd keep the computers, and the books of course, but not those stupid Mills and Boon that Podge's mum reads. Maybe he'd keep them if Podge wanted him to. He was deep in thought, making a list of what would stay and what would go, when Nel knocked on his door.

"I'm going to make pancakes this morning. Would you like some?"

He didn't move and breathed slowly, hoping she might go away.

"Joe? Oi, wake up. Wake up!"

She was hammering on his door. It was going to be one of those mornings. He didn't want any of her stupid pancakes. He grunted loudly enough to be heard through the door, and then sighed to himself. He looked around the room. The floor was covered in clothes and books. There was only a small patch of blue carpet visible, over near the window. His empty suitcase was on top of the wardrobe where he'd hung up his two smart shirts, and there was a chair where he'd arranged his 'things' – a model red Ferrari, his lucky pebble, and a battered plastic superman figure. He'd had these objects for years and took them everywhere, always arranging them in the same way, and when he looked at them it made him feel calmer. Emmie came round the other day and she nearly sat on them – he yelled at her and made both of them jump.

The sunlight was piercing the gap in the curtains. The dust was dancing. It occurred to him that this dust-made-visible must surround him – he was breathing it in all the time. Did it clog up anywhere in his body? Is that what the hairs on the inside of his nose were for, to keep it out?

As he watched the specks of light he started feeling sleepy again, and snuggled back down under his duvet. He was letting his eyes droop when he heard Nel clanging saucepans in the kitchen. He felt sure she was doing it on purpose. He sighed again, deeply, and dragged himself out of bed to see what he could find to wear. Nel had shown him how to do his own washing, but he's been putting it off. He sighed yet again at the thought that he might have to do it today. Why couldn't she just leave him alone?

He found Nel bouncing around in the kitchen. She was singing a song in Dutch, and Joe kept hearing his own name so assumed it was one she'd made up. If he hadn't felt so tired and grumpy, he would have asked her to translate it for him. There was no mention of the boyfriend conversation over the pancakes, and Joe wondered if she even remembered it.

She asked him three times why he was so quiet. He was still thinking about how he could fix Nel's love life. Maybe that was why she was in such a good mood. She'd fed Joe all that information on purpose, because she'd seen how brilliant he was at logical thinking. She knew he'd come up with a solution before long. He couldn't let her down.

The next day, Joe's mum came to the phone. She sounded small and distant and didn't seem to know what to say. She asked him twice what the weather was like. He pretended he wanted to ask his dad something, as a way of cutting their conversation short. Joe's dad sounded strained too, asking him nervously how his mum had sounded. After the call he felt glad to be in Amsterdam and not in Milton Keynes.

He continued to surreptitiously gather data on Nel's love life. He asked Nel to buy him a cardboard folder so he could keep all his research together – he told her he was doing a project on European weather satellites. Before he started, he thought he ought to organise the project into sections with subheadings – that was how they did it at school. But what should the subheadings be? The problems seemed to be interlocking – how could Nel afford to support herself and her art? Should she be with Jeroen, or Henk, or somebody different, or maybe even nobody?

First he wrote down everything he could remember from their conversation the night before. Then he decided on a couple of hypotheses to begin with (his dad had taught him about hypotheses) – he could always change them as time went on.

No. 1 – Nel needs to do her painting
No. 2 – Nel doesn't want to be lonely

Writing these down instantly complicated everything. The first depended on the second, didn't it? Which was more important to her – doing her paintings or having a boyfriend? He wrote this unanswered question on a different piece of paper, and added to it as he thought of other questions, planning to drop them into conversation casually.

He cunningly approached his first question while they were watching television. "If you could only have one which would you have, a chocolate biscuit or a cheese biscuit?" and then, "In your next life would you rather be a cat or a dog?" She got into the spirit of things and gave him a few too – silly ones like, "Would you rather do your washing or fall off a cliff?" Then he hit her with, "If you had to choose between your art and a boyfriend which would you want?" She seemed taken aback and stopped to think. "It's like asking a mother to choose between her children, Joe," she said, and sighed. "My art," she said. "But I don't know if my art would be very good if I was unhappy all of the time. I don't get lonely very often, but when I do it's terrible." He waited for one more round and then pretended he needed the toilet, so he could scribble down what she'd said.

As the day wore on, Joe's list of unanswered questions kept growing longer. Nel was restless too, flicking through magazines, and wandering between the living room and the kitchen. She'd return with an olive or a handful of nuts, or sometimes nothing at all. As the clock struck five, she jumped up from the sofa again and went to get her jacket. As she was pulling it on she instructed Joe.

"Put down your project, darling. I'm going to show you my space. We can eat there if you like, they have a little café."

Joe had heard a lot about Nel's 'space', where her first ever exhibition would take place in less than a week's time. She kept mentioning to Joe that this particular gallery only accepted you if they really liked your work. There was 'a lot of competition', and she'd had to work hard on her portfolio before they accepted her. She reminded him of a child waiting for Christmas.

As Joe started tying his laces, the buzzer rang. Joe heard Jeroen's voice over the intercom, and Nel spoke to him in

Dutch. She looked back at Joe and said, "Hurry up, then. We'll just have to take him along with us."

There was a tension between Nel and Jeroen as the three of them walked along the canal paths. He tried to take Nel's hand once and she pulled away. Jeroen said something angrily in Dutch, and Nel snapped back. Joe missed all the good stuff, not knowing Dutch. He was starting to recognise the occasional word from his lessons with Emmie, but when she taught him, she said the words individually and clearly. It was like a different language when people talked at their usual speed. The words all blurred together and the vowel sounds changed, and they left the ends off words or even left whole words out. Maybe he could carry on learning it when he went back to Milton Keynes. He could be fluent by the time he came back for his next visit.

On the train, a pretty girl wearing a red beret sat opposite Jeroen and he seemed to perk up. Joe watched Nel watching Jeroen. She looked angry, and whispered something in his ear. He looked even more cheerful after that, although Nel was in an even worse mood. Joe thought about his project, and relationships. It wasn't anything like the chemistry experiments they did at school – add this chemical to that chemical, and this happens. After a while Joe gave up trying to work out what was going on between them, and looked out of the window.

Jeroen was in such good spirits when they got off the tram that he put his arm around Joe's shoulders. Joe didn't like the feeling of it there at all. He had a strong urge to shrug it off, but he didn't want to cause any more trouble for Nel and so he kept quiet. He focussed on counting backwards in sevens to take his mind off it.

They walked right through the centre of Rembrantplein with its touristy bars and hotdog stands, and turned into a side alley. They emerged at a wide canal, and Joe counted the bicycles chained to the black railings as they passed. They all looked ancient – where did all the new bicycles go to in Amsterdam? Did people take their new ones straight home to batter them and scratch the paint so they fitted in with everyone else's? Jeroen finally took his arm off Joe's shoulder and tried to take Nel's hand again. She didn't pull it away this time, but she didn't look at him. She smoked a cigarette with her other hand.

They arrived at the gallery. From the outside it looked like an ordinary canal house – the front door was painted red, and there were red shutters framing the windows on the upper floors. On either side of the large windows were small round ones, like portholes – Joe liked the idea that he'd be looking through them from inside, out at the canal, in a minute. Nel ruffled Joe's hair (he wished she'd stop doing that) and they went inside.

Joe wasn't sure what he'd been expecting, but this was a disappointment. The gallery was just like a normal house inside too, without any furniture and with more paintings than usual hung on the walls. He watched Nel and Jeroen, who were pausing in front of each painting for ages. He walked over to look at one of them more closely. It consisted of different coloured squiggles and shapes, something he could easily have done himself. He stood there for a while and tried to copy Nel. It was boring to stare at it. Maybe he should be an artist and make lots of money and then he could buy Nel a flat.

As a general rule, art held no interest for him. He couldn't see the point of it. If you could take a photo of something, then why spend hours with a paintbrush trying to copy it? Once he'd seen some cool paintings on a school trip – they looked exactly like photos until you got up really close. What were they called – photo-realistic? That was a clever trick, although it would still be quicker to take a photo…

Nel was rabbiting on in Dutch to Jeroen. She kept sticking out both her thumbs and first fingers at right angles, making a rectangle, and looking through them at the paintings. It seemed like a silly thing to be doing. Joe wandered off by himself to explore. At the back there was another smaller room, which contained sculptures of strange animals. There was a big sign on the wall as you came in. Joe watched three separate people look around, see the sign, and then start to run their fingertips over the sculptures, so he guessed it said you were allowed to touch them.

The surface of the sculptures was cool, as if they were made of stone. He wanted to pick one up to see how heavy it was, but he was worried that they might be stuck down with glue and he might snap them off. They were all roughly the size of a cat, and consisted of body parts from different animals melded together. One had a pug's head and a fat lizard's body, and one looked like a kangaroo from the neck down but had a bird's head with a long sharp beak. The animals were very realistic – there were feathers carved on the bird's head, and fur on the furry ones.

Joe found his favourite. It had a seal's body, claws like a hawk where the tail should have been, and a cat's face. The face looked like a seal's face, and it was only when you looked closer that you realised it didn't quite fit. The body was so smooth – he stood next to it and stroked it for a long time. They were really spooky. He liked them, even more than he would if they were ordinary animals. He got out his notepad and made a note of all the different body parts – he wanted to tell Podge about them, and he thought Emmie might be interested too.

After what felt like a long time, he wandered up the stairs. He found the small café – round tables circled by uncomfortable looking metal chairs, and a long counter with food on display under the glass. Here were the porthole windows. He hovered at the doorway, wanting to go and look out of them. Nel came up behind him and put her arms around his shoulders.

"You want a piece of cake? It always makes me hungry, looking at art."

Her voice sounded croaky, and the rims of her eyes were red.

"It's okay, they were happy tears."

Her voice started to crack, and she sighed as if amused and exasperated. She squeezed her eyes shut and rubbed them with her fists.

"I just can't believe I'm getting a whole exhibition to myself. You see that couple over there, drinking coffee?"

Joe nodded.

"They could be looking at my paintings next week. And that man there?"

She was pointing to a middle aged man with the biggest moustache Joe had ever seen. He was scribbling things down in a leather-bound notebook.

"He writes for De Telegraaf, their art section. I talked to him downstairs. Next week people will be looking at my art and writing things down. Isn't that wonderful? No, it's not wonderful, it's terrifying!"

Jeroen arrived and pinched her bottom. Nel put a hand on each of their backs. "Shall we see what we think of the café in my gallery, then?"

They chose a table by the big window, and Jeroen jumped into the seat that Joe wanted. Joe went to the counter to choose his cake, and then left Nel to wait in the long queue which snaked alongside the counter. After Joe had watched the boats and bikes from the portholes for a few minutes, he sat down at the table with Jeroen. He wished he didn't have to, but he didn't want Nel to think him rude. As soon as he sat down, Jeroen asked him a question.

"So what does she say about me, then?"

"Who?"

"Your aunt, of course, you idiot. What does she say about me when I'm gone?"

Joe looked over at Nel, who was still at the back of the queue. The woman behind the counter seemed to be taking forever. Nel waved gaily, her bright smile reminding him instantly of his mother. His mother, who he hadn't spoken to since that last time when she sounded small and frightened. His dad kept telling him she was 'upstairs in the bath' or 'out seeing her friend', but he didn't believe him. He was starting to wonder if he'd done something terrible to annoy her, and she wasn't speaking to him, but what? Joe thought about Jeroen's question. He didn't want to get Nel into any trouble.

"Umm, she says you are a promising artist."

"Promising? She said promising?"

Jeroen was lost in thought for a minute. Joe crossed his fingers under the table – hoping that was the end of it – but before long Jeroen put his hand on Joe's arm.

"Does she like me? Does she like me more than Henk? It's very important – think hard now, what does she say when she talks about both of us?"

After their long talk the other night, Joe knew exactly how she compared Jeroen with Henk. He could remember her precise words about Jeroen – 'Even if Jeroen could support me, I could never live happily ever after with him'. He couldn't say that. He tried something milder.

"It's very complicated, because she doesn't really know what she wants."

Jeroen frowned, and so Joe kept going.

"She says there are problems with everyone, and maybe she'd be better off without Henk, or anyone."

Joe realised that 'anyone' meant Jeroen too. Jeroen's face darkened and he leant forward and asked another question. He said it so quietly that Joe could hardly hear him.

"Does she want me or Henk? Just tell me."

Joe looked at him, desperately trying to find the right thing to say. Jeroen changed tack, and tried to be solicitous.

"Look, I know you don't want to get your aunt into trouble. It's okay, I already know the answer, I just want to hear it from you."

It was as if Joe's maths teacher from last year was asking him a question in front of the whole class again. A question he didn't know the answer to. Eventually he stammered, "I don't know." To his horror, Jeroen looked furious and took Joe's chin roughly in one of his hands.

"Tell me, you idiot!"

Jeroen was hurting him. He looked around and saw Nel chatting with someone in the queue, oblivious. An elderly woman across from them caught his eye and looked alarmed, nudging her husband. Jeroen leant right up to Joe's face and hissed into his ear.

"Your mother doesn't want you. You're driving her crazy. Who would want someone like you as a son?"

With this, he pushed his chair back violently, and left the café. Nel turned round to catch his back disappearing, and looked over at Joe with a question. Joe wanted to smile to reassure her, but he couldn't manage it. She started to look worried so he mouthed to her, "He's gone to the toilet". He wasn't sure why he lied. She made another expression with raised eyebrows, meaning, 'Are you sure everything is okay?' and he nodded. She shrugged at him and turned to the woman behind the counter, who was about to take her order.

Joe's chin had started to smart. He felt a muddle of different emotions – guilt at not handling it better, fear of what Nel would say if she knew what had happened, and anger at Jeroen for humiliating him. Mostly, he felt afraid. There was a sensation as if Jeroen was still gripping him, and he touched his chin to make sure there was nothing there. He rubbed at his skin and tears sprung to his eyes. He didn't have long to pull himself together, Nel was making her way towards him with her laden tray. He imagined what he'd write to Podge about Jeroen, and called him a few names under his breath. This made him feel angry again and the tears dried up. By the time Nel had arrived, he had a cover story.

"He said he wasn't well, he's gone home."

"I thought you said he'd gone to the toilet?"

"Umm, he went to the toilet first, he said. He said he ate something bad."

Nel looked worried.

"I'd better go and see if he's all right."

"He said he was fine, to say sorry."

Nel looked at him weirdly. "Is everything okay, Joe? What's happened to your chin?"

Joe hadn't realised he was still rubbing it. He took his hand away from his face and shrugged.

"Well, I'll just check and see if he's still there. You're okay here for a minute?"

Joe grunted.

She was back soon enough.

"Well – he wasn't there. I'm sure he'll survive. I'll call him when I get home. I suppose that means I'll have to drink his coffee as well as mine. What a shame he didn't want cake, eh?"

Joe snorted. Nel stirred sugar into her coffee. She brightened as if she'd just remembered something.

"Here's to me. Here's to my exhibition."

She held up her coffee cup, and Joe picked up his glass of Orangina. They clinked, and Joe wished that Jeroen was dead. Henk too. Nel didn't need anyone else. He could look after her much better than they could. Then he blushed, and looked out of the window so Nel wouldn't notice. When his cheeks returned to their normal colour he ate his cake, which was delicious.

It was ten in the morning, and the phone was ringing again. Since their trip to Nel's parents the phone had been ringing at this time every day. Joe was still in bed, flicking through his folder on Nel's love life. He'd continued to work on the problem, and had slipped other unanswered questions into conversation; "Might you change your mind about wanting to be a painter?" (no), "How long could you wait to be a full-time artist?" (forever), "Do you want children?" (no), and "How much money do you make in Amsterdam if you're a famous artist?" (no idea).

He tried to spread the questions out but Nel started getting suspicious. His cardboard folder had got fatter, and he tried to supplement his investigations with information from library books. He read an entire book about 'how to have a happy marriage' (and found himself none the wiser), and another one about the children of alcoholic parents. He recognised his mum in some of the case studies, but not really Nel. He still had a long way to go before he could come up with any solutions.

The phone was still ringing, and eventually he heard Nel come out of her room to answer it. He listened to her speaking quietly in Dutch. He was learning more and more words from Emmie, but he still couldn't make sense of much Nel said. He heard 'Ja' for yes, and 'Vaarwel' for goodbye. Moments after hanging up, she knocked on his door.

"Come!" he ordered.

This was what Joe's dad said when you knocked on his office door. It had always made him giggle. Nel opened the door and stood in the doorway.

"You're probably wondering who's calling every day. Or haven't you noticed?"

Joe nodded.

"Can I come in?"

He shrugged. She sat on the bottom of his bed and looked around the room as if she'd never been in there before. She got up again and went over to the window, bent to a pile of books and read the spines.

"Meteorology for Scientists and Engineers, eh?"

Joe shrugged again and went back to reading his book. If she had something to say he wanted to hear it, but she was taking ages. He might as well make use of this silence while she faffed about.

"Well..." Nel said, as if she was about to launch into a long speech.

He looked up from his book. She didn't continue so he started reading again.

"Look, will you put that book down for a minute?"

She sounded exactly like his mum. It gave him an odd pang in his stomach. He put his book down and tried (not entirely successfully) to stifle a sigh. Nel sat on his bed again, arranged her skirt, and then looked at her hands as she spoke.

"It's been your grandfather on the phone. Well, your grandmother is behind it. I wouldn't be surprised if she's been giving him a piece of paper with his lines on..."

She paused again.

"I've never been very good at keeping the peace with my mother. She just makes me so mad. She's always asking me questions about my life, it's never good enough for her. I always disappointed her."

"Is that what you were fighting about?"

"Oh, that. It's difficult to explain."

"Is it because I'm fourteen? Nobody tells me anything. It's what Mum always says, 'When you're older'. I keep getting older and older and it hasn't made any difference, she still doesn't tell me anything."

Nel looked taken aback at the length of Joe's speech. "No, it's not that. I haven't really told anyone what happened when I was growing up. Your mum knows, because she was there too, but we don't talk about it either. It feels like it's best left in the past. It would be better if I just never saw Mum again, but then I miss my dad and he keeps talking about how much Mum misses me and trying to make me feel guilty. Ninety nine percent of me never wants to see her again. I'd be happy if she just died. But then one percent of me…"

Nel's confessional tone loosened Joe's tongue.

"I hate my mum sometimes. But I still… she's okay sometimes, I suppose." Joe had nearly said he'd missed her. Nel reached over and ruffled his hair.

"What happened growing up then?"

The directness of Joe's question took both of them by surprise. Nel fiddled with her skirt, folding it over and then smoothing it out.

"Well, there was lots of stuff. She was mean to Dad, that's one of the things. Really mean. Evil. He couldn't help himself when he got drunk, he'd fall asleep on the sofa in the afternoon sometimes, and Mum would draw a moustache on him, or put her knickers on his head. She made me join in, and we were both laughing about it, but even then it didn't feel right.

There was this odd feeling, a sort of guilt… Dad never found it funny either, and once he even slapped her.

"It didn't stop her though. One time she locked him out of the house and he fell asleep on the front lawn. When I went to school the next morning she'd stuck a stupid sign up next to him, on a post, where everyone could see it. It said, "Beware, drunken husband". All my friends saw it, and nobody said anything. It was even worse than being teased about it – everyone just avoided me as if I had the plague or something. Your mum never really had many friends at school anyway, she was always the quiet one, spent a lot of time by herself, but I was popular – I worked so hard to get people to like me."

"What happened when he woke up?"

"I don't know Joe – I just got home and everything was normal again. She was mean to me too, in a weird way – I couldn't be sure of it. She'd give me these looks sometimes, like I was stupid. She said things to put me down, make me feel like an idiot. She never did anything in front of dad, and when I told him about it he said to stop being silly, which made me feel even worse, like it was all in my mind… Is this okay, Joe?"

Joe nodded and grunted. He knew exactly what she was talking about. Mum did that to him sometimes. Made him feel like an idiot. He'd always just assumed that she was right. He did get things wrong all the time.

"When your mum said you were an idiot, was she right?" Joe asked.

"What do you mean?"

"Well, were you doing stupid things?"

"Oh, sometimes. It doesn't matter, Joe. Parents shouldn't make their children feel stupid even when they are doing stupid things. Children get things wrong – they're children.

When a parent is mean like that, it's because they're taking something out on them. Something they're struggling with themselves, you know, getting wrong somehow. Do you ever feel annoyed at your friend, what do you call him, Pidge?"

Joe snorted. "Podge."

"Podge. Are you ever mean to him? Do you lose your patience?"

Joe blushed. How did she know? He shrugged.

"Well, I can guarantee that whenever that happens, you've just had an argument at home, or you've got something wrong and are angry at yourself. Otherwise he wouldn't annoy you so much."

Joe thought about this. He could remember the last time he'd shouted at Podge, a few nights before he left for Amsterdam. Podge had gone on and on about how bored he was going to be without Joe there, and it had made Joe madder and madder. He was so whiny. It made him feel angry even when he started thinking about it now. He couldn't remember any arguments he'd had at home. Nel interrupted with, "Or sometimes I'm annoyed at people who do something I don't want to admit doing myself."

Joe would never whine about anything, especially missing Podge. Although. Maybe he had been worried about going away and being on his own. He had wished he could take Podge with him. Maybe he'd been angry at Podge because he didn't want to admit to feeling lonely. It was an uncomfortable thought, and so he thought about Nel again.

"So what does your mum do that you don't want to admit doing?"

Nel kept staring at her skirt, and he wasn't sure she'd heard him. Then all of a sudden she got up, moved a stray book onto the top of the towering pile, and took a deep breath.

"Well, we're going to see them again today. Not at their house, but at this place they have nearby – a kind of adventure playground. I've swapped my shift at work. We're leaving in an hour or two – make sure you're wearing something you don't mind getting dirty."

She hadn't answered his question. Maybe the being-annoyed-at-someone-because-they-remind-you-of-you rule doesn't work all the time.

This time, the trip passed more smoothly. Nel spent most of the time talking to her dad, but she did talk to her mum as well. Joe was too old for the playground climbing frames, but because he was in Amsterdam he didn't have to worry about the cool gang at school seeing him. He could act however he wanted to out here. His grandfather even pushed him on the swings – he was fourteen now, it was ridiculous! But he loved the infusion of energy when his grandfather pressed his hands on his back, and he loved soaring into the air without having to make all the effort himself.

Later they went to a café with bright yellow walls, and all the adults complained about how weak the coffee was. Eventually Nel took the tray back and they swapped their coffees for different ones. When Nel's mother tasted the new one she said something kind to Nel in Dutch that made her whole face go slack. It reminded Joe of how she looked when she was facing the easel. She made other expressions when she was painting – a fierce concentration like a small girl trying to tie her own shoelaces, or confusion. But when it was going well, her whole body went floppy.

His grandfather gulped his coffee down quickly, and got up to buy another. When he returned, Joe watched as he took his silver flask from the inside of his jacket and sloshed in the amber liquid again. He kept pouring and pouring. He tried to catch Nel's eye, but she wouldn't look at him. Joe was suddenly glad that his father wasn't an alcoholic. His grandmother turned to Joe with a bright smile and asked him if he'd like to play a game of cards. Joe shrugged. They cleared a space on the table and she took a pack out of her handbag. She explained the rules to Nel in Dutch, who translated them for Joe. Nel's mother interrupted when she heard a word or phrase she understood, repeating it.

"First of all you deal the cards, sharing them all out," said Nel. "Then the first person takes a card…"

"Take a card," said Nel's mother.

"… then you see if it's more or less than the card on the pile. The first person to lose all their cards is the winner."

"The winner!" said Nel's mother, triumphantly.

They also taught Joe to say 'troef' (trump in Dutch) and had a great time making fun of his pronunciation. He got the last laugh by saying, "Sorry, I don't speak Dutch very well" with a near perfect accent – a phrase he'd asked Emmie to teach him phonetically. His grandfather was delighted. They enjoyed their game of cards, and then another. When Joe's grandfather got his silver flask out again, Joe noticed Nel looking at her watch and looking anxious. She kept her eyes on him, and exchanged glances with her mother. When her dad got up and said he was going to get more drinks for everyone, Nel said no thank you and they said their goodbyes.

The next day, Joe was woken up by Nel clattering about in the kitchen. It sounded as if she was making lots of noise on purpose. He felt grumpy, and then when he swallowed, it hurt. He hated having a sore throat. It's what he always got when he was ill. It never went away until the evening, or the next day. It wasn't like he could just stop swallowing for the day. Although he did try that once, collecting his dribble in a glass instead, but it was so viscous and full of bubbles that it made him feel queasy. Every time he swallowed, it was like knowing you had to rip off an old plaster. You could either get the pain over and done with in one sharp *rip*, or spread it out for longer with a long slow pull... the pain added up to the same in the end.

His head ached too. He wanted his mum. When he was ill, she'd come and sit with him and read from whatever book he was in the middle of. She tended to get a lot of the words wrong, and read in a monotone, but it didn't really matter – her boring voice was good for sending him back to sleep. He liked to go to sleep with her perched on his bed like that. He wondered how long she carried on reading after he'd drifted off. Once he'd woken up after what felt like ages, and she was still reading. Maybe she could read something to him over the phone? Although he didn't want to speak to her again if her voice was weird and small.

He managed to drift off again, and was filled with an instant rage when he woke to Nel knocking loudly on the door.

"What?!"

The word hurt his throat. Losing his temper at Nel made him even more annoyed, and so when she opened the door and peered in he just turned his back to her and pretended to be asleep.

"What's up, Joey?"

Usually he quite liked it when she called him Joey, but this morning it sounded patronising. He had the urge to call her 'Nelly' in a snide voice but didn't dare. He was such a coward.

"Joe?" She sounded on the edge of annoyance.

He sighed loudly, and turned round to face her. He put on his best ill voice.

"I'm not feeling very well. I've got a bad throat."

"Oh dear. Would you like me to get you anything?"

She didn't sound very sympathetic. He wanted his mum again. He shook his head and sighed.

"I needed to tell you that I'm going to see Henk today, about the exhibition – he's helping me with all the publicity and things like that. Then Jeroen is coming round later, I was going to ask if you could go and see Emmie, but you don't have to come out of your room if you don't want to."

She wanted to get rid of him. Tears started pricking his eyes. He pulled the duvet over his head.

"What's wrong with you today? Are you in a bad mood?" she said, angrily.

"No!" he said, equally angrily. "I don't feel well!"

Did she expect him to say yes? Does anyone ever admit to being in a bad mood? It was like when adults talked about children in front of them, saying, "Oh, he's just tired. You're tired, aren't you?" Joe always wants to say, "What's your excuse when you're being an idiot? Are you over-tired, Dad? Do you need a nap?" This wasn't allowed though – only adults were allowed to moan about the children.

Now Nel sighed. "Look, Joe, I'm only trying to help here."

That's what his mum always said. He hated being in Amsterdam. He hated the smell of this room, which just wasn't like his room. He hated the noise outside the window all the time – all those stupid Dutch people going backwards and forwards along the street. All those stupid bicycles. He hated the food, the weather, Henk, Jeroen – he especially hated Jeroen, and if he was coming round later then he definitely wasn't going to come out of his room. He hated Emmie too – he just couldn't think of a good reason at the moment. And he hated Nel. No – he didn't hate her – he just really didn't like her right now. He let the silence hang and hang. When would she just go and leave him alone?

"Okay – I'm not going to force you to talk to me. I'll be off out in five minutes – let me know if I can get you anything before then. Do you want a pain–killer?"

"Do you have chewy orange ones?"

"No, just the tablets."

He couldn't take the tablets. They stuck in his throat and made him gag. Everything here was wrong. He felt like crying again. Nel softened her voice.

"Would you like to talk to your father?"

"I want Mum."

"Well, I'm not sure about that… You can ask your father. I'll bring the phone in and write the number down for you. I'll bring you some squash too, just in case you get thirsty, and a sandwich. Okay Joey?"

She ruffled his hair and left his room. He did cry then. Three fat tears splashed onto his pillow in quick succession, and then he squashed the feeling back down again. He was an expert at squashing it all back down. He imagined a big flat wooden implement – pushed downwards, and the tears and upset compressed until they became a small black pellet. He didn't know where these black pellets went, but he did wonder how many of them there were by now.

He'd stopped crying by the time Nel came back in. She'd written down his home number with the international code, and also the number for the restaurant she was going to with Henk. She'd written Maartje's number down too, in case he couldn't get hold of her for any reason. She made double sure he was happy for her to go, and then she kissed him on the forehead.

Joe heard the front door shut and cried some more. When he'd stopped (it hurt his throat to cry) he dialled home. His dad answered the phone, and Joe told him he was ill and he wanted to speak to his mum. His dad said he couldn't. Joe asked why. When his dad gave him some stupid excuse, Joe started crying. He hadn't cried in front of his dad for years. He was embarrassed, and said, "I have to go now", and put the phone down. The phone rang, then rang again five minutes later. He didn't answer it. He drifted back into sleep.

Joe woke up in the middle of a desert. He tried swallowing, and discovered the sore feeling had completely gone. There was a new problem, though – when he looked down he didn't have any feet. His ankles ended in stumps. The skin had a few clefts in it, like dimples. He wanted to poke his fingers into the folds but he was afraid the skin might give way into flesh. He looked around him, and found a glass containing a couple of inches of slightly murky water. As soon as he saw it he realised how thirsty he was. He looked beyond the glass and there was nothing but sand – nothing for miles and miles. He drank the bitter-tasting water in one gulp and it left him thirstier than he was before.

He needed more water. How would he get anywhere without any feet? He saw a small dot on the horizon – it grew bigger and bigger, it was travelling faster than a train. Eventually he made out a golf cart, driven by Nel. The rest of the cart was crammed with men – they didn't look like Jeroen or Henk in the dream, but Joe knew that's who they were – the current two, and all the others Nel had told him about. She shouted out, "Sorry, no room!" and rode past him, looking cheerful. He wanted to make her understand how important it was that she give him a ride, but when he opened his mouth and yelled there wasn't any sound. The golf cart disappeared even more quickly than it had arrived – soon it was only a dot on the horizon again, and then it was gone.

After it had gone, Joe realised that two of the passengers on the golf cart had actually been his Mum and Dad, in disguise as Nel's old boyfriends. Why hadn't they said anything? He felt a rising sense of desperation. Then a big black bird flapped down from above. It had a bald head like a monk, and although it didn't look quite right, Joe knew it was meant to be a vulture. He shoo-ed it away with his hands, and it flapped away from him and then started hopping back towards him. It was trying to peck at his ankles. It got less and less scared of Joe's frantic hand-flapping, and just as it was about to make contact with the soft flesh of his ankle stump the dream stopped.

He woke up frightened, and bathed in sweat. It took him a while to realise that he wasn't in his room in Milton Keynes, but in Amsterdam. His throat was hurting even more than it had been before he went to sleep. He was thirsty, and he drank the whole glass of squash that Nel had left by the side of his bed in a series of gulps. Each one hurt – ouch – ouch – but the squash tasted good.

He touched his forehead with the back of his hand, like his mother did. He was hot, feverish. He wanted his mum! He drifted in and out of sleep. His dreams all had a fractious, anxious quality. There was too much happening, too many things he had to remember.

He was woken from one of these dreams by the phone ringing. He nearly didn't answer it, thinking it might be Jeroen, but when he did it was his father.

"Joe? I've got her here. She's not feeling well so she might not be able to talk for very long. Okay?"

After a muffled sound, he heard a woman's voice.

"Joe? Are you ill, Joe?"

"I have a sore throat." He didn't know who this woman was, but he thought it polite to answer her question.

"Oh, oh dear. Oh dear, my poor Joe. So far away in Amsterdam."

As Joe listened to her quavering voice and the way she inflected the word 'Amsterdam', he realised that this woman was his mother.

"Mum?"

"Yes?"

"What's wrong? You sound funny."

"Oh, your father will explain all that. I've missed you. I've really missed you."

As she spoke, her voice cracked, and Joe was horrified to realise that she was crying. She continued to cry, softly, and he felt his body become alert, the sleepiness draining away. He didn't know what to say to get her to stop.

"Don't, Mum."

His voice was whiny. His mum hated it when he used that voice, but rather than telling him off, she sniffed a big sniff and then let out her breath in a sigh.

"Sorry."

Where was his dad? Was he standing there next to his mum, listening? Why didn't he take the phone back? Joe felt like crying himself. He waited with the silent phone pressed up against his ear, and eventually his mum spoke again.

"I haven't been myself, love. I'll get better for when you come home, I promise. Are you missing me?"

Joe nodded, and then realised that she couldn't see him. He was thinking about the word 'love'. His mother had never called him love before. It was something their next door neighbour called him. Where was his mother? What had they done to her?

"Is Dad there?"

"Yes, I'll put you back onto him. Joe. Tell me that you miss me." Her voice took on a sudden desperation. "Joe! Tell me!" Before he could say anything she repeated it again. "Joe! Tell me!"

He held the phone away from his ear as her voice rose to a shriek. It was as bad as the nightmare. Behind his mother's crying, he could hear his father in the background, saying, "It's okay, Ineke, just give me the phone. It's okay…" Then Joe thought he heard someone else, a man with a deep voice. He couldn't make out what he was saying. His mother became quieter.

"Boy?"

His dad sounded out of breath and panicky.

"Dad, what's happening? What's wrong with Mum?"

"I can't explain now, Boy, I need to… It'll all be okay, we just need to… Joe? Is Nel there?"

"Yes." He wasn't sure why he'd lied.

"Look, go and… tell her to…"

"Dad?"

Joe could hear someone speaking to his dad in a low voice. It was a woman this time. Who were these people? Was his mum in hospital? In prison? What had she done?

"Dad, where are you?"

"I've got to go, Joe – I'll call you as soon as I can, I promise. Everything is going to be… you're okay, aren't you? You're a strong boy, aren't you?"

Joe nodded, and again remembered that his dad couldn't see him. He didn't know what his father meant. He tried to reassure him.

"Yes, Dad."

But he was speaking to an empty phone.

Joe spent a fitful day in bed. He ate a few bites of the sandwich Nel had left him, and went to the kitchen twice to get himself some water. When he went to the bathroom to pee, he felt so wobbly he had to concentrate hard on his aim. He tried to pick up a book later in the afternoon, but the white of the paper hurt his eyes so he put it down again. Later on, Nel called to ask him how he was feeling. She told him she'd arranged to go and see Jeroen at his place so she didn't have to bring him back to the flat. He managed to read for an hour in the evening before falling asleep again at eight.

He was woken by a crash at the front door, as if someone had fallen into it. His throat still hurt. The skin on his face felt tight and his eyes were sore. Joe heard a key in the front door and prayed that Nel didn't have Jeroen with her. He heard her noisily making her way through the flat, talking all the way, and then going into the kitchen. He listened for a while before he realised that no one was replying, and that she must be talking to herself. He looked at his watch – it was nearly two in the morning.

Five minutes later, she knocked on his door – so gently that he could hardly hear it. It was in such contrast to all the noise she'd made before, it made him smile. He'd guessed she was drunk, even before she'd made her way over to his bed and breathed clouds of warm alcohol over him.

"Is everything okay, Joey?"

She was talking in a theatrical whisper, as if she didn't want to wake him up, but when he didn't respond she shook his shoulder gently.

"Joey? I don't want to wake you up. How are you feeling?"

He grunted, hoping that might be enough to make her leave him alone. He'd been desperate to speak to her ever since the phone call, to ask her questions, but she was no good to him like this. He hadn't seen her properly drunk before. Why tonight, of all nights? She knew he was ill. It was typical of adults – they were there for you when it suited them, but when something happened in their own lives they completely forgot about you.

"Okay, Joey. I'll leave you alone now, I'll see you in the morning. I love you, Joey. I love you."

She'd never said she loved him before. He couldn't remember either of his parents ever saying it either. He grunted again, and she kissed him on the forehead, sloppily, before stumbling out of his room.

Joe slept badly for a few hours – he kept waking up covered in sweat. He thought he heard someone being sick in the bathroom a couple of times, and felt muddled about whether it was his mum or someone else. His sleep evened out towards the morning, and he woke at ten to the light streaming in through the gap between the curtains. He swallowed experimentally, and was pleased to find only a faint echo of yesterday's pain. His head wasn't aching either.

He was about to get out of bed when he felt a sinking sensation. The phone call with his mum. He thought about hiding under the duvet again, but as if on cue his stomach made a gurgling noise and he realised how ravishingly hungry he was. He thought he'd to sneak into the kitchen and make a sandwich and then come back to bed.

He was amazed to find Nel already at the kitchen table. She was fresh out of the shower and her wet hair was in ringlets. She was wearing her smart jacket, and Joe wondered if she was going somewhere. The kitchen smelt of brewing coffee, and the radio was playing softly. There was toast in the silver toast rack. She turned around to him, smiling. It was then that he saw the colours around her eye.

"What happened to you?"

She touched her face distractedly with her fingertips, as if she hadn't realised there was anything wrong with it.

"Oh, never mind that. I want to know how you are this morning, Joe."

A strong tension gripped him, rose up. The shout burst out of him before he could stop it.

"I can't bear all these FUCKING SECRETS!"

He felt like throwing himself onto the floor or taking a knife to cut his arm. Instead, he sat on a kitchen chair, rested his head on his folded arms, and sobbed.

He hadn't cried like that for ages. It used to happen all the time – his mum used to call him the Tantrum King. He could remember the last tantrum he had, when he was eleven. He was in Toy City, and he'd had a terrible day at school. He'd wanted a pack of Star Wars cards, they only cost a pound, and his dad had said no. He couldn't bear it, and he fell onto the floor. He was mortified afterwards, and so was his dad.

He felt the same now. He just wasn't able to stop crying, like when you're sick. He hated it when his parents said it was just a way of getting attention, of getting his own way. These crying jags left him exhausted, and they never changed anything anyway. Why would he do that to himself on purpose? The sobs shook through him, and he felt Nel's hand come to rest gently on the top of one of his arms. He shook her away, but she put her hand back, and he let it stay there. It made him cry even harder. She didn't say anything sarcastic, like his mum did sometimes – "It's such a hard life being a child", or "Quick, David, we should change our minds at once and buy Joe the toy after all". Nel didn't say anything impatient-sounding like his dad either – "How long is this going to continue?" or, "Is this *really* necessary?" She just sat silently next to him, and when Joe finally felt able to lift his head from his arms he saw through his tears that she looked sad. He wiped at his face with one of his arms.

"Wait a minute, I'll get some tissue for you," she said, and returned with a roll of toilet paper.

Joe was having those sudden intakes of breath that took you by surprise – he always got them after he'd cried that hard. They were like hiccups, but more violent. It hurt to swallow again. He couldn't see anything through his glasses, they were smeared with tears and snot. He took them off and wiped them with a piece of tissue. He concentrated hard on this, and found that it took his attention away from his upset, and his embarrassment, which was growing by the second. He was far too old to cry like that. What was Nel thinking of him? And he'd sworn at her too – the 'f' word. He'd never sworn at home, except a 'bloody hell' once that got him grounded for a week. Then he looked at her black eye again and the shame dissolved into a fresh spurt of anger. It was exhausting; he could hardly keep up with it.

"Would you like a cup of tea with lots of sugar?"

As soon as Nel made the offer, he realised that this was exactly what he'd needed all along. Maybe if he'd drunk his tea first he wouldn't have got so angry. Maybe that was what it was like for alcoholics. He waited, making occasional hiccupping noises, while Nel re-boiled the kettle and stirred in sugar and milk. He cupped the hot mug between his palms and the gaps between his sudden in-breaths got longer and longer before they disappeared altogether. Nel poured herself a fresh cup of coffee and they both sat there, sipping. Joe took a longer look at her eye.

"Does it hurt?"

"Oh, a little. I'm more worried about looking like an idiot at my opening, it's only the day after tomorrow."

Joe grunted. After a short silence he said, "You can put some make-up on it, can't you?"

Nel smiled. She took a deep breath and blew the air out slowly.

"Jeroen hit me."

Joe's eyes widened.

"I suppose it serves me right for knocking him unconscious last month," she said, and it took Joe a second to realise that she was joking. She caught his expression. "No, you're right – it's nothing to laugh about. We were both very drunk, and we both misbehaved, but then he took it too far. It hasn't happened before. Well, not very often."

Joe looked away from her. He wasn't sure he wanted to know the truth anymore. When Nel spoke again, she sounded like a little girl.

"I've told him it's over. I left him a note, just in case he doesn't remember everything this morning. Although I'm not sure what I wrote in it, exactly. I can't remember."

Joe seized the chance to confess.

"He said something to me in the café, when we were at your gallery."

"What?"

"He asked me what you thought of him. I wouldn't tell him, and he kind of threatened me. I didn't tell you because… well, I don't know. It was embarrassing. And because you liked him I suppose. That's why my chin was all red – he'd…"

Nel looked upset. She put her hand on the side of his cheek.

"Oh, Joe. I'm so sorry."

"It's not your fault."

"It is, it is. It's all my fault. What a mess. What a mess."

She looked so sad. He wanted to cheer her up somehow, but then he remembered.

"Nel?"

"Yes?"

"I spoke to Mum yesterday."

"Oh."

He heard from her 'oh' that she knew much more than she'd been telling him.

"What's wrong with her?"

"I don't know if I should…"

"Dad said that you'd tell me about it – he had to go in the middle of the call, something happened. She sounds like she's really ill or something, she was acting all strange."

Now Nel leant forward into her crooked arms, elbows on the table. She pushed her fingers through her hair and rested her head forwards. She shut her eyes and spoke in a monotone.

"Your mum has been having emotional, ah, mental problems, Joe. She's been finding it harder and harder to cope with life. It's been going on for some time, but she's managed to keep it hidden from you, and also from your dad for a long time. She told me things, now and then, but I always hoped she was exaggerating, or that things would just get better on their own. It's why you're here for the summer – things had got very bad, and she'd been seeing the doctor. He'd given her stronger tablets than she was taking before, but they weren't working well enough. The week after you arrived here, your dad decided it would be better for her to go to hospital to try and get her better. The kind of hospital people go to when they're not coping with things. Do you understand?"

Joe tried to take it in. This had been happening in front of his eyes. Why hadn't he noticed that something was wrong?

"Will I ever see her again?"

"Oh Joe, darling, of course you will. I'm sure she'll get better, she's getting the right kind of help now. She'll be back to normal in no time."

"What if she's still in hospital when it's time for me to go home?"

"Your dad will be there."

His next question felt like the most important one, but for some reason he couldn't get it out of his mouth. It sat on his tongue like coal – bitter, hard. Is it my fault? Is it my fault? Is it my fault?

Nel looked beautiful. She was wearing a deep green dress, one that went all the way down to the floor and skimmed the carpet as she walked. The silk undulated whenever she moved. She'd piled her hair up on top of her head, and she was even wearing a little bit of make-up. Henk had bought her the dress, of course. And the necklace she was wearing, which she fussed with as she waited for Joe to get ready to leave the house. She shouted at the closed bathroom door.

"What are you doing in there?"

"Nothing!" he said, annoyed. Everyone was always hassling him. He was actually standing at the mirror with a pot of gel he'd bought yesterday. His first attempt had failed – he'd put too much of the gunky stuff on and it looked like he'd been out in the rain. He'd had to wash it all off in the sink and dry his hair with a towel and start again. He thought he was almost there, but every time he pulled a lock of hair between his thumb and forefingers it moved a different clump out, or made his head look unbalanced... He'd vowed never to use the stupid stuff again. He'd got a spot too, right on the end of his nose. It hadn't matured enough to get a white tip, and he knew it would be pointless to try and squeeze it – you just get an even redder mess for even longer. He had a sudden flash of inspiration.

"Where's the make-up you used on your eye?" he yelled.

He heard Nel try the door, which was locked, and he let her in. She got it down from the bathroom cabinet.

"What's it for?"

"My spot." It was embarrassing to admit.

She peered at his face, and made a play of not being able to see anything.

"Let me give you something proper to cover up," she said, making fists and getting ready to box him. He snorted, but he still wasn't sure they should be laughing about Jeroen hitting her. You couldn't see the colours behind her make-up, but if you looked really close you could still see that something was wrong. She noticed him peering at her.

"Do you think Henk will notice?" she asked nervously. Joe thought about lying but decided against it – he always got found out. Instead he said, "You could tell him you fell over."

Nel smiled.

"Look what an example I'm setting you. I should be ashamed."

As they'd been talking, she'd unscrewed her small tube of cover-up and had squeezed a small blob of cream onto the tip of her finger. She smeared it over the tip of his nose, rubbing it in and then standing back to admire her handiwork.

"There." She took Joe's wrist so she could look at his watch. "Aargh – it's nearly six! He'll be here any second! Are you nearly…"

Before she finished her sentence, the buzzer rang.

"Oh – he hates it when I'm not waiting outside! Come on, let's go, let's go!"

The phone started ringing again as they were leaving the house. It had been ringing for a couple of days now, on and off. Nel said it was Jeroen. She answered it the first couple of times and told him to go away, but she said it was just impossible to talk to him. She said she was worried he might have gone a bit mad. Yesterday Jeroen turned up on the doorstep and wouldn't give up and go away for hours. She made them stay in the house like prisoners, even though Joe wanted to go round and see Emmie. Nel hurried Joe out into the hall, slamming the door shut behind them.

Henk was in an especially good mood. He greeted Joe warmly and went on and on about how nice Nel looked. He was wearing a suit himself, a dark grey one, and looked quite dapper. He made Nel sit in the front with the chauffeur, because she was 'the star', and he got in the back with Joe. Nel fretted on the journey to Emmie's house that they'd be late – she said she was always late for everything. When they pulled up at her apartment there was an older girl stood outside on the pavement, and when Joe jumped out of the car to press the buzzer to Emmie's flat the girl looked over at him as if he was mad.

It took Joe more than a second glance to realise that it was Emmie. She was wearing a dress! Not only that but her hair, which was always pulled back into a tight ponytail, was loose and full. It seemed to be curlier than usual too – maybe she'd done one of those girl things to it.

She smiled at him and he noticed a new expression on her face. Could she really be shy? Stupid spot, why did it have to ruin his night? But then he remembered the cover-up, and he felt a new confidence. He'd got his cover-up, he'd got his spiky hair – he swaggered over and offered her his arm. It might have worked if he hadn't stumbled on a cracked paving stone and almost fallen on his face. Emmie burst into her usual ugly laughter, a kind of hee-haw-ing, completely ruining the effect of her hair and the pretty dress. Joe snorted and Henk beeped the horn. They piled into the back seat, and the four of them spent the rest of the journey in a nervous silence.

When they arrived at the gallery, the street was teeming with people. Joe guessed that someone had been mugged. A few weeks ago, Joe and Nel were out shopping when a tourist was mugged, and there had been a great commotion. As the chauffeur was pulling over Emmie squealed. She said a phrase in Dutch and kept repeating it, tugging on Joe's sleeve to try and make him understand. It sounded like it could be a name. And then Joe spotted the photographers – three of them, snapping away at a short man with thick spiked blonde hair. He'd arranged his spikes much better than Joe had, and he was annoyed – how could he hope to get Emmie's attention now? Emmie and Nel spoke in Dutch, and then Nel turned to him.

"That man is a big soap star, he's just released a record. Henk knew his agent and asked him along. He's got a reputation for being a bit stupid, so his people are trying to make him look cultured at the moment. That's why he's come to my show. He's invited a few famous friends, and told the press they're coming. It's like bees to a honey-pot."

Joe realised that this man, and this crowd, were actually here for Nel's show. He felt nervous for her, but she looked happy.

"Are you still nervous, Nel?"

"I'm not, darling. I feel just great. I hope the world is ready for me!"

She looked at Henk and he smiled. Joe wondered if Henk would mind having his photo taken – wouldn't his wife see them in the paper? He wanted to ask Nel about it but he couldn't with Henk there. Nel turned to him and Emmie.

"Are you both ready to dazzle? Got your best smiles on?"

Emmie put on a broad fake grin, and Joe snorted and tried to copy her, which made her laugh her ugly laugh again.

"Let's go, then!"

As they got out of the car, one of the photographers recognised Henk, and turned his attention from the blonde guy to the four of them. Joe expected Nel to take Henk's arm like she'd seen him do before, but instead she stood apart from him as Henk whispered something into the photographer's ear. They started taking photos of her, and she posed for them as if she'd been doing it all her life. After a few shots she beckoned to Joe, who shook his head furiously, blushing crimson. Emmie tried to push him towards her but he backed away and went to stand by Henk.

Henk put an arm round Joe's shoulder and smiled, saying, "Silly people, eh?" It was the first time Henk had stuck up for him. Joe remembered that he'd arranged all of this for Nel. Maybe he was okay. He couldn't be as bad as Jeroen, anyway. If only he didn't have a wife, maybe Nel could live with him happily ever after. Maybe they could get rid of his wife somehow. He thought back to his attempts at deciding whether Nel should be with Jeroen or Henk. His silly project.

Emmie came over to tug Joe's sleeve and point at a red-headed woman getting out of her car. The photographers started snapping her. He'd never really understood the concept of celebrities. They were just normal people, weren't they? Maybe some of them were better looking than average people, but why did everyone get so excited about them?

It was just like the popular boys at school. They seemed to have a special talent for attracting attention. If you listened hard to what they said, they weren't really any funnier. People just laughed more loudly at their jokes. It was all very unfair. Joe knew he'd never be one of the popular boys, and it didn't really bother him most of the time. Podge didn't care about stuff like that either. They were all idiots anyway, as Joe would endlessly tell Podge – why would they want to join a crowd like that?

Joe was surprised when Emmie slipped her arm through his, especially with all the celebrities there. He didn't think she'd want to be seen with someone like him. Maybe he'd been more successful at gelling his hair than he thought. He felt the skin on the underside of her arm brush against his wrists and it sent shivers through him. It was cool, and so smooth... He could smell her too, her perfume, and something else – something fruity... He leant in closer. It was coming from her hair – lemons. The smell was so acidic, it made his mouth water. He was worried about getting an erection, and so focussed instead on the thought of his grandfather's train set.

He didn't like to think about Emmie in that way. After he met her for the first time, she floated into his mind that night as he reached down under the duvet, but she seemed too pure for him to think about as he masturbated. Although he'd read the leaflets at school about masturbation not making you blind, he still couldn't get rid of the thought that it was dirty. Maybe it would feel less weird if he didn't do it so often, or if he had a girlfriend to kiss. He couldn't imagine ever getting a girlfriend, and so his solo sexual experiences were already a substitute for something he'd never be able to have. Pathetic.

Emmie had been banned from his sexual fantasies, but sometimes he did allow himself to think about a segment of her, like her little red top that showed off her belly button, or her ankles. The feel of her skin against his was almost too much. He felt sure she'd feel the heat radiating from him in a halo.

As they walked inside, following Henk and Nel who were still walking separately, a man approached Nel and kissed her hand. Joe guessed he was the gallery owner. He took Nel's coat and handed it to one of his staff, and took her through into the downstairs space. Loud music was playing – electronic, with a pulsing drum beat, and violins and strings. There was something sad about it, the word his mum might use was 'maudlin'.

The rooms were filled with people. They were an odd mix. Half of them were dressed smartly, like Henk and Nel, with proper suits and cocktail dresses. The other half looked like hippies to Joe – there was a man with a spike through his nasal septum, and a woman with pink hair and a big tattoo on her back. When Nel came in, lots of people stopped talking and turned round to look at her. Joe felt nervous for her again. She didn't look intimidated at all – she looked like she was loving the attention, and she'd started flirting with Henk, nudging him with her shoulder.

A scattering of waiters were carrying around trays of what looked like sculptures. When Joe looked more closely, he could see that they were canapés. There were black blobs topping tiny pancakes, miniature red tarts with sugar cages balanced on top, and a pink jelly studded with prawns. He certainly didn't want to eat any of it, but it did all look exquisite.

Joe looked past all of the chit-chatting people and the food. Nel's paintings! He moved towards them, sliding free from Emmie's arm so he could get a better look. They looked so different in here. In her makeshift bedroom studio the colours fought with everything else in the room – the duvet cover, the bright curtains – but here each painting was surrounded by a swathe of white space. The white hemmed the colours in, kept them concentrated. He looked for the ones he was already familiar with – the two paintings Nel had been working on over the summer. The deadline had been a couple of weeks ago, and Nel had stayed up most of the night making last minute changes, although Joe couldn't tell the difference in the morning.

He found one of them in the small adjoining room. Joe recognised a few words of the title. He took a few paces backwards and stood in front of the canvas. He saw the painting as a whole, and then his eyes drifted towards a tiny fish-shape. He noticed a streak of green in the middle of the orange. And then he noticed a bird-like shape in the background. Did Nel paint it that way on purpose? Did the bird have anything to do with the tall building? He made a mental note to ask her later. He was still looking, feeling like he'd gone into a kind of trance, when he smelt lemons and heard someone breathing next to him.

"What's the word 'mus' mean?"

She corrected his pronunciation. "It means sparrow.'

They viewed the remaining paintings together, Joe translating as much as he could of the titles, and Emmie filling in the rest. Joe managed to guess some of the words that Emmie hadn't taught him. He'd been watching TV in Dutch, and he wondered if some of the words had seeped into him. Maybe the Dutch he'd heard when he was very small was still stored somewhere in the recesses of his brain too. He imagined the old neural pathways reconnecting, like strings of fairy lights. He couldn't wait to speak to Emmie and Nel in their own language. He'd started having short conversations with Nel already – asking her if she wanted a coffee in the mornings, and attempting to talk to her about the weather.

As they stood in front of Nel's last painting, the chatter of voices dropped to a murmur, and then silence. They walked back into the main room, where all eyes were on Nel. She did look very beautiful. She started talking, and Joe tried to concentrate on the Dutch.

After less than a minute, they all heard a man in the entrance hall, shouting. The noise moved towards them, and Jeroen appeared, followed closely by the man from behind the front desk. The man was talking quietly and had his hand on Jeroen's arm, but Jeroen shook him off without looking at him, mumbling all the time. He looked dreadful – his shirt was crumpled, and he had a few days growth of beard. One of his eyes was bloodshot and the skin around it was swollen. Joe thought of Nel's make-up, and wondered if she had done that to him. He hoped so. He looked at Nel, who was open-mouthed and wide eyed. The room shifted their eyes between Jeroen and Nel, waiting for her lead. Before she could do anything, Jeroen saw her and started shouting again. Then he whipped something out of his pocket. Joe saw it glint in the light.

Fear rippled through the room. People moved backwards in a wave. A man pushed into Joe, squashing his foot. A woman screamed. Someone dropped a full glass of wine, and Joe saw bright red, splashing on the polished white floor. Lots of red. It was too much red to just be the wine. Jeroen dropped to the ground and his head hit the floor with a sickening 'thud'. And then Emmie fell beside Joe, crumpled without a sound, and he saw more red. Joe thought it might have been her blood. He thought she'd been shot.

Everybody was barging past him now. He wanted to make sure it wasn't Emmie's blood, but people kept getting between him and her, pushing, shoving. He managed to grab onto an older woman as she moved past him and pointed down at Emmie, saying 'help'. He didn't know the word in Dutch. The woman helped Joe to lift Emmie and they half-lifted and half-dragged her into the second room at the back, which was deserted. Everyone else was trying to move in the opposite direction, clotting the exit. Joe looked behind them before the woman shut the wide door. He saw Jeroen flat on his back, with three more people bending over him. He couldn't see Nel.

They lay Emmie on the floor, and Joe checked her over – he couldn't find any wound. He realised that there hadn't been any bangs, so there can't have been any bullets. Unless Jeroen had used a silencer. The woman didn't speak any English, and she was gabbling in Dutch. A man burst into the room and then backed out, slamming the door.

As Joe checked once more for blood Emmie started to come round, moving her head gently from side to side. She opened her eyes and looked up at Joe. Warm relief rushed through him. He said to her, "There was blood." She nodded, and started to push herself up into a sitting position. After the woman said something to her in Dutch, she rested her head between her knees. They helped Emmie scooch over to the edge of the room. All three of them sat down with their backs to the wall, Nel's paintings surrounding them.

They didn't speak. Joe listened to the commotion in the next room, trying to make sense of it, and after a few minutes they heard the sound of sirens approaching down the road and stopping outside the gallery. Emmie lifted her head from between her knees and got up, supporting herself at first with a hand on the wall. She walked over to the small window at the side of the room, and Joe followed her. They could see a small overgrown garden, and a dilapidated garden shed. The light had started to fail, and it was drizzling. Joe wanted to feel it on his face – it was stuffy in the room. He imagined everybody else out on the street at the front, milling about, jostling against each other. Maybe the photographers were snapping away. He imagined the back of the ambulance opening, and two paramedics coming out, rolling a gurney. Would Jeroen leave a trail of blood behind him?

The woman said something to Emmie in Dutch.

"She wants to know who that man was. Should I tell her?"

Joe shook his head. He didn't think they should give away any of Nel's secrets. Emmie nodded and spoke to the woman, shrugging. They could hear voices inside the building again now, in the next room. Where was Nel? Was she with Jeroen now, getting all covered in his blood? Joe hoped Jeroen wouldn't say anything to the ambulance men about Nel hitting him over the head. Although he had hit her too… He touched his chin with his fingertips and felt a stab of anger. Jeroen had ruined Nel's opening night. She'd been looking forward to it her whole life. Joe hoped he was dead.

Emmie and Joe watched a tabby cat balancing along the fence at the bottom of the garden. She placed each paw carefully and then she leapt out of sight. Time passed, and Emmie started pacing the room. She asked the Dutch woman something, but the woman shook her head. She walked around the perimeter of the room like a lion in a cage. Eventually she persuaded Joe to play I Spy with her out of the window.

Joe heard the sirens start up again, and Nel burst into the room. She ran over to Joe and crushed him into a hug. He let out a sob or two into her shoulder and hoped no one else would hear. She pulled Emmie into the hug too. Then Nel spoke to the woman, clasping her hands – Joe recognised the word 'thank you'. When the woman had gone, Nel started talking to Joe in Dutch. When she realised what she was doing she laughed. Joe noticed that her hands were trembling. They heard more sirens.

"Can we go home now?" Joe asked.

"Henk says they need to ask me questions. The police. That's them, I guess."

Joe furrowed his brows, and Nel put her hand on his shoulder.

"It's okay, it's just to fill in the background. They're not going to put me in prison! I'll call Maartje and get her to pick you both up. I shouldn't be too long. Let's get out of here now, are you ready?"

They both nodded, and Nel took them both by the hand. Neither of them pulled away from her.

"Try not to look now, there's a lot of mess out here," Nel said.

Nel opened the door and neither of them could take their eyes off the 'mess'. At the centre of the room was a large pool of blood, darkening and smeared at the edges. There were dark drops and spatters further away, as if the blood had spurted. For a moment Joe admired a perfectly circular drop against the pale floor. It was like art. There were bloody footprints leading to and fro the door, and empty wrappers, white gauze and cellophane scattered across the floor. The room was cluttered with empty glasses, some set neatly onto the floor but most of them on their sides or smashed, and there were several platters of crushed food. The strangest object was a single red stiletto, and later Joe wondered if he'd really seen this or if he'd imagined it.

Emmie put her hand over her mouth and stopped. Nel cupped a hand by Emmie's eyes to shield her from the blood pool, and encouraged her to keep walking. Nel warned them both to be careful not to step on any broken glass. Joe had never seen that much blood at the same time before. He'd seen a couple of gory playground accidents in his time, but nothing like this. Jeroen must have been completely drained. As they left the room, Joe looked at the walls. There they all were – Nel's paintings. Were they damaged?

"Your paintings…" he said.

"Oh, they're only paintings," said Nel, "I'll come back for them." She squeezed Joe's hand, and they walked out onto the street.

The morning after the exhibition, Joe was dragged from his dreams by a wailing sound from the living room. He pulled on his dressing gown and stumbled out to see what was going on. He was half expecting to see another body, face down on the carpet. Instead he found Nel sitting cross-legged on the floor, with the morning paper open in front of her. She didn't look up at him but carried on reading, her face full of horror. Joe perched on the arm of the sofa while he waited for her to look up. The room smelt of stale smoke. Finally she looked up at him, despairingly.

"They've printed everything, Joe."

"What?"

"Everything. They've printed everything. That Jeroen was my lover, that I broke up with him before the show, that Henk arranged the exhibition, that he was financially supporting me, that he... They didn't actually say he was having an affair with me, but you'd have to be stupid not to guess."

"Oh."

"What am I going to do, Joey?"

"Did they say about you hitting Jeroen?"

"Oh, no, of course not. They made him sound completely crazy, though. They said our relationship was violent. They said he was on drugs."

"Oh. It was violent, wasn't it?"

"Oh, not... I suppose... That's not the point. It makes us both sound like...."

She couldn't find the word she wanted. Joe searched for something to say.

"Did they say anything about your paintings?"

Nel looked stricken, as if she was about to cry. She massaged her forehead.

"Nothing. Fucking nothing. They put all those stupid celebrities in, and they even described my stupid dress. Not a single fucking thing."

Joe was alarmed by her swearing.

"What are you going to do next?"

"I don't know, Joe. I really don't know."

"But what's going to happen?"

She just shrugged, and continued rubbing her forehead. He gave up. He was annoyed at her, for not knowing what to do, but he knew it was a selfish thing to feel. He wished he could just feel sad for her, like a normal person would. He felt so useless when other people were upset. He never knew what to do, and when he did try to be comforting he usually ended up making it worse.

Nel finally tilted her hand away from her eyes, as if she was shading herself from bright sunshine. She squinted up at him.

"Oh Joey, don't frown. It makes you look ugly. Make me some coffee, will you?"

He wanted to go over and hug her. In theory, he could just take three steps across the room. Should he bend over or just stand up with his arms open? He needed a shower – would she be able to smell his armpits? He gave up on the idea and grunted instead. As he went to the kitchen he could hear his mum's voice in his head. "Useless lump."

As they were finishing breakfast, the phone rang. Joe watched her pick up the receiver and then put it back down again, looking shocked. She told Joe it was Henk's wife, asking calmly for confirmation that he was really having an affair with her. Joe didn't know what to say, and so he went back to washing up the breakfast things. An hour later the phone rang again. This conversation went on for a long time, and Nel alternated between sounding angry and apologetic. Eventually she got upset and hung up, going straight into her room and slamming the door. Joe imagined her getting back under her duvet like he'd seen her do after that argument with her mum. He tried to go back to his book, but he couldn't concentrate. He even tried to write a letter to Podge, but after three attempts he abandoned that too. He just didn't know where to start.

Nel didn't come out until early afternoon. Her eyes looked sore. She told Joe she wasn't hungry, but insisted on making him a ham and cheese sandwich. As he ate, she told Joe it had been Henk on the phone earlier, calling from his office. His wife had just called him, and told him that she wanted him to move out. He'd been disappointed in Nel for hiding her relationship with Jeroen. He was also furious that his reputation might be tarnished by the stories in the papers. Nel spoke up for herself, saying she didn't think it was fair to blame the whole business on her, and he exploded. She'd never heard him so angry before – he was usually so calm and sensible. It had scared her. When he'd finished shouting at her, she'd told him she never wanted to see him again, and had put the phone down on him. Once again, Joe didn't know what to say. He picked up his sandwich and forced himself to keep eating.

A few hours later Nel told Joe she was going to visit Jeroen in hospital. Joe was incredulous. He thought Jeroen would be the last person she'd want to see – he was the reason for all this mess. He'd got her into trouble with Henk, and it was his fault that she was in the papers for all the wrong reasons. He'd completely ruined everything. He was tempted to point this all out to Nel, but she must have already known. Maybe Nel felt guilty about him trying to kill himself, even though their break up was Jeroen's own stupid fault.

When she'd gone, the flat was too quiet. It was as if he was the only person in the whole building, in the whole street. He went back into his room and tried to read, but nothing held his interest. The nest building behaviour of goldcrests seemed utterly irrelevant. He was considering trying to sleep when he noticed his bookmark. It was the scrap of paper Nel had used to write out his home number. He'd be flying home in just over a week's time, away from all this confusion. He thought about home. He wanted to know what the weather was like there, and what was on English TV. He wanted to hear his dad's voice, and picture him standing in their hallway, next to the barometer and those ugly watercolours of dogs that his mum kept buying. He took the scrap of paper into the living room.

As soon as his dad answered the phone, Joe regretted making the call. He sounded so weary. Joe pictured him holding the phone with both hands, which he sometimes did when he didn't really want to speak to anyone. It was as if the phone had become too heavy for him to lift. His dad sounded as if he was in the middle of something important. When Joe asked if his mum would be meeting him at the airport he said, "Probably not, son, no, probably not."

Joe wanted to ask how long she was going to stay in hospital for – surely a fortnight would be enough to get her better? A boy in the class below him was only in hospital for a week when he had his appendix out, and that was a major operation. He didn't tell his dad anything about the exhibition or about Jeroen. He didn't want to give his dad a bad impression of Nel. None of this was her fault. The call ended awkwardly, with Joe's dad telling him that he loved him. First Nel, and now his dad. He just grunted back. He felt guilty for the rest of the afternoon. He should have said it back. Why didn't he say it back?

On the second and third days after the exhibition Nel moped around in her dressing gown, puffing endlessly on her foul cigarettes. The phone kept ringing but she didn't answer it, and when Joe asked who it was she was evasive. Joe spent as much time as he could at Emmie's house.

He'd put off going there at first. Seeing her in that slinky dress with her hair down had changed things. She had entered his masturbatory fantasies with a vengeance. The slight swell of her cleavage, or the way she flicked her hair, or the shape of her bottom through her skirt. He'd been having other fantasies too, where she'd come back to England with him and he'd show her round Milton Keynes, or they'd go travelling around Europe together. He'd take her into his bedroom, sit next to her on his bed, put his arm around her back and kiss her gently on her soft, sweet lips…

He felt awkward when he first saw her after the exhibition. Would she know he'd been thinking about her? He made an effort to put all his lascivious thoughts on hold, but even so caught himself gazing at her legs once, and trying to manoeuvre on the sofa so their arms were touching…

On the fourth day Nel borrowed Maartje's car and took Joe to see his grandparents. On the drive she told him she was going to leave him there so she could visit Jeroen in hospital again. Afterwards she was going to meet Henk so they could 'discuss things'. She expected it was the last time she'd see Henk. He'd always told her he didn't want to leave his wife and children, and now that his wife knew about Nel it would be impossible for him to carry on seeing her. That would mean she'd lose the money he paid her as well. If she lost her money she would probably lose her flat, and she would definitely lose the luxury of having the time to paint. She said she didn't even know if her parents had read the papers. When they arrived she deposited him on the pavement and sped off.

Joe hoped his grandfather might give him a miniature figure to paint, or show him how some of the wiring worked. He enjoyed talking to his grandfather. It was a challenge to use the sprinkling of English words his grandfather understood plus the few Dutch ones that Joe knew.

Joe had been increasing his vocabulary fast, using a book he'd found in a second hand shop. The words were listed in the order of the most commonly used. He'd set himself a target of learning fifty a day, and he'd already got up to nearly five hundred. He got Emmie to test him, and she suggested a way to make it more interesting. They started with a small pile of jelly beans. If he got ten words right in a row he would get one of Emmie's jelly beans, and every time he got a word wrong he had to give her one of his. He wasn't really very keen on jelly beans – they were sickly sweet and most of them tasted of chemicals – but he wanted to beat her very much. After he ended up with all of her jelly beans several times in a row, they changed the rules so it was every fifteen words, and this evened things out a bit.

He'd even learnt some specialist words so he could communicate with his grandfather – signal, tracks, paint, engine…

His grandmother answered the door, and Joe knew that something was wrong as soon as he saw her face. She ushered him into the living room, where his grandfather was half-asleep on a chair. There was a glass of something clear in front of him. He jumped up when he saw Joe and lurched over to hug him. He smelt rotten, and Joe couldn't help veering away. His grandfather squinted at Joe and his face grew dark. He opened his arms again and Joe hugged him politely, but it seemed to be too late. His grandfather looked angry, and started muttering something under his breath. Joe was frightened by his behaviour, and looked over to his grandmother for reassurance. She wouldn't catch his eye, and she looked even more anxious than he was.

Joe remembered what Nel had said about her mum. "She never did anything. She'd moan and complain and humiliate him in front of other people, but she never *stopped* it." His grandfather gave him a final dark look before stumbling out of the room, slamming the door hard behind him. Joe sat and played cards with his grandmother for a while, and then he brought out his book. He ate the sandwiches and drank the juice his grandmother provided, and thanked her politely. His grandfather never reappeared. He kept one ear open for the sound of Nel's car returning, and was flooded with relief when he heard it pull up. He'd said goodbye to his grandmother and was out into the street before Nel had a chance to knock on the front door.

Nel didn't speak on the way home. Joe didn't want to hear anything about Jeroen or Henk anyway. As soon as he got home he went to his room and started writing a letter to Podge.

He'd be seeing him in less than a week and he wasn't sure if the letter would arrive before he did, but there was too much going on in his head and he wanted to spill some of it out onto paper. He told Podge about his grandfather and about how pretty Emmie looked at the show. He told him about the stories in the newspapers, and the bad mood Nel had been in. He told him about everything except the phone calls with his mum.

When he'd finished writing, he felt grateful that he had Podge as a friend. He could imagine him reading the letter, biting the tip of his little finger, and caring about what Joe had written. Joe wasn't very nice to his friend a lot of the time. When Joe thought about it now, he couldn't remember exactly what was so annoying about Podge. When they went to the cinema together and there was a funny bit, Podge would sometimes turn to Joe and smile, wanting to share the joke with someone. Joe could see him doing it out of the corner of his eye. But Joe never turned to Podge and smiled back. He just sat there, staring straight ahead as if he hadn't seen him. Eventually Podge would just turn away again. Why didn't Joe just turn and smile?

He could be horrible sometimes. His mum was right. And here was the thought he'd been trying to avoid. He was the reason she was ill. He didn't do the things she asked him to, he never asked her how she was, he didn't even tidy his room. He could even remember her saying it once, a few years ago, when he was having a tantrum. "You'll make me ill, if you carry on like this." Joe had always thought she meant a physical illness – a cold, or maybe the shingles like his Grandma Pearl had had. Not this. It was his fault. Would he make things worse, by going back to England? Wouldn't she be better off without him?

On the fifth morning after the exhibition, Joe woke to the smell of bacon. He went into the kitchen and found Nel singing to herself. There was a fine spatter of pale blue paint on her cheek.

"Morning Joey!"

Joe grunted.

"Sit down and let me make you some bacon and eggs."

Joe's stomach gurgled. He was ravenous. What had he eaten over the past few days? He couldn't remember anything except endless rounds of toast and chocolate spread, both at Nel's and at Emmie's, and the sandwiches at his grandmother's.

"Can I have two eggs?"

"You can have as many eggs as you like, darling."

"Yum."

Nel looked pleased. After she cracked the eggs into the pan she turned to him and crossed her arms.

"Do you want to hear how I've sorted my life out, then?"

Joe nodded.

"Well, I couldn't sleep again last night and I started thinking. Something I read in a book once about failures being opportunities for success. I thought about the stories in the papers, about being exposed. What if it wasn't such a terrible thing at all, Joe? What if it was an opportunity for me to come clean, and to live my life as if it isn't a secret? I'm not ashamed of it, but I've been acting as though I am."

She opened the oven door and flipped the bacon over with her fingers before continuing. The delicious smell was making Joe's stomach go crazy.

"So I've made three important decisions. The first is to break off contact with Jeroen. I've got to do it, even though I don't want to. The second is to talk to Henk and to make a new proposal – that we keep our business relationship, if he still wants to help me with my art. He can be my agent, and take a commission from the paintings I sell in return for a smaller monthly payment. I've worked out that I can just about survive without him if I take on some extra shifts anyway. And the last thing is that I'm going to get serious about selling my art, not just leaving everything to Henk. I need to learn to be a businesswoman, Joe. I owe it to my paintings."

"Wow."

Nel beamed. "You think so? Wow?"

"Definitely. Definitely wow."

Nel ruffled his hair enthusiastically, and Joe shrugged her off.

"Good, Joe. That is what I shall do. Two eggs coming up."

Later that afternoon, there was another call. Joe could hear from Nel's voice that this one was different to the others. Joe could see her excitement mounting as the call progressed, and when she put the phone down she started dancing around the room.

"I've sold two of my paintings! Someone wants to buy two together! Joe – they want to buy them!"

She caught him and swept him into a waltz. And the afternoon got even better. Henk called, saying he'd had enquiries from three other galleries who wanted to show some of her work. Three! He told her that the bad publicity had worked after all – everybody was talking about the gallery where 'someone nearly died'. They were going to the exhibition to look for blood spots on the floor, and ended up admiring Nel's paintings instead. Henk told her that nobody expected her paintings to be so good.

Nel took Joe out to dinner to celebrate that night. He had his favourite meal in the world – cheeseburger and chips (without any green stuff in the burger, of course). As he ate, he watched Nel flirt with the waiter. If Nel was happy, then so was Joe.

Joe's last week in Amsterdam was clotted with goodbyes. His grandparents were first. Nel came inside the house with him this time, and managed to have a civilised conversation with her mum. Joe was starting to see how Nel always took her dad's side, even though he was usually the one doing something embarrassing or annoying. They all sat downstairs in the living room and there was a fine spread, just like the first time he'd visited. When it was time to go, Joe's grandmother pecked him on the cheeks as if she'd only just met him, but his grandfather swept him up into a suffocating hug and wouldn't let him go for ages. When he did finally pull away his eyes were glistening, and Joe felt sad too. He'd enjoyed their times together in the train room and at the adventure playground.

At the door Joe's grandfather said, "Last time, last time," and Nel told him not to be silly. On the drive home, Joe asked Nel what his grandfather had meant. She said his grandfather thought he'd never see Joe again because he'd be dead soon. Nel told Joe he was always saying things like that, and to not pay any attention to it.

Joe and Nel met with Henk in the posh café to say goodbye. They still had to work out the details, but Henk had agreed to a smaller monthly stipend in return for a percentage of her sales. Nel said she was surprised Henk's wife had agreed to it, but apparently he'd told her everything, and she'd decided to trust him. Nel and Henk had both wondered if maybe the whole thing had been for the best. Henk seemed to be in good spirits when they met up. He even made a few jokes in English that made Joe snort.

Joe also said goodbye to the staff at the café (including his friend the dog), one of the friendliest librarians, the old woman who lived in the flat downstairs, Nel's friends Anouk and Mariela, and the owner of the local shop. All of them said they looked forward to seeing Joe again on his next visit. Joe couldn't remember saying goodbye to this many people when he'd left England.

The only person he didn't say goodbye to was Jeroen. Nel had said her own goodbye after making her decision to cut off contact with him. She told Joe he'd taken it surprisingly well. Maybe it was all the happy pills they were dosing him up with. She said he was going to stay in hospital for a while, and so she knew he'd be in safe hands.

His goodbye to Emmie took an unexpected turn. Sometimes they'd hung out at a park a short walk from her place, and she'd asked him to meet her there rather than at hers. When he got there she led him to their favourite bench. It was in an isolated spot overlooking the pond, and sometimes they would play a counting game with the ducks. They walked towards the bench in silence, both of them with their hands in their pockets. It was unusual for Emmie not to be talking. She usually gave him a running commentary on the workings of her mind – "I still haven't done my Geography project" or, "Do you think cows ever get cold?" Joe thought the phrase was 'stream of consciousness'. Or maybe it was more like a raging river of consciousness. When they reached the bench, Emmie gestured that Joe should sit down. She sat so close to him that he could smell the mint on her breath. He was about to make a sarcastic comment about her silence when she draped an arm around him and leant in to kiss him on the lips.

He reared back in shock, and she laughed.

"Don't you like it?" she asked.

"You think… I didn't… It was just a bit of…" he started stammering, but before he could finish a sentence she had leant in again. Her lips were silky soft, and surprisingly warm. He could taste mint. He was still rigid with fear, but he managed to shift his body so it was in a more comfortable position, and parted his lips, pushing towards her. How was he meant to do this? Emmie moved her mouth too, it reminded him of cows pulling at the grass with their big lips, or the way his baby cousin suckled on your finger when you offered it to her. He wasn't sure how long they kissed, but it felt like a long time. His body started to thaw. He became bold enough to place a hand on her waist, just at the crook of it above her hip, and he felt himself getting hard. This alarmed him – what if she noticed? But he was enjoying it too much to stop now. He leant into her, hungrier. Suddenly Emmie leant back.

"There. You understand now, don't you?"

She spoke in Dutch, and he understood every word. He replied in Dutch.

"Thank you. Good."

He would rather have said 'nice' than 'good', but in the heat of the moment he couldn't remember the word. There was an echo of mint on his tongue. She was looking at him intensely, and he felt himself blushing. He looked away, towards the pond.

"Shall we count the ducks?"

Once he'd said this it sounded ridiculous, and he felt even more embarrassed.

Emmie switched to English too. "No, I've got to go now Joe. I have to meet a friend. I wanted to say goodbye to you properly."

"I liked your goodbye better than…" He nearly said his grandmother. It felt weird to mention her so soon after the kiss. "Better than anyone else's."

He wasn't sure what to say anymore. Everything sounded wrong. She smiled at him indulgently and ruffled his hair, just like Nel. How did she get to be so confident? She probably kissed boys all the time, he was probably her fifth this week. He didn't care. He'd rather be the fiftieth than not be on the list at all. He started composing a letter to Podge in his head before remembering that he'd be seeing him in a few days. Maybe even the day after tomorrow, if his dad let him out.

"Can I write to you?"

She shook her head. "I don't like writing letters. You can write to me if you want, but I won't write back. But when you come and see Nel next, you promise you'll come and see me again?"

Joe nodded. She was getting ready to go.

"One more kiss before you go?" He can't believe he dared to ask.

She smiled and put her finger on his lips.

"Always leave them wanting more, that's what my mum says. You'll remember me better that way."

She kissed him on the forehead, and he got a glimpse of her cleavage. He tried to freeze it in his memory. He started to feel turned on again, and forced himself to think about toads. Toads always halted his erections, he guessed it was something to do with their warty skin.

He offered to walk Emmie to her bus. As they walked across the park, she slipped her hand into his. He squeezed it, and she squeezed back. They had a conversation as they walked: he'd squeeze once, she'd squeeze back twice. She squeezed once, and he'd squeeze back twice. He wasn't sure what they were saying to each other, but it wasn't in Dutch or English. They didn't look at each other, and they didn't speak. The last image he had of her was through the back window of the bus. She put two fingers up at him, and then blew him a kiss.

Joe had been dreading his very last goodbye. He and Nel spent a cosy last night together. It was just the two of them as Joe had requested, and they stayed up late watching Dutch horror movies and eating popcorn. Joe learnt the Dutch words for 'hell', 'blood' and 'flesh-eating zombie'.

It was an early flight. When the alarm went off at 4.30 a.m., Joe succumbed to an irresistible urge to go back to sleep. Ten minutes later he felt Nel shaking his shoulder.

"Wake up, slaapkop."

When he opened his eyes he half expected to see his mum standing there. He'd been in the middle of a dream about Emmie (she was heavily pregnant with his baby) and it took him a few seconds to orientate himself. Nel looked exhausted – her eyes were puffy and her hair was all sticking up. The sky was completely black in the gap between his curtains.

"Half an hour before we need to leave, Joey. You might want a bit of toast – I'll see you when you come out of the bathroom."

Nel's voice was husky, and her breath smelt of coffee. There was the scent of coffee on the air too, wafting through from the pot brewing in the kitchen. He snorted.

"What?"

"Even at four thirty in the morning you can't go without your coffee."

She growled at him and whacked him gently with a pillow.

"Come on, up you get. See you in the kitchen."

His stomach felt unsettled and empty when he was pulling on his jeans and spraying deodorant under his arms, but by the time he'd brushed his teeth he'd found his appetite. He called out to Nel, "I'll have marmalade on mine, please!" She shouted back "Yes sir!" He'd miss these little routines they'd developed over the summer – the phrases they used with each other, the in-jokes that nobody else would find funny. They'd already agreed that he'd come back at Christmas to stay for a week, but that seemed so far away.

Would Nel still have the same luminous pink toothbrush when he came back? Would this 'DON'T FORGET TO PAY THE GAS BILL' note, which had been pinned to the kitchen fridge for the duration of his visit, still be here? Would Nel have new clothes? A new boyfriend? Would Henk still be around, and would he ever see Jeroen again? All those things would be carrying on without him here. He'd have his old Milton Keynes life back. His own bloody boring life.

He was looking forward to seeing Podge, and Podge's cat Brutus. He had missed his books – he kept wanting to look things up, and then remembering that his bookshelves were hundreds of miles away. He'd even missed his stupid old school, but he'd give up all of that if it meant he could stay in

Amsterdam. In a second. Maybe Nel would adopt him, and he could live with her forever. He sighed and looked at himself in the mirror. There was a spot blossoming on his chin, but his hair didn't look too bad.

He remembered Emmie's kiss again, and a warm glow spread through his body. He'd glowed all yesterday evening, and Nel said he looked like the cat who'd eaten the canary. Joe laughed at her and told her it should have been the cat who'd got the cream, but apparently she'd heard it on American TV. She got the truth out of him eventually, by firing questions at him until he surrendered. She was so proud of him, she'd glowed for the rest of the evening too. Joe wondered if the girls from school would recognise something new about him. Maybe they would want to kiss him too, now he knew how to kiss.

In the kitchen Joe found that Nel had cut his toast into eight pieces for him. He'd watched her cut her own slices into neat eighths at the beginning of the summer. It was so she could eat toast when she was painting without having to take a bite and put the piece down again. She said she ate less paint that way, although Joe wasn't convinced by the logic of this. She had arranged it symmetrically on the plate, just how he liked it. It was too much for him. He tried to wipe the tear away before she saw it, but Nel never missed anything. She biffed him gently on the arm before pulling him into a hug, and he allowed three more tears to roll down his cheeks before he took a deep breath and sighed.

"You silly old thing. You're as bad as me," Nel said, although she wasn't crying. "There, eat your beautifully arranged toast. This is only 'au revoir', you know, not goodbye."

He frowned and opened his mouth, but Nel slotted a piece of toast between his lips before he could disagree.

The taxi had been waiting for ten minutes by the time they left the apartment. Joe wasn't surprised – he couldn't remember arriving anywhere on time with Nel for the duration of the summer. Except for her exhibition. He tried to pay extra attention to the scenery as the taxi drove them through the dark streets of Amsterdam. He wouldn't get to see it again for a while. The dark blue sky was reflected in the flat canal water, criss-crossed with the black shadows of branches. The bicycles waited patiently for their sleeping owners. An older woman sat out on her balcony, wrapped in a blanket, reading a book. He tried to concentrate on what he was seeing, but his thoughts kept straying towards Emmie instead – her minty breath, his fingers in the hair at the nape of her neck. If he never ever kissed another girl, this memory would be enough to sustain him for the rest of his life.

He glanced across at Nel, who'd sat in the back to keep him company. She was caught up in her own world. He wondered if she was thinking about the two commissions she'd been offered through contacts of Henk's. She'd already sold five of her paintings from the exhibition. She said she'd be getting enough money to keep her going for a few months at least. Joe was relieved that things were working out for her. Some of the tangles in her love life seemed to have untangled all by themselves. He thought again about his project to try and sort her life out – he'd thrown the whole folder into the bin a few days ago. He wouldn't need to worry about her so much now.

The airport was bigger than Joe remembered. Joe wasn't keen for Nel to come all the way through to the Departure Lounge with him. He hated stringing out goodbyes, and would rather have let her take the same taxi straight back to her flat again. She assumed she was coming with him, though, and he didn't have the energy to protest. At least she could make sure he was in the right place. He didn't want to end up on the wrong plane, and touchdown in Zimbabwe rather than Gatwick.

There was a long queue at the check-in desk, but after his suitcase had been labelled and ferried away on the conveyor belt they still had half an hour to kill. Nel said she'd buy him his last Dutch coffee. Joe's stomach was feeling wonky again, so he chose a bottle of lemonade instead. Nel had coffee, of course, and a huge round pastry. Joe carried their tray to a plastic table and set it down roughly, sloshing her coffee. After they settled down, Nel peered at his face. He guessed she was looking at his spot.

"Yes, I think you look more healthy now. You've got a bit of colour, and your hair is much better."

He did feel different. He felt cool. Or a little less nerdy, at least. He just needed some new glasses now. He was going to ask his dad when he got home. He'd had these ones for years – the optician changed the lenses in them when his prescription changed. He wanted some of those trendy glasses, the round ones. Emmie's kiss had definitely helped too.

Nel looked down at her hands.

"So this is it, then. The end of the Summer."

Joe looked down too. Sad words. Maybe he'd never spend a whole summer in Amsterdam again. He might never see Emmie again, and she was sure to have a boyfriend by the time he returned anyway. He wouldn't be able to talk to Nel about what he was reading anymore, or what he was thinking. There would be no more chats while she made the dinner.

"I hate the phone."

Nel nodded her head.

"It's not the same, is it? Not the same as watching awful films together."

"Can I write instead?"

"Of course you can, Joey. I'd be very happy to get a letter from you. But once you're home you might forget about me. Other things will be much more exciting – school, your friends, girlfriends…"

Joe shook his head. "Not likely."

"Why not?"

He just shrugged, and took tiny sips of his drink. It was making him feel better. A small girl at the next table started screaming, and dropped herself onto the carpet where she banged her legs up and down against the floor. Her mother tried to pacify her, embarrassed. A large man in a turban was lying across three chairs just along from their table – Joe watched him open one eye and then go back to sleep. All these people, moving from one country to another. Where were they all going? Who were they going to see?

Joe sighed.

"That's a big sigh."

"I don't want to go home. With Mum, you know, it'll be…"

Nel nodded and looked off into the distance. She didn't say anything for a while and so Joe continued.

"If it gets out at school I'll be history. And I'm scared she's going to be weird. How should I act around her? How can I not make her any worse?"

Nel looked at him directly.

"That's not your job, darling. You can't make her better or worse – she's a grown-up – she has to do that herself. This is nothing to do with you, you do know that, don't you?"

Joe shrugged.

"Your mother made choices in her life, and some of them might have been the wrong ones. That's all. She'll get through it, I'm sure. But it's not your fault. It's nothing to do with you. You've got to remember that, do you believe me?"

She put her hands on his shoulders. "Do you believe me, Joe?"

Joe nodded. Secretly, he wasn't convinced. It did feel good to hear Nel say it.

Now Nel sighed. "I don't like saying goodbye. It feels so final. We'll meet again soon, won't we? Can we just say 'see you soon' instead?"

Joe nodded. There were things he wanted to say, but he couldn't find the words. He wasn't even sure what the things were, exactly. Maybe he could write them down in a letter. They finished their drinks and followed the signs to the Departure Lounge. Before they parted, Nel hugged him fiercely. Joe didn't turn back.

As the plane's engines started roaring and the plane prepared to takeoff, Joe remembered one of the things he wanted to say to Nel. It was too late now. He couldn't put it in a letter. He'd really wanted to say it to her face. He'd wanted to say thank you.

PART TWO

As the plane shuddered down the runway and then pushed, screaming, into the air, Joe's ears popped. It happened at every takeoff and touchdown, no matter how many boiled sweets he sucked, or how often he swallowed. This time, the sensation made him want to cry. He shifted his body in his seat, turning away from the teenage girl sitting next to him and facing the small window. He wished he could have some privacy.

He didn't know where this fresh wave of upset had come from. Tears of a mysterious origin had become a common occurrence for Joe in the preceding months. It had started at work, almost six weeks ago. He'd been working at the European Meteorological Centre as an Analyst for eighteen months now. He was a cloud formation expert in the Satellite Data Section, and his theoretical calculations contributed to the unimaginably complex model for predicting the weather that his colleagues had nicknamed 'The Beast'.

His research should be contributing to the accuracy of the model. But it hadn't been going very well. Joe's working days had been getting longer and longer. One of his colleagues, Thierry, had started making snide remarks about Joe's lack of tangible results. Helle, the woman Joe shared an office with, said that Thierry was only trying to be funny and to ignore him. Joe had tried, but then one lunchtime in the canteen Thierry had joked that maybe Joe had numerical dyslexia. He'd said it in front of everyone. Joe had burst into tears. A twenty nine year old

Analyst at the top weather centre in Europe, snivelling like a schoolboy.

Thierry was mortified, of course, and didn't know where to look. Joe cried, and his colleagues froze with their forks mid-air and gawped. Eventually his manager Herman noticed what had happened from the next table, and led Joe off to a meeting room. Joe left his untouched Thai green curry behind him. Herman didn't tell Joe to stop crying, which was just as well, as Joe found that he wasn't in control of himself. His boss went off to fetch a length of toilet paper and Joe was left alone, sobbing into his hands. He had the ridiculous thought that he'd never be able to stop, and that they'd have to put him on a drip to stop him from getting dehydrated. Maybe he'd wither away completely. Maybe he'd die.

He had eventually managed to stop crying, and Herman sent him home early. He started up again as soon as he shut the front door behind him, and then again the next day when Helle left him alone in their office at lunchtime. He'd gone to his dad's for a visit a few days later, and had broken down in front of his dad's girlfriend, Pam. After work he would return to his flat and go straight to his room, closing his bedroom door so his flatmate Rick couldn't hear him. He'd lie on his bed and cry, and then wait until Rick had gone to bed so he could emerge to cook himself Super Noodles without his red and swollen eyes being seen.

He became even more isolated than usual. He refused Paul's offer to go out for a beer three times in a row, and turned down all Podge and Sarah's invitations. He tossed and turned at night, numbers swarming through his dreams like ants, and felt listless all day. He lost his appetite. He missed four days of work within three weeks, because he simply couldn't face getting out of bed. After the crying incident Joe's manager had referred him to the HR manager, who'd told him to go and see his doctor. When the appointment finally came around, Joe's G.P. had asked him to fill in a form with questions like, "How often do you think about suicide?" and promptly signed him off work for six weeks. Six whole weeks! His G.P. told him he needed a complete break. A complete break from what? Joe didn't understand what was wrong with him.

It would have made more sense if this emotional cloud had descended upon him when he was fourteen. He remembered getting back from Amsterdam to find his house in chaos – his mum an inpatient at the mental health unit, and his dad utterly failing to look after himself properly, never mind Joe. He remembered the botched sandwiches he got in his lunchbox at school, and his dad's creased shirts, and what his classmates used to say about his mum.

He wouldn't have been surprised if it had happened at seventeen, when his mum had her second breakdown and then Dad was in hospital with shingles and he was at home alone all the time, trying to work out how to use the washing machine, and dealing with trips to that awful place to visit his mum. He might have been pushed over the edge at the end of his undergraduate degree, when he had to leave his beloved tutor Dr. McKie behind and set off into the big wide world, a world he was still entirely unequipped to deal with.

He would even have understood if it had happened at the end of last year, when his work started going wrong, and when his old manager Susan was leaning heavily on him, and when he had to deal with his mum's mental health deteriorating (again). Oh, and his relationship with Meg was in its final death throes. He acknowledged that there wasn't much of a relationship to break down, but they had lived together for nearly three years. That was still a long time to have a non-relationship. Especially when it was the closest he'd got to a proper relationship since that fumbled affair with Jenny when he was nineteen.

Since then, his work had been showing signs of improvement, and his new boss Herman had been very supportive. His mum had improved again, and was back in her flat with the support of the community psychiatric nurses. He'd even stopped feeling so sad about Meg. That was around the time that the dreams had started. The nightmares.

In the dreams, he kept turning invisible. He would be talking with his dad in the day room in hospital where his mum stayed when she was ill, or holding hands with Meg, and he'd look down and notice his skin becoming translucent. As soon as he noticed he was fading away, he became powerless – he couldn't make a noise, or any movements. The dreams always ended with his complete disappearance. His dad would look round the room for him, calling "Joe?" or even worse, Meg would notice he'd gone and look relieved.

The dreams reminded him of a film, where Will Smith was the only person left alive in New York. Three years ago everyone else had been wiped out by a virus that turned people into zombies. Smith had a big dog, Samantha, and she went everywhere with him. You saw him washing the dog in the bath, and riding in the car with the dog grinning at the open window. Smith talked to her all day long – she was his link to sanity. Halfway through the film, the dog turned into a zombie and Smith had to kill her. The grief was too much for Joe to hold.

As Joe remembered Samantha now, his body clenched and threatened to shake. He stayed facing the window and let the tears roll down. It was ridiculous, getting so upset over a fictional character. The dog didn't really die, it probably went on to film a comedy cop movie, and he was sure Will Smith had gone home to a beautiful wife and glittery showbiz friends. But he couldn't stop thinking about that dog dying. He couldn't help thinking that, if he were Smith, he would've had to kill himself straight afterwards. Before he had time to feel any of that grief. He would have to put a bullet through his brain.

His invisibility dreams didn't sound terrifying to anyone else. Podge said it sounded really cool to be invisible, and advised him to go and find some women's changing rooms or a lesbian orgy. He even tried to tell his doctor about them, but she didn't seem to know how to respond and changed the subject. He couldn't explain the horror. What would be the point of living, if nobody could see him or hear him? Every so often, when there was no mail on the doormat for him yet again, or when someone passed him in the corridor at work without acknowledging him, he'd have the chilling thought that maybe his dream was already coming true.

He took a quiet, deep breath. He was desperately hoping that nobody would start asking him if he was okay. In his current state of mind, he was worried he might tell them to fuck off and mind their own business. These alarming bursts of anger had started at the same time as the tears. He wouldn't describe himself as an angry person. He was sarcastic, and Podge often accused him of moodiness, but he very rarely let his anger out directly. He was surprised at how suddenly the fury had been rising up, and at how quickly it drained away again. Sometimes he wasn't able to keep a hold on it, and it came out in spikes and hurt people.

He'd upset his mother last week. His dad was forever saying, "Don't upset your mother." It was his mantra for Joe's teenage years. Joe had gone round to visit her in her mouldy flat, and she'd started to do that stupid rocking thing at her kitchen table. It had always driven Joe mad. He didn't care if it was a side-effect of her medications or not, he was convinced she did it on purpose when she wanted attention. It burst out of him: "Stop that fucking rocking!" and she did stop, for five shocked seconds. She pushed back her chair and exited, leaving Joe to the empty kitchen's burning disapproval. He took another deep breath. He'd stopped crying now. He blew his nose into a tissue. Man-size.

Joe could hardly remember what it was like, before his summer with Nel. He thought about her, all those years ago. He had such a good time that summer. The freedom of being able to wander the streets of Amsterdam, of helping himself to books from the library whenever he wanted. The late night conversations with a slightly-drunk-Nel about her complicated love life. She always took him so seriously. Sometimes he thought she must have been the first person ever to treat him like a real person, a person in his own right. And that kiss! He could only remember a couple of the details now – running his fingers through the hair at the nape of Emmie's neck, and the taste of mint in her mouth. He still felt warm and squishy whenever he thought about it. He knew he'd only been fourteen, and that Emmie hardly knew him, but when he thought about that moment, he felt lovable.

He'd never had that warm squishy feeling with Meg. He didn't know if it was because of their arid sex life. 'Our sexual dysfunction', as Meg referred to it. She always made it sound so clinical. He didn't know why it was always 'our' and not 'my' –

she was the one with the phobia of 'sexual intercourse', as she called it. He could cope with not having penetrative sex with her. She'd let him rub himself against her stomach or her thigh until he climaxed, so he wasn't sexually frustrated. The worst thing was that Joe couldn't be sure if she enjoyed any of their physical relationship together. Even when they kissed. He knew that she made an effort, and that she felt terribly guilty about not being able to offer him more. But whenever Joe touched her waist when he passed her in the kitchen, or cuddled up with her on the sofa, he felt her shrinking back.

How could anyone take any pleasure from another person's body, knowing that they were merely enduring the whole episode? Joe could. That was the shameful truth – he did take his pleasure whenever he could. It was only afterwards, when he looked into Meg's empty eyes, that he'd feel sick with guilt.

He was still a virgin, technically. A twenty nine year old virgin. As he had this thought, he wasn't sure whether to laugh or cry. How did he arrive at the cusp of his third decade without being allowed inside a woman, not even once? What was wrong with him? He was a hopeless case, hopeless. He put his head in his hands, in a parody of despair. After a few minutes he fished his iPod out and fiddled about with it. A good dose of Sigur Ros – that's what he needed. Some other-worldly music to take him away from this stupid plane that smelt of stale farts, and these stupid air hostesses with their fixed grins. Most of all, to take him away from himself. His stupid bloody life.

Joe drifted off into sleep, and woke up with a jolt when the girl next to him folded up her table with a loud 'bang'. The plane had begun to make its descent. He looked at his watch – it was nearly seven, but the sky was still bright outside. They were sliding down through the clouds. Joe recognised forms and features like old friends: cirrus spissatus, altocumulus lenticularis, cumulus mediocris, and, in the far distance, even an impressive cumulus congestus. Sigur Ros was still playing on his iPod, and he listened to the sweeping strings for a while before unhooking the earpieces from his ears. He glanced sideways at his teenage neighbour – she was reading a Stephanie Meyer book with glazed eyes.

He loved the precise moment when the plane touched down. He always wondered how gently the pilot would manage it. Maybe pilots prided themselves on the smoothness of their touchdowns, and boasted about it to their wives. He would, if he was a pilot. This landing was a little bit jerky, but too not bad. He listened to the roar of the reverse thrust after they hit the runway. He was thirsty, but it was too late now. The doctor had told him it was a common side effect of the anti-depressants he'd started taking a few weeks ago – dry mouth, nausea, insomnia... The list of side-effects sounded worse than the depression.

He didn't trust drugs, after his family's experience with his mum's medication over the years. His G.P. insisted, though, and he didn't have the strength to protest. Maybe he'd just stop taking them, when he got to Holland. He could see what Nel thought, or maybe he'd do some reading about it. He was surprised he hadn't been woken up to be offered a coffee or a beer during the flight. He wasn't expecting a meal, but he thought he'd at least get a free cold drink and a mini packet of peanuts as part of the deal. It wasn't like the old days. You had to pay for everything separately now, even your bloody luggage.

It was good of Nel to offer to put him up for the summer. Joe hadn't spoken to her properly for ages. They both hated the phone. He had emailed her to check she was sure, and to warn her that he wasn't in the mood to be sociable. She had plenty of room now, she told him, and he'd be free to suit himself. He hadn't even seen her new place yet. The latest one. She's still right in the middle of the city, next to the canal, but she's got a whole house to herself now, all four floors. It sounded huge, especially for Amsterdam. Her houses had grown in size over the years, in tandem with her reputation as an artist.

As he walked through the airport, the anxiety rose. He hadn't seen Nel for ages. How many years? She'd come to stay with his parents that time, but Joe was busy at work and he only saw her for lunch one day. And before that, maybe four years? The last time he visited her in Amsterdam, he had just met Meg. He didn't know much about her life recently, only what his mum passed on, and his mum wasn't the most reliable of messengers.

He knew that Henk had been ill, and that Nel had spent a lot of time visiting him at his house. She'd become good friends with Henk's wife over the years. His mum had told Joe that there was a new man on the scene too – another young one, another Jeroen. He knew one of her beloved cats had been run over last year. That was all. He should have kept in better touch. He'd been selfish. But this thought led him to a sudden crushing attack of self pity. He hadn't had any energy to worry about anyone else, lately. He'd put everything into trying to make it work with Meg. He'd put everything into worrying about his mum, and work – especially work. Look where it had got him.

Joe collected his orange suitcase (always easy to spot on the luggage conveyor belt) and passed through Arrivals. He thought of Podge, who would have made a predictable joke about internal searches for drugs. As he rounded the corner he spotted Nel in the crowd, waving like a maniac. A grin appeared on his face, the first one he could remember for a long time.

"Joey!"

Nobody called him that in England. It felt good to hear it.

"Nel – good to see you, you are looking well." He said this in perfect Dutch, wanting to impress her.

"Ah, your accent is coming along nicely! What a clever boy!" Nel replied, also in Dutch. She pulled him into a hug, fierce and brief.

He was pleased to have his accent praised. He'd worked hard on his Dutch. It had helped him to keep his mind off work, and Meg. It was the only leisure activity he allowed himself. He'd been listening to Dutch radio on the internet to get comprehension practice, and reading Dutch novels to improve his vocabulary. Conversational Dutch practice was more difficult to come by. Ordinarily he would have relished the thought of all this real life opportunity to practice, but he couldn't raise any enthusiasm for it at the moment. He lapsed back into English straight away.

"How is Henk?"

"Oh, not so good, not so good. I'll tell you all about it later. Let's get you home, shall we? Oh, you do look thin, Joe. I'll have to feed you up."

He frowned, and she smiled at him affectionately, ruffling his hair.

"I am twenty nine now, you know."

She looked sad. "Twenty nine. No, you are still fourteen to me. You'll always be fourteen, and then I can be twenty nine again. Everything was simple then. Do you want to have a coffee somewhere?"

Joe shrugged. He was eager to get out of this too-bright, too-busy place. People kept knocking up against him or his orange suitcase, and he might tell one of them to fuck off if they did it again. He didn't want to lose his temper in front of his aunt.

"You look tired, Joey. Come on, let's go home."

Once they were in the car, Joe had a chance to get a proper look at her. She was wittering away, telling him about the weather, and a friend who'd put herself forward for the local elections. Nothing important, he could afford to fade her out. She had thickened up over the years, and her body reminded him of his mother's, or even their own mother. There were wrinkles radiating from her eyes, but she didn't have the deep creases across her forehead that his mum had. He had a few wrinkles of his own now, and he was afraid of getting them on his own forehead. Seeing Nel's smooth forehead gave him hope – maybe if he used his face in a different way then he'd be okay. He'd have to start paying attention to his expressions.

Nel's clothes were similar to the kind of things she'd always worn. She was dressed in a pink embroidered silk tunic over wide culottes, and long silver necklaces garlanded her neck. She still looked 'arty', but somehow Joe could tell that her clothes had come from fancy 'ethnic' boutiques at great expense. How odd that she had pots of money now, but she still bought the kind of clothes she'd find in second hand shops or hippy markets when she was poor.

Joe's dad went on and on about how rich Nel was now. He was incredulous that someone could make so much money from paintings that 'didn't even look like real people'. Money had never really been important to Joe. He never knew what he should spend his wages on, and the excess just built up in his current account. He kept thinking he ought to do something with it – put it in a savings account or something. His dad said that Joe wasn't worried about money because he'd never had to go without anything, not like his own impoverished childhood. Maybe he was right. What did other people spend their money on?

Nel was saying something about her neighbours now. Joe looked out at the drizzly street. The ever present bicyclists were getting wet. He recognised a few of the buildings now from his previous trips. Here was an elderly couple holding hands, and here were a handful of teenagers – probably gossiping about who snogged who at the party last night. There was a mother, bending over to help her small boy open his packet of crisps. Joe could see her face. She looked so kind. Joe started crying again. He let the tears run down his face, silently. When he sniffed, Nel turned to glance at him and then looked again, harder.

"Joe, what's wrong?" She sounded horrified.

He sniffed again, and shrugged. "I just keep crying all the time. I don't know why." He considered telling her about the mother and child, but was worried he might sound crazy.

Nel was quiet. The crying eased off, and Joe extracted a tissue from his bag and blew his nose noisily. When he blew his nose in public, he sometimes thought about something Podge's wife Sarah had said to him once. He'd been in the middle of a horrendous cold, and after a particularly energetic mucus-evacuation session she'd said fondly, "No wonder you haven't got a girlfriend". He kept forgetting to ask Podge what she'd meant.

Good old Podge. Joe hadn't found an opportunity to talk to Podge about how he was feeling. He didn't think Podge had ever been depressed in his life. He got grumpy often enough, and Joe had seen him upset – millions of times when he was younger, and then at his mum's funeral, or whenever Manchester United lost. When Joe tried to describe how his flat mood could pin him to his bed for entire weekends, Podge just didn't seem to get it. He kept saying, "But why don't you just remember all the good things in your life", or, "Just give it a few days, you'll feel better". This advice hadn't been of any help to Joe at all. Although, to be fair, it wasn't just Podge's advice that was useless. Nobody had said anything yet that had made him feel any better. He slid the snot-filled tissue back into his bag.

"There, I've finished now."

He felt embarrassed, and snorted, which embarrassed him further. He wasn't a teenager anymore, he was a grown man. A grown man, with a place of his own and a proper job. A man with an ex-girlfriend. Nel put a hand on his knee, and squeezed it.

"I've been talking on and on, and I haven't even asked how you are," she said, sounding disappointed in herself.

"Oh, I don't want to get into that now. You'd be bored to death, anyway."

"No I wouldn't."

"OH yes you would…"

She smiled at his intonation. Five years ago during a trip to England, Nel had arranged to see an old artist friend of hers who'd moved to London with her young family. They'd arranged an outing to a pantomime, and Nel had persuaded Joe to come along with them. Nel had loved it – joining in with all the children with the, "OH no you're not"s and the, "He's

BEHIND you!"'s. Joe hated every second. He felt pressured to join in with all the fake jollity, and spent the whole performance in dread that he'd be picked out of the audience and asked up onto the stage.

"OH no I WOULDN'T. Don't forget, Joey, you're talking to the woman with the most complicated private life in all of Holland."

Joe grunted. Waves of tiredness were sweeping through him. It was the kind of fatigue that hits your body as well as your mind. His eyelids ached to close.

"I'm really sleepy," he said, through a yawn.

"We're nearly there now, and you can have a nap as soon as we get in if you want. We can go out for dinner later if you have the energy. Or I can order some food in. Whatever you like. This is your recuperation holiday. Your wish is my command!"

Joe had an image of her in a pink tutu with wings and a wand. His fairy godmother. He looked out of the window again and tried to keep his eyes open. The car swished on through the rain.

Joe woke to Nel shaking him gently. He stretched and yawned, and looked out at Nel's house, which he recognised from the pictures she'd posted on Facebook. It was much more impressive in real life. It was red brick, and seemed somehow more solid than the houses to either side of it, which had both been converted to high end flats. Nel's front door was heavy blue-painted wood, studded with iron nails – you could see the history in it. Joe admired the neat blue shutters, and the white painted bricks that made an arc above every window. There was a mosaic in black and white tiles saying '1903', and Joe wondered for a moment about all the people who had lived in this house since it was built. Had anyone been born here? Had anyone died?

Nel told him to leave his suitcase in the boot – the driver would take it up to Joe's room for him. She opened the door wide and ushered him in.

"Welcome to my palace!" she announced.

She took off her coat and chucked it over the staircase balustrade as Joe looked around. The hallway was very Nel-ish: a mixture of order and chaos. A table pushed against the wall held a few objects arranged neatly and symmetrically – a phone, a letter rack, a pot of pens, a pad of paper. It wouldn't have been out of place in Joe's dad's ultra-neat office. The effect of this tidy spot was ruined by Nel's coat rack, which was heaving with coats, scarves and hats, hovering above a jumble of shoes, wellies and slippers… It was as if it might come alive at any moment. A coat-monster. It would surge and billow towards them both, arms out, and sweep them both up into its musty embrace before swallowing them whole. Joe smiled to himself. His own insane thoughts were just about the only thing that amused him these days.

Nel led him through to the kitchen, so she could make herself a ubiquitous coffee. It was a big room, full of shiny implements and devices that looked like they hadn't been used. A row of saucepans and frying pans hung from a long metal rod on the wall, hooked on big metal 'S's. The silver clock on the wall (with a silently sweeping second hand) said it was nearly eight – to Joe it felt hours later. He sat at the wooden table, sinking back gratefully into the cushioned chair.

"What can I get you, munchkin?"

Joe wondered where on earth she'd got that. Munchkin?

"Do you have any cocoa?"

Joe had fond memories of Nel's cocoa. He remembered a one afternoon when they both decided to 'go on strike' and watch trashy TV from the sofa with a blanket covering their knees. Nel called in sick to work. It felt so naughty. Joe thought about sharing this memory with Nel, but as he watched her busy herself at the stove the words melted away on his tongue. Slipped back down his throat.

Words had been doing that, lately. A few weeks ago, before the crying at work, Helle had teased Joe about speaking more and more quietly. She'd said that soon they'd only be able to see Joe's mouth moving, and that only dogs would be able to hear him.

That reminded him. The report he was responsible for. He'd left one unfinished, a fortnight ago. It was the very first one he hadn't finished on time. A flush of shame moved through him, and he felt the itch of fresh tears. He wondered who was dealing with his workload. He was completely useless to them now. Although maybe he'd been completely useless when he was at work anyway. Maybe nobody was missing him. His thoughts kept swinging between these two extremes. One minute he was the only one who knew the password for a spreadsheet that, when it couldn't be opened, would bring the whole place to a complete standstill. And then he swung to the other extreme. His boss knew all the passwords. That bloke in the next office, who didn't seem to do anything all day except play Solitaire and call his mother, could easily take most of his workload. His research was going nowhere anyway. How could he possibly justify the level of his pay? He earned far too much. He'd been fooling them all.

There was a sharp 'clock' as Nel put a mug down in front of him onto a deep blue porcelain coaster.

"So, Joey, what shall we talk about now?"

Joe shrugged. He thought he might try to smile, but instead he lifted his mug and wafted it under his nose. The hot steam and the rich chocolaty smell rose up. His vision clouded as condensation bloomed on his glasses. He thought about his optician, and the small dark room where he took his sight tests. She was a nice stout Asian woman, with one of those bosoms where the boobs joined up to become a single shelf. He couldn't help wondering what kind of bra she was wearing underneath her blouse. Did it even have separate compartments for the left and right breasts?

Breasts. Usually even thinking about the word would be enough to raise a twitch. He didn't know where his sexual appetite had disappeared to. He hadn't even been masturbating, lately. A fortnight ago, as an experiment, he dug out one of his old porn magazines from the back of the cupboard, but the images had left him cold. He'd thought about trying to tell his G.P., thinking it might be important information, but he was too embarrassed. A twenty nine year old impotent virgin. If he couldn't get it up anymore, then he might as well be dead.

There it was again. He might as well be dead. 'Suicidal thoughts', as the G.P. described them. They kept appearing in his brain, nagging at him. It wasn't a matter of whether he should kill himself. He gave that only brief consideration, before acknowledging how much better off the world would be without him. Thierry at work would finally step into his job, which would make him the happiest man alive. Not to mention the effect the pay rise would have on his three children.

Would anyone miss him? He'd been a constant disappointment to his dad. He wasn't sure if his mum was bothered one way or the other, but she had started mentioning grandchildren a lot recently, and he was sure to fail at that. Podge would miss him, and Sarah, but he only saw them a couple of times a month anyway. They were such nice people, Joe was sure they could find a replacement friend in no time.

The thoughts that plagued him were more a matter of when, and how. Asking his G.P. for help had complicated matters. He didn't want her to lose sleep, wondering if she could have done something more to prevent his death. Now he felt obligated to practise 'thinking positively', and to take the bloody pills for a while (or pretend to). He'd need to convince her that he's made a full recovery, and then wait a good couple of weeks. Surely then she'll be able to think, "Well, it was nothing to do with me." It meant he'd have to wait longer, though. Bide his time.

As far as the method went, he'd settled on pills so far. He had already stashed away some anti-depressants at home, and he could also use the bottle he had with him now. His only worry was that an overdose wasn't very manly. He had heard somewhere that more men succeed in killing themselves than women because they chose more direct methods – shooting, hanging, jumping in front of trains. Taking pills did seem cowardly. He wouldn't be able to bear it if he survived, and was then accused of attention seeking. He'd just have to make really sure he swallowed enough of them, so he wasn't around to deal with any consequences. He'd get his calculations right.

The silky texture of the cocoa distracted him. It was delicious. He could feel it warming his stomach, and the heat radiated out to his hands, his toes, to the tip of his nose. He wanted to thank Nel, but again the words got stuck in his throat. She was looking expectant. Had she said something to him? She was looking into his eyes, searchingly. His mum used to look at him like that when he was younger, in the quiet aftermath of his stormy tantrums. Nel brushed against his hair with the back of her hand. Joe liked the feel of it, and angled his head towards her as her hand moved away. Like a cat.

"It doesn't matter, Joe. You've had a long journey, eh? Maybe you don't want to talk about anything tonight. We can just sit here and drink. Is it good?"

He nodded gratefully. The words 'thank you' were still sitting in his mouth. He was stupidly grateful to her, for making him this mug of cocoa. When was the last time someone had made him a drink? Except Sarah, of course. Sarah was always kind. He was happy for his friend, for having found such a lovely wife, but sometimes it didn't feel fair. Podge was just so... so ordinary. He had an ordinary job, an ordinary car, an ordinary everything. Wasn't Joe equally deserving of a nice girlfriend? He had a proper job, at the Weather Centre, and he knew all kinds of things about all kinds of subjects.

Podge had picked up the rules of relationships from somewhere. Everyone else seemed to know them too. How did he miss out? Was it because he grew up with his head in a book? Or maybe he was just born broken. Something had snapped inside him when he was cosseted in his mum's belly. He wasn't sure that you could fix that kind of damage. He'd always be broken, just like Jeroen was.

Joe drained the last of his cocoa and looked around at Nel's kitchen. The walls were painted a dark burgundy colour, and scattered with framed art postcards. A tall dresser stood against the end wall holding row upon row of milk jugs, mugs and bowls, all in mismatched colours. There was a blue glass bowl full of bright lemons in the middle of the table, and plants lined the windowsill behind the sink. Sitting there was like sitting inside a hug. He wanted to remember everything about it – catalogue every object, memorise every postcard. He wanted to tuck it all away somewhere safe, like the facts he still gobbled from books.

Maybe he could write a letter to Podge, and describe it all. He hadn't written a letter to anyone for years. He sent emails to Nel, and sometimes they talked on Instant Messenger. Nel had the annoying habit of using the winking face at the end of practically everything she said. He sniffed the air in the kitchen. It smelt overwhelmingly of Nel's coffee – the one she was drinking now, and all the thousands of previous cups. There was also a faint rotting vegetable smell. Maybe it was coming from Nel's compost bin – she'd told him she'd just started making it for the tomatoes she grew in her tiny back yard. And there was something else. It was in the background – something warm and musty. It reminded him of freshly baked bread, or snuff. Something comforting. He sniffed audibly, and Nel looked over at him.

"Are you crying again?"

He snorted. "No, I'm just trying to work out what that smell is. I remember it from somewhere…" He trailed off in concentration before saying, "It just smells like home."

Nel smiled. There was such warmth in her face. As if she really cared about him, stupid idiot that he was, social failure and career wrecker and bad son and failed boyfriend. Her look washed through him like the cocoa, and for a sweet moment he sucked it in, allowed himself to bathe in it. A sweet moment, before something shut – a wall slid down, like the metal cages that protect shop fronts at night. She was still smiling at him, but when he looked at her, he felt nothing. She could have been anyone.

The next morning, Joe woke to an empty house. Nel had told him she had a meeting in Utrecht – complaining that her career demanded more meetings from her now than it did actual painting. At first, Joe didn't know where he was. He hadn't seen his room properly last night, through his haze of sleepiness and the lack of light. He had half expected to wake up in the makeshift bed on the floor of Nel's little studio in her old flat. Her studio, which she'd given up for a whole six weeks that summer while she painted in a cramped corner of her bedroom. At the time, he hadn't realised what an inconvenience it must have been. He can't imagine she'd welcomed the thought of entertaining a sullen fourteen year old for all that time. Although maybe it wasn't as much bother as hosting a depressed nephew.

It was a spacious room, with a high ceiling, and decorated in a palette of pale greens and a dark purple colour that reminded Joe of aubergines. There was a big pile of cushions on the floor that Joe could remember chucking off the bed – he'd never understood the concept of putting cushions on a bed. Two of the walls were almost completely lined with tall bookcases, and the dark grey carpet looked thick and soft. The lush curtains traced the shape of a bay window, and two antique chairs faced a view of the canal. They were upholstered in pale green silk, with a silver embroidered pattern. Joe briefly considered getting out of bed to go over and touch his cheek to the material, but decided he couldn't be bothered. He couldn't be bothered to do anything anymore. Even reading had lost its juice.

He heard a slow creak, and looked across to his bedroom door, which was slowly opening of its own accord. First whiskers appeared, and then a delicate pink nose and slanted eyes. The cat paused for a second, appraising this new man in her favourite bedroom, before leaping lightly into the room and onto the bed. She landed on the plump duvet with a 'whoomph', and proceeded to ignore Joe completely as she pushed her claws in and out of the material with great concentration. That explained the snagged threads, scattered across this expensive looking throw.

"So you must be Tante Truus. Hello, pussycat. Hello, Truus."

Joe brought a hand from under the duvet and held it out towards the cat, making a kissing noise with his mouth, but she had far more important things to attend to. Her only concession to his attention was to put one ear back in a gesture of mild annoyance. When he leaned back into his pillows he saw her relax, her shoulders still pumping. After a few minutes she followed her tail in three circles like a dog, curled into a tight ball and shut her eyes.

Joe stretched his feet down to the bottom of the bed and looked at the silver clock on his bedside table. Ten forty five. Since he'd been off work, he'd started sleeping late again. It was as if there was some kind of glue keeping him in his bed in the mornings. He woke up exhausted, as if half his blood had been drained from him in the night. It was much easier to slide back into sleep, and return to his dreams. His dreams had been a comfort to him recently. He didn't have to deal with people in his dreams, or try to get anything right for anyone. He wasn't a disappointment to anyone.

He'd never known how to say the right thing. He remembered Nel confiding in him that summer, telling him all about her love life. What was she thinking, giving so much intimate information to a completely clueless teenager? Hadn't he had some ridiculous notion at the time that he could work things out for her? He knew better now. He'd never dare to imagine he'd have anything useful to add to a conversation about relationships. At fourteen, he held out hope that relationships could be reduced to logic – the same kind of logic that he applied to everything else. He thought he'd be able to suss them out as soon as he gathered enough facts, arranged them into categories, and applied the right analysis. Like learning a new language. Since then, everything he'd thought he knew about relationships had been shattered. Over and over again.

Nel getting back together with Jeroen was one of the facts he couldn't make fit. It was after Jeroen had got out of hospital, after she'd promised Joe it was over forever. Nel didn't admit it to Joe for ages. He started getting the feeling that there was something she was leaving out of her letters. He had enough of his own problems at the time, with his mum still in hospital and his dad struggling to hold things together at home. The relationship had only lasted another four months, but how could she, after what Jeroen had done to her? It shook Joe's faith in her.

After Nel broke up with him for a final time, Jeroen started stalking her – making phone calls in the middle of the night, turning up at her work. Eventually she had to get a restraining order against him. He got into trouble with the police, and continued taking too many drugs. He died three years after

Joe saw him slit his wrists, from head injuries after he fell off a wall. Nobody knows whether he jumped or fell. There were drugs in his system when he died. Nel hadn't seen him for over a year by that point. She'd spent so long feeling furious at him. She went to his funeral through duty, but told Joe that she was surprised by how affected she was when she saw his coffin.

Another surprise to Joe was Nel's refusal of Henk's serious offer to leave his wife and move in with her. Henk had even asked his wife for a divorce, in a desperate attempt to win Nel over. Desperate – not something Joe could imagine of the Henk he remembered. Accepting Henk's offer would have solved her money problems forever – she could have painted all day long. Henk had gone back to his wife soon enough, and they'd had couples counselling and mostly lived happily together ever since.

Nel solved her money problems for herself, eventually. It took her another nine years of hard work. She lost her flat after refusing Henk's offer (he withdrew all his financial support despite their previous agreement), and had to move in with a landlady, taking a single room at the top of the house with barely enough room for a bed, never mind her canvases. She was determined not to accept any money from her parents. When Joe went to visit her when he was seventeen, just for a couple of nights, he had to sleep on a camp bed in the hallway. She tried to put a brave face on, cooing about how sweet her landlady was, but she looked tired and drawn. There were long years of poverty, but her art triumphed. She told Joe she always knew she'd get there, eventually. It was only a matter of time.

Tante Truus stirred, and positioned herself like Jabba the Hut so she could wash her generous belly. It wasn't a very dignified position. It almost raised a smile in Joe, but just before it formed he remembered that he was depressed. He immediately felt crushed. And then a familiar thought arrived. Could he be making this all up? Was he choosing to be so miserable, choosing not to cope? It was a terrible thought, and it always left him feeling uneasy and guilty. All these people he was inconveniencing. It would be like pretending to have a broken leg – getting the hospital to plaster him up, taking time off work, and his colleagues having to take up the slack of his workload… No. The only way he could bear this illness was to see it as completely out of his control. If he thought about the depression as a virus, as something physical, then he could just about manage to live with himself.

He let his head drop back into the hollow in the pillow. Nel had told him she was coming back at lunchtime to take him somewhere, 'a surprise'. He didn't feel up to surprises at the moment, but he didn't want to hurt her feelings. He could try and make an effort for today. The thought of making an effort brought on a fresh wave of exhaustion. He was hungry, but if he relaxed into feeling sleepy he was sure he could drop off again. He'd become quite an expert at it, sleeping when his body didn't really need any more sleep. If he really put his mind to it, he could sleep through his entire time in Amsterdam. His entire life.

Joe was woken up by a loud knocking on his door. When he opened his eyes, Nel was standing at the side of his bed and peering down at him, a perplexed look on her face.

"Are you ill? I thought you might be dead."

Tante Truus was still curled up on the bed, keeping an eye on proceedings. Joe made a brief attempt to smooth down his hair. He felt self conscious of his bare arms and so slid his hands back underneath, which made him think about masturbating, so he took his hands out from under the duvet again and crossed his arms behind his head, yawning self-consciously.

"There – there is some life in there. Have you had anything to eat?"

He shook his head.

"Would you like me to bring something in? There are some good chocolate croissants…"

"I don't really eat breakfast anymore, Nel. I don't seem to have the appetite before lunchtime."

"It is lunchtime! Are you sure?"

Joe nodded.

"Well, we'll see what we can do about that. Okay then, off into the shower, and we can get going in half an hour. I'll see you downstairs dressed. You know how to work everything?"

He nodded and she left the room. Tante Truus put her head back down onto her paws and closed her eyes. Bloody lucky cat. He hadn't planned on having a shower, but Nel would notice if his hair wasn't wet. He hadn't been washing as often as usual, not lately. There didn't seem to be much point. He'd get dirty again anyway, wouldn't he? And nobody ever got close enough to him to smell his armpits, or his greasy hair…

He lifted his arm and took a tentative sniff. The smell hadn't taken on that rotten aroma yet, but it was certainly pungent. He sighed heavily, and launched himself up from the pillows to a sitting position. Tante Truus was most alarmed, so he spent a minute tickling her ears and stroking the short hair on her nose to settle her back down before easing himself out of bed.

There was a tall mirror next to the shower, and Joe caught sight of his naked body. He paused to pose like Popeye, flexing an arm and trying to find the muscles. It was a pretty unremarkable body. Pale, but not ghostly. Thin, but not skinny – he liked to use the word 'lean'. Pretty hair-free, apart from the dark mass of curls at his crotch, and a few stragglers around his nipples which he usually plucked out with the tweezers Meg had left behind. He inspected the smooth skin around his aureoles – a few had grown back. Another sign of his current dilapidated state.

He turned around and twisted his neck so he could look at his bottom. It was the part of himself he felt most confident about – Meg had always said he had a good bottom. She used to squeeze it sometimes – it was most unlike her. She praised it so often that Joe had started to believe her. And he was pleased with his penis – man-sized. After puberty he'd always thought his genitals looked as if they didn't quite belong to the rest of his boyish body. Although he didn't like the way that one of his testicles hung lower than the other – it wasn't symmetrical. If he wasn't careful he'd start obsessing over it – doing searches on the internet, thinking about cosmetic surgery. He knew that women got their vaginas fiddled about with these days – what were they called, designer vaginas?

He wouldn't know a designer vagina if it was staring him in the face. He'd never got up close to Meg's. He might recognise them from porn, although he suspected that porn stars were a different breed of women altogether. All hairless and sanitised and bulging red and swollen. He ought to find those vaginas a massive turn on – porn wasn't a multi-billion industry for nothing. But somehow he'd always preferred to look at women's breasts – normal sized ones, not those bulging balloons filled with silicone. The curve of their bottoms. The squishy bits at the top of their thighs. And at these thoughts, his penis came to life with a twitch. Had he got time…? But the arousal faded before he could be bothered to act upon it, and by the time he got into the shower, he was thinking about his mother.

Once he was washed and dressed, he couldn't find Nel. There were so many rooms in this new place. He knocked and opened doors onto empty bedrooms, an empty study, and what looked like a second living room. Eventually he opened a door and found himself in a large, bright room full of windows and paintings.

Nel was over by the corner, studying a canvas. She glanced up, as if dragging herself from a reverie. What was it like for her to carry on painting, now that she didn't need to sell any more work? Or maybe she wasn't quite that rich yet. He gestured with raised eyebrows and a cocked head to ask if it was okay to come in, and she nodded and put her paintbrush down. When he got closer she shut her eyes and sniffed at the air.

"Mmm, you found that shampoo?"

"I didn't remember to bring any, sorry… is it —"

"No, I put it there for you. I just love the smell of it. Don't you think it's wonderful?"

Joe hadn't noticed but he nodded anyway. Most of the time it was simpler to go along with the things people said.

"Come here, Joey."

He bent his head in closer so she could smell his hair. When she called him Joey he had a tight feeling in his chest. He wasn't going to cry again, was he? He moved around to look at her canvas to distract himself.

It was a naked man. A close-up of his trunk and legs. Joe's eyes flashed over it quickly – the fleshy tones, the dark purple penis, the auburn pubes. Nel was looking right at him, amused, and so he walked over to the window and feigned interest in the scene outside. After a minute or two he broke the silence with, "I'm ready to go now, if you are."

They travelled by taxi – Nel told Joe she hardly used public transport anymore, that she'd been spoilt. Nel got in the front with the driver and chattered away with him. She turned her head a couple of times to ask Joe questions, but he gave short dead-end answers. As the taxi pulled up outside Artis, the city zoo, he felt his spirits sink. There were crowds at the entrance, and a small boy was screaming his head off. He'd never liked crowds, but it had got much worse recently. He couldn't help feeling that everyone was looking at him. He swore that people could tell that there was something odd about him. He emitted oddness, like a strange smell.

He looked at Nel. She didn't look very happy, either. They joined the snaking queue, forced into single file by a system of barriers. He fought the urge to start baaaa-ing. Once they'd reached the booth, they tussled over who would buy the tickets – Nel won. Joe wanted to pay his own way – he was an adult now, not a teenager. But in truth he was worried about money.

Work had agreed to pay him his full salary for the next six weeks, but then they said they'd 'review it'. What if he wasn't ready to go back? He had a mental image of holding onto the frame of the office door, with his manager pushing at him from behind. He felt panicky when he had these thoughts. He wouldn't know how to do any other job. He'd have to move back home, into his tiny box room. He'd have to sit in the living room with his dad and Pam while they watched the news, twice every evening, and suffer Pam's clumsy cooking. He'd rather live on the streets.

Nel stopped to study the signpost at the entrance and Joe retreated into fretting and planning. He'd always spent a lot of time inside his head, but recently it had been getting ridiculous. There was a room in his mind, and the lock had got stronger and the door had got thicker. He could still hear people outside the door, shouting at him, but their voices were so faint he could hardly make out the words. He didn't really care what they were saying anyway. They'd give up, eventually.

There was always plenty to keep him busy in this room. He felt like an administrator sometimes, with a desk piled high with papers. A lot of his work seemed to be checking back over things he'd already done, to make sure he'd done them properly. Had he offended Sarah when he'd called her a clever clogs? She had looked shocked. Had he made a mistake on that last report he'd handed in to Herman? These thoughts mostly went round and round in circles, but it still gave him a kind of comfort to think them.

Joe noticed a silence, and realised he was staring at a miniature donkey with great concentration.

"Well, Joe, what shall we do with you?"

He looked at his feet, scraping circles with the tip of one of his trainers.

Nel shrugged. "Okay, the penguins. Maybe they'll cheer you up."

She muttered something under her breath in Dutch which he didn't understand. His Dutch was pretty passable now, but people still sometimes spoke too fast – he knew all the words but he couldn't get his ears around them quickly enough. Nel linked her arm through his, and swerved him around a slow-walking elderly woman.

As they walked, he was conscious of the bare skin of her arm pressing against his. It was a hot day, and Nel's arm was cool. He focussed on it, this patch of skin. There were papers piling up in his head that were waiting to be processed. Concentrating on this place of contact seemed to keep the thoughts at bay. Where had Nel said they were going?

"Can we go and see the giraffes instead, Nel? I'm not sure about penguins. They give me the creeps."

Nel smiled. "Of course, darling, of course."

When they returned from the zoo, Nel disappeared into the kitchen and Joe retreated to his bedroom for a snooze. When he woke up a few hours later, she was still cooking and told him to wait in the dining room. Joe circled the table as he waited for his muzzy head to clear. It had been laid with two places; elegant silver cutlery, square white plates and scarlet napkins. Nel had emailed him before he'd arrived to double check his latest food requirements. His list of forbidden food had got shorter over the years, but it still contained prawns, olives, feta cheese, cooked mushrooms, grapefruit… He'd made a special mention of his horror of soup with lumps in. It had to be pureed until it was completely smooth, as any lumps reminded him of vomit.

The previous evening, Nel had shown Joe her fridge and encouraged him to help himself. It was stuffed with things she didn't have to cook. There were pineapple rings in plastic packages, cartons of salads, and ready prepared meals from a Dutch company she told him cost 'handen vol geld' which she translated as 'handfuls of money'. She said that the most complicated food preparation she did these days was mixing milk and sugar into her coffee. She seemed proud of her lack of competence.

Nel often spoke to Joe about food in her emails – teasing him about what his 'meal of the month' was. As Joe was still a fussy eater (although he preferred to use the word 'particular' these days), when he found a meal he liked, he tended to eat it over and over until he got thoroughly sick of it. The current favourite was a breaded chicken breast with cheese sauce inside from Waitrose, petit pois, and a particular brand of frozen French fries. It wasn't that he was lacking in cooking skills. When he'd lived with Meg, he had cooked for them both most nights as she had a demanding job in London and arrived home late. He always followed recipes to the very last milligram, and got pretty good at all the required techniques – Delia was his favourite.

He sat down at the table when Nel came in, carrying their starters. The meal she served Joe was mostly a success. He even ate the sauce, despite suspecting it contained a hint of garlic. It actually tasted pretty good. She brought Joe up to date on her love life, which sounded incredibly complicated as usual. She also spoke about her old friend, Willem. Joe recognised his name from Nel's emails over the years. Willem's longtime partner Theo wasn't interested in art (or parties) at all, and so Willem often accompanied Nel to her glitzy functions.

Nel said she really appreciated being able to ask Willem to come over when she was feeling depressed without having to make conversation with him. Some days she'd go round and fall asleep on their sofa in the middle of the afternoon. "I suppose you could say he's the nearest thing I've got to a best friend," she said.

Nel kept filling up Joe's glass with burgundy wine, and he kept drinking it. After dessert he curled up on his side on the sofa, and Nel brought him a soft pink blanket. He wrapped himself up like a burrito. Nel had built a real fire in the modern marble hearth, and the flames hypnotised him. She talked to him quietly about her life – the joy of having her work recognised by the art world, a growing sense of feeling settled in herself, the recent loss of her mother and her new status as an orphan. When she stopped talking about herself and started asking him frank questions, it felt like the most natural thing in the world to answer them. The words poured out of him, like sand through a sieve. He talked and talked until he was empty.

His wine glass was empty too. His eyes started flickering shut. Nel walked him up to his bedroom, and tucked him in as if he were a small boy.

"Oh, we have a visitor tomorrow, Joey."

"Mmmhhmm?"

"We do. You'll be pleased."

Nel came back into the room and smiled mysteriously. She stroked Joe's hair back from his forehead, kissed him softly, three times, and then disappeared.

Joe had a terrible night. It was as if something was waking him up every twenty minutes, and then it took him seventeen minutes to get back to sleep. The bed was too hot, and then too cold. His dreams were fragmented, anxious – a bear was chasing him and he kept stepping on thorns with his bare feet, or he had to carry a frog down to the stream at the bottom of the garden to safety, but it kept jumping out of his hands before he got there.

He wondered if it was his medication, mixed with all that wine. He imagined the alien chemicals riding in his blood, altering the biochemistry of his brain. He hadn't taken a pill since he'd arrived in Amsterdam, and he wasn't going to take another one. He lay half-awake and tried not to think about his mum, but it was like trying not to see the elephant in the room.

He wished she were dead. That was the truth of it. It was a familiar thought but it stung him every time. He was a cruel person to think it. It wasn't her fault that she left him at fourteen. Back then, his hatred for her was at a peak. He'd fantasise about her taking an overdose, just like she kept threatening to do, when he and his dad would go and visit her in the hospital. His dad gave up trying to stop her saying it. At the time Joe was afraid that it would burst out of him: "Go on then. Why don't you just hurry up and do it, we'd all be better off without you." Sometimes he went to the toilets and locked himself into a stall so he could mouth it over and over. "Kill yourself, kill yourself, just fucking do it."

At fourteen, Joe had wished that his father would die too. He wasn't as furious with his dad, despite his incompetencies, but if his dad died it would mean that Joe could go and live with Nel full time. And he'd been angry at Nel, for sending him back to Milton Keynes. All that bitterness, all that anger. It didn't have anywhere to go. It dulled over the years, and eventually his mum became a burden – nothing more. Joe guessed that his dad was angry at her too, although he'd never said it. He'd wasted most of his life, waiting for her to get better. Thank God he'd finally given up, and got himself a girlfriend. At least Pam seemed to make him happy.

Joe drifted back to sleep, and the next time he looked at his clock it was midday. He felt grateful that Nel had left him alone. Last night, she'd threatened to wake him up early. She wanted to take him out for breakfast, said she knew the 'perfect place'. He groaned and turned over, wanting to sink back into the oblivion of sleep, but his long lie-in had already squeezed all the sleepiness out of him.

He reluctantly got out of bed and pulled on his old dressing gown. He felt dirty after his fractious night, coated in a sheen of dried sweat. As he soaped it away in the shower, he discovered that his head felt clearer than it had for a while. Maybe it had helped to talk to Nel last night. He heard his doctor's voice in his head – "You must *talk* to people". Talk to people – that made it sound simple. As he strapped on his watch he wondered if it was too late for him and Nel to go out for breakfast. Would they still be serving it at this time of day?

The house was silent. There was no sign of Nel's Peruvian cleaner, Claudia. Maybe it was her day off. Thinking of coffee drew Joe to the kitchen, where he spent some time trying to work out the coffee machine. As he was stirring in the milk he remembered that he should have taken Nel a cup. Why was it so hard for him to hold other people in mind? How did others do it? It must be that part of him that was broken. He'd go and find her now, and he could offer to make her a fresh batch. He carried his cup with him, taking a premature sip and scalding the roof of his mouth. He held it underneath his nose as he walked, taking in drafts of the robust, earthy smell.

He tried her studio first. The door was pulled to, and he called out as he opened it wide: "Good morning, Auntie," but it was empty. He spent a few minutes wandering around and looking at the canvases. He took a closer look at the men's penises. He looked at the veins on the shafts, the foreskins. He'd only learnt the biological name of the opening at the tip of the penis recently – the 'meatus'. He heard a noise and looked behind him. There was nobody there, but even with no one watching he felt voyeuristic, examining the details of these men's cocks. He couldn't imagine how anyone could find a man's body attractive. Their bodies were so boring, straight up and down, and men's genitalia were a bit of a dog's dinner. Although maybe vaginas were too, when you got a good close look at them.

He wandered out, touching one of the painted penises with the tip of his finger as he passed it. He tried the living room, the small back yard, and the room Nel had kitted out as a gym. She told him she never used it. There was nobody there. Then he went back upstairs.

The door to Nel's bedroom was ajar, and Joe called out a long "Hello?" as he put his hand on the doorknob, not wanting to disturb her in a moment of privacy. He swung the door open. It revealed the expanse of Nel's king-sized bed, with a curved dark wood headboard. Her sheets were bunched up over her feet, and her fuchsia duvet was on the floor. Nel was in the centre of the bed, on her back.

He knew at once. Another part of him calmly carried on looking, taking it in. He walked into the room and stood at the foot of her bed. She was wearing a long green silk nightdress, rucked up on one side and exposing a plump knee. Her eyes were almost closed, white slivers. Joe couldn't see her pupils, and he had an image of them rolled back inside her head. As if they were like the balls in deodorant bottles, completely smooth, not attached to anything. Her lips were parted, and her head was arched back a little, her neck lifted. He looked around and saw her pillows on the floor, as if they'd been flung there. Maybe she didn't like to sleep with pillows. The rest of the room looked ordinary – the curtains were still pulled shut. He wanted more light. He walked over and pulled them wide.

He looked at his watch. Maybe he'd be asked this, later. Eighteen minutes past one. He didn't want to think about later. He wanted to have a good look at her first. He wanted to stay with her. He walked further into the room, towards her head. Did she look peaceful? He couldn't decide. It crossed his mind that he ought to be sure, and so he watched her chest intently for a few minutes. Nothing. He was meant to hold a mirror against her mouth, wasn't he? Instead he touched her on the shoulder, and then on the face. She was clammy, and cold. Her skin was a creamy colour. He looked around the room. There was a chair over by the window, and he brought it over so he could sit next to her. He was aware of his own breathing.

He looked closely at her face. There were fine hairs on the skin above her top lip, and he wondered if she bleached them like his ex–girlfriend Meg used to. Nel's face was a statue, a still-life. There were wrinkles – around her eyes, joining the creases of her mouth to her nose – but she still looked beautiful to him. Even with her eyes half shut. Although the thin strip of white was unnerving him, and he wondered if he could shut them, like he'd seen people do in films. He was irrationally worried about hurting her, and so he left them as they were. Her lashes were pale, stripped of mascara.

Her hair was mussed up, it looked all tangled. He had the urge to fetch a brush and brush it out – would that be wrong? No, she'd want to look her best. He found one in her en-suite bathroom. He started by brushing the hair at the sides, but then had to lift her up to get at the back. He was amazed at how heavy her head was. It reminded him of when he held a baby for the first time, Podge's daughter, Anne-Marie. His god-daughter. Joe was gentle with Nel, as if she were a baby, as if he were teasing the tangles out of five year old Anne-Marie's hair. He was an expert at it. Anne-Marie liked the way Joe did it, and when he was at Podge's house she would fetch her brush and put it into his hands. He hadn't seen Anne-Marie recently. He had kept saying no to the invitations. Had his god-daughter missed him?

Joe tried not to touch Nel's face too much. He didn't like the way it felt, but he was also thinking about the evidence. Meg used to watch those crime scene investigation programmes endlessly, and every so often Joe would look up from his book to see a flayed body or a pretty blonde woman looking down a microscope. They were always going on about 'contaminating the scene'. He might be a suspect, especially as he'd been depressed. Maybe she was murdered, or maybe she killed herself. They'd need to find these things out. He didn't want to mess things up.

When Nel's tangles were brushed out, he noticed a fragment of sleep in the corner of her right eye. He replaced the brush and fetched a piece of toilet paper, dampened under the tap. He twisted the tissue paper into a point and wiped the sleep gently away from her eye. As he was doing this, he felt overwhelmed by sadness. He felt something tickling his cheek, and when he brushed it, his fingers came away wet. It didn't feel like he was crying. It was more like filling your mouth with water and then parting your lips. He dropped the tissue on the floor and picked up one of Nel's pillows, hugging it to himself. He folded over. He sniffed at the pillow, and let the water out.

He only responded to the doorbell when it rang for the third time. He didn't want to leave Nel, but he thought it might be the police, and so he kissed her on the forehead (cold, clammy) and went downstairs. When he opened the door, someone was walking away – a slight figure, with cropped dark blue hair. The person turned back when they heard the door, and he saw that it wasn't a boy, but a woman. She had a silver ring through her nose, and her eyes widened when she saw Joe.

"Joe! Look at you!"

He stared blankly at her. The woman stared at his face as she got up closer.

"What, have you been crying?"

She put a hand on his arm and he flinched, so she removed it. There was something about her voice… it was as if he'd heard it somewhere before.

"Nel told me you were feeling down. It's good to cry sometimes, eh?"

As she said the word 'Nel', he recognised her. It was the hair that had confused him. In the last photo he'd seen of her, on Facebook, she had long copper-coloured hair.

"Nel is dead."

Once the words were out of his mouth, they sounded blunt. Maybe he should have asked Emmie to sit down first, like they did on TV – but he'd never really understood why they did that. Emmie laughed.

"What, like 'God is dead'? Nel is dead, long live Nel? Let me in, you silly thing, don't leave me standing on the doorstep like this."

She made to push him aside but he held her by one shoulder, gently. He tried another tactic, and said the same words in Dutch.

"Nel is dood, Emmie."

This time, Emmie looked into his face. She searched his eyes for a sign that he was joking. She looked and looked. Eventually, her own eyes started to change. The amusement drained away, and so did the colour from her cheeks. And then Joe realised why they asked people to sit down, as she fainted into his arms.

She was surprisingly light. Joe turned her around and lifted her under her arms. It was difficult to get a proper purchase on her. He carried her through into the living room, where he lay her out on the sofa and put her in the recovery position as best he could. This was what the orderlies at the hospital used to do with his mum, when she had panic attacks and passed out. She only got to the point of actually fainting a couple of times – usually they caught her when she'd started to hyperventilate, and Joe's dad would stay with her while Joe fetched a paper bag for her to breathe in and out of. If they couldn't find a bag they made her cup her hands up against her nose and mouth.

Fainting didn't alarm Joe as much as it did some people. When he was fifteen, Podge had gone through a weird stage of fainting all the time. Joe was convinced that he did it to get attention. He'd got used to spotting the signs that he was about to go, and became adept at catching him. Podge had been much heavier than Emmie – a dead weight. He watched her closed eyes, and remembered the last time Emmie had fainted on him.

Emmie started to come round, and Joe told her in Dutch to keep her head down for a bit longer. He realised he hadn't used his Dutch with Nel since he arrived. He added the word 'yet' to this in his head, and then removed it. His fluency had improved so much since he'd last seen her, he'd really been looking forward to showing it off. After a few minutes Emmie slowly raised her head. There were two red dots on her pale cheeks. He kept watching her, just in case she went again. She spoke to him in Dutch.

"What happened?"

"I just went in there this morning, to her bedroom, and she was dead."

"When? How did you know?"

"She was…" He couldn't find the Dutch word for 'still', and so he used the English one. Emmie repeated it, as if she was in a dream.

"Still. Still." Her eyes widened. "Where is she?"

"Still in her bedroom."

It occurred to Joe that he'd used the word 'still' again, and that it meant both 'motionless' and 'remaining'. He hadn't realised it was the same word. This had happened to him before at University, when he used the word 'nucleus' in biology and then realised he used it in chemistry as well. Should he be thinking thoughts like that now? Should he be feeling sad? Surely he should be concentrating on what had happened? He started to think about what he needed to do next, but Emmie had got up and left the room. He rushed after her, calling.

"Emmie. Wait. Are you sure?"

She didn't answer, and before he could catch up with her she was approaching the door to Nel's room, which Joe had left wide open. She stopped as if she had banged into an invisible wall, and Joe heard her take a sharp breath. She stepped into the room, three steps, four, standing on tiptoes so she could look at Nel's face without getting any closer, and then she turned and stumbled back towards Joe out in the hallway, wrapping her arms around him and burrowing her face into his chest. He looked down at her blue hair and noticed her darker roots. After a few moments, he remembered to put his own arms around her back, and he felt her shuddering. Rhythmic shudders. He waited for her to stop. He tried not to feel impatient. They really ought to call someone official soon. He was feeling guilty about leaving it so long, about sitting beside her. Although it felt good to have Emmie in his arms.

The shuddering slowed down and Emmie raised her face to him.

"She's definitely fucking dead."

This made Joe laugh, but he stopped when he saw the look on Emmie's face. Instead he said, "We need to make some calls". He sounded to himself like a character in an American soap opera, and felt the urge to laugh again. He started off down the stairs before Emmie could see his face, calling behind him, "What's the number for the police here? Would it be the police, or the ambulance?"

She started to follow him. "I don't fucking know. I haven't experienced many deaths this past week, I can't remember."

This was the Emmie he remembered. Crude, and rude. They went back to the living room and sat with the phone on the table between them. Joe waited to see if Emmie would offer to call – it was her country after all – but she didn't so he picked up the receiver himself. He felt as if he could do anything that needed to be done. He'd always thought he'd fall to pieces in a crisis.

"I'll try the police first. What is their number?"

"112. What are you going to say?"

Joe shrugged and dialled the number.

"Hello, I'd like to report a death."

The police told Joe that they needed to call Nel's doctor, and then the undertaker. They used the words 'de overledene' for Nel, which Joe had to repeat and Emmie translated as 'the deceased'. Emmie found the number for Nel's doctor in her address book, which was next to the phone, and again Joe made the call. Nel's doctor sounded shocked. She said she was in the area, and that she could be there within half an hour.

Emmie couldn't stop crying. Once Joe had brought her a box of tissues and offered her a drink, which she refused, he wasn't sure what else to do. He felt awful listening to her jagged breathing, as if he was responsible for her upset. Eventually he asked her if there was anyone she could call, and she nodded mutely. At the start of the call she seemed even more upset, but the person on the other end of the phone must have said something helpful, because she did start to sound calmer. As they waited, Joe counted the dots in the design on the sofa.

When the doorbell rang, he'd reached 328. Emmie was still sniffling. It was so quiet in the house. Joe showed the doctor upstairs, while Emmie made coffee for them both. Just before going into Nel's bedroom, Joe had the bizarre thought that Nel might have moved – that maybe she was still alive after all. He had a vivid image of her stretched out on the floor, having tried to get some help, and felt so spooked by this that he refused the doctor's invitation to come in with her. He went downstairs to help Emmie, and did the washing up that was waiting in the bowl. It felt good to have something to do with his hands, and the hot water soothed him.

When Nel's doctor came back downstairs, she seemed genuinely upset. He'd imagined that she saw death every day, that she'd be immune to it. She accepted her coffee gratefully, and they went through to the living room while she finished off the paperwork. She told Joe that it needed to be passed on to the Registrar's, but that the undertaker usually took care of that. And there would be a post-mortem. She could only guess at what had happened – a heart problem, an aneurysm… Joe noticed that the doctor was speaking to him as if he was in charge. He supposed he was. She offered to call an undertaker for them, and Joe accepted – two official phone calls in Dutch felt like enough for the day. After she'd made the phone call, she sat down again and drained the dregs of her coffee before looking at Joe and Emmie. She sighed.

"I will miss her, you know."

This set Emmie off again. Her crying wasn't as dramatic as her laughter. She made quiet snuffling noises that reminded Joe of a dog sniffing out a scent trail. The doctor put down her cup and went to Emmie, sitting next to her on the sofa and putting her arm around her. Joe realised he should have thought of that earlier, rather than suggesting she call someone else.

While the two women sat and talked in Dutch, he interrupted to say he was going to the toilet. They didn't look up at him as he left the room. He went upstairs and into the main bathroom which nobody ever seemed to use – Nel had her own shower and had said she rarely took baths. The air in the room was cool. He put the toilet seat down and sat on it. He looked around. Everything was white or silver – white bath, silver old-fashioned taps, fluffy white carpet. Even the toothbrushes were white. It was too much. Whose idea had it been to decorate the room like this? If it had been used, it would never have stayed this clean. Joe imagined the stains – a splash of vivid blue mouthwash, dribbles of dark yellow piss, a single drop of menstrual blood. Our bodies are too messy for this white palace, he thought. It made him feel dirty.

He went back into his own room instead, where there was more colour, more clutter, more chaos. More life. He spotted Tante Truus, curled up on one of the chairs in the bay window. She made a neat circle in the absolute centre of the square of the cushion, and when she saw him she curled up tighter and tipped her bristly chin upwards. Joe stroked the silky hair on her throat, gently, gently. He imagined stroking Emmie's hair, smoothing it down, rubbing his hand backwards across the hair at the nape of her neck. Soothing her as she cried. He wished he could be downstairs with her, in place of Nel's doctor, but he'd probably just be mucking things up. She was better off with the doctor. He lay on his back on his bed, stared at the ceiling, and let his mind go completely blank until he heard Emmie calling him downstairs.

Joe didn't realise a death would cause so much activity. He said goodbye to the doctor and then had to answer the door to Nel's cleaning lady, Claudia, who was completely unaware of what she was walking into. When Emmie told her about Nel she became hysterical, and so Emmie sat with her while Joe made more coffee. The undertakers arrived before they could get rid of Claudia, and of course they all wanted coffee too.

They started asking Joe questions he couldn't answer (What kind of casket? Did he want them to send out cards to her relatives?) but Emmie helped him make the decisions that were immediately necessary and put off all the others. They decided the undertakers should take Nel away to the crematorium rather than leave her in the house with Joe. He didn't want to be left alone with her. Everything else, they said, could wait until the next day.

Next, they made the final phone calls that they knew they couldn't put off. Emmie used her mobile to call her mum, and a good friend of hers who was Nel's god-daughter. Joe called his father first – he was relieved to be able to leave a message on the answer phone asking him to call back urgently. He then found Willem's number in Nel's address book. When they'd spoken last night, Nel had said he was the closest thing she had to a best friend.

A man with a deep rough voice answered the phone.

"Hallo met Willem?"

"Hello, is that Willem?"

Joe spoke in his native language without thinking, and was grateful when the man switched to English.

"Hello?"

"Oh, I'm Nel's nephew." There was a silence, and so he added "Joe?"

"Ah, Joe! I've heard so much about you, I'm looking forward to meeting you, Nel said that we could have dinner later in the week?"

Joe felt terrible. He sounded so happy.

"I'm sorry but, I've... There's something... I've got to..." He didn't know how to say it, and trailed off into silence. Emmie was crying again, on the phone to Nel's god-daughter.

"Are you okay, Joe? Where is Nel? Who's that crying?"

Joe realised that if he didn't just say it he might not be able to speak at all.

"Willem, Nel is dead."

It sounded just as blunt as when he'd told Emmie. What were the right words? How could he help to cushion people from the shock? The phone went quiet. After a while Joe said "Hello?" and then "Willem?" When Willem spoke again his voice was tight, as if his throat had closed up.

"Dead? O, mijn God."

Joe waited for Willem to speak again.

"What happened?"

"The doctor doesn't know yet, Nel's just in her bed. She didn't... I found her this morning."

"Where is she now?"

Joe gave him the name and the telephone number of the undertaker.

"O, mijn God, Nel. I'm going to go and be with her, Joe."

Joe was wondering if he should have travelled with her. He couldn't remember the undertakers giving him that option, but he hadn't understood everything they'd said. He suddenly hated the idea of Nel alone, without anyone she knew.

"Please, Willem. I don't want her to..." His voice cracked, and he took a deep breath. "Please go with her."

"Are you okay, Joe? Are you alone?"

"Emmie is here. I've just called my dad."

"Good. Everything will be all right. I'll come to you after I've seen Nel, and then we'll sort everything out together, okay? You won't be on your own."

Joe felt Willem's warm strength envelop him.

Willem sighed. "Okay Joe. I'll see you soon. Stay calm. Doei."

Joe hung up, and a few minutes later Emmie ended her own call. She looked exhausted. Joe told her she should go and see whoever it was she'd phoned (he was secretly hoping it wasn't a boyfriend), and he assured her that he'd be okay until Willem got there. He was impatient for her to go, as he was so tired he could hardly stay awake. The exhaustion was a physical urge, like being desperate to urinate. As soon as he'd shut the front door he went upstairs two at a time, pausing to shut Nel's bedroom door, the room which contained her empty bed. He climbed into bed fully clothed, pulled the duvet up under his chin, and fell immediately into a deep sleep.

Joe was woken a few hours later by a high-pitched sound. For a few moments he thought he was at home in his flat in Reading. The sound continued, and it became a cat's impatient miaows. Tante Truus. He placed himself in Amsterdam, and then in Nel's new house. Hadn't she been fed? Where was Nel? And that was when he remembered.

The memory began as a thought, a plain fact – "Nel is dead" – but it quickly became physical and reverberated throughout his body. It was as if he were a gong. His stomach swooped, his heart pounded, his mouth felt dry. He marvelled at the speed of the chemicals flooding his body, imagined puffs of neurotransmitters firing across his synapses. Would it be like this every time he woke up? Tante Truus mewed again, more loudly. Joe peered over the side of the bed. Her green eyes fixed on him, her white-tipped tail lashing.

"Hello, little one. You don't know what's happened, do you?" he said to her, as he swung out of bed and followed her downstairs towards her food bowl. The belt of his jeans had pressed into him as he slept, and he rubbed at the itchy red indent in his skin. Although he opened every cupboard in the kitchen twice, he couldn't find any cat food. Maybe Nel had run out. He splashed a dollop of yoghurt into the cat's bowl to keep her going, and left her lapping at it while he went in search of a shop.

The shop he found at the end of the Nel's street was part of a chain – Albert Heijn. It reminded him of his local

Tesco Metro. Soulless, and staffed with bored and probably underpaid men and women from a wide variety of ethnic backgrounds. He found the right aisle and browsed the different varieties of cat food – Brokjes, Felix, supermarket own… He wondered what Tante Truus's usual brand was, and whether she'd turn up her nose at the cheap stuff. In the end he chose the most expensive tins in three different flavours. He even bought her a carton of Kattenmelk. He was worried that she'd miss Nel and start to pine – he'd heard that animals could stop eating and starve to death when their owners died. Although maybe that was just dogs.

On his way to pay, he caught sight of some Choco Chippies, and added a packet to his basket. Choco Chippies. They were exactly the kind of unhealthy food item that Meg would have been appalled by. He also wondered what he might want to eat for dinner, but the cereal (and a couple of packets of crisps he added at the checkout) was as far ahead as he could think. He felt frightened at the prospect of going home to the huge empty house, and at the thought of having to look after himself. He had to remind himself that he was perfectly capable of being an adult, and that he'd looked after himself for many years back in the UK. Although, admittedly, he hadn't been doing such a good job lately. On his walk back he tried to breathe slowly, like his G.P. had suggested. It was meant to calm him down, but whenever Joe tried it, it just left him more out of breath than before.

As Joe was forking out the smelly meat to a grateful Tante Truus, the doorbell sounded again. He left her eating, and opened it to a man in his fifties with a shaved head and unruly eyebrows. He was wearing bright blue glasses. His clothes looked expensive – a dark grey suit and a glossy purple shirt that strained over his substantial belly. Behind him was a skinnier man, about the same age but with deeper wrinkles, and dyed yellow hair.

The bigger man was looking at Joe with such genuine sympathy that he found himself getting upset. When the man opened his arms, Joe allowed himself to be held as if it was completely natural, as if he'd known this man for years. His aftershave was strong and woody. It was only when he pulled away that Joe found himself still grasping the cat fork. He'd been holding it instinctively away from the man's body. He didn't want to draw attention to it by putting it down, and so he held it behind his back and waited for the man to speak.

"Joe. Oh, Joe." He sounded tired and sad. "This is my partner, Theo."

The man stepped forward without smiling, and Joe shook his proffered hand. His fingers felt calloused. He realised that they were still standing on the doorstep and he stepped back, inviting them both in. The man with yellow hair wouldn't meet his eyes, just nodded and disappeared into the living room. His body lolled from side to side as he walked, reminding Joe of a penguin. He watched Willem hang his coat on a hook and kick his shoes off as if it were his own hall. When was the last time he'd been here? What had he and Nel talked about?

"I can hardly believe it. If I hadn't seen her with…" Willem's eyes shone. "A tragedy, it is such a tragedy. You don't know… if only… If only she'd lived for another few weeks."

Willem took Joe by his shoulders to illustrate the point. Joe didn't know what Willem meant, but he nodded anyway. He felt embarrassed about their hug – a complete stranger. Joe offered the men something to drink, and left them in the living room, refusing Willem's offer of help. He wanted to play the host – it was his job to look after them now. He found an unopened packet of biscuits in a cupboard – Kip and Rijst. Would they want to eat at a time like this? He got them out anyway, and arranged them onto a plate. This was what his mum used to do when they had visitors round – they never ate them straight from the packet. When the coffee was ready, he poured it into mugs and put the sugar bowl and some spoons out. He couldn't find a jug, and so poured some milk into a spare mug. He'd seen a tray somewhere… ah, there it was – a blowsy red O'Keefe flower. He loaded everything onto the tray and carried it precariously through into the living room. Willem and his partner were sitting next to each other on the sofa, their knees touching. They looked up when he entered the room and Willem smiled. His eyes were still watery.

"What a fine tray, thank you."

The penguin man nodded in agreement. Joe hadn't heard him say a single word yet. Joe sat down and sipped at his own mug of coffee – the taste comforted him. Coffee had always reminded him of Nel. He felt the steam rise up and start to condense on his top lip. After a time he distractedly wiped it away, and felt the rough stubble under his fingers. When had he last shaved?

"I must look a mess."

Willem made a dismissive gesture with his hand. "How long have you been here?"

Before Joe could answer, Willem was interrupted by his partner, who whispered something into his ear. It was like having a child in the room. Willem nodded at him and turned back to Joe.

"Theo would like to go and spend some time in Nel's bedroom. That is where you found her? He would like to absorb some of the, how do you say it, vibes. And he would like to look in her studio too, and see where she'd got to with her latest painting. Is that okay with you, Joe?"

Joe nodded. It felt odd that these men were asking his permission. He felt like an imposter.

Willem put a hand tenderly on his partner's cheek before he left the room.

"He is a bit shy about speaking English. I hope you don't find him rude."

Joe shook his head.

"This is such a terrible shock. It must be a shock for you, Joe."

"I didn't know she was ill. Was she ill?"

"I knew nothing about it. Nel told me everything – the state of her love life, her fears about her career… I don't think she would have kept anything from me." He frowned, looked troubled. There was a silence which Joe began to find awkward. He was hopeless at thinking of things to say, he always had been. He waited for Willem to speak, but he just sat there, tapping his foot, fiddling with the coffee cup. Eventually he looked up.

"How long have you been here?"

"Oh, only a couple of days."

Willem tutted, as if this made everything much worse.

"How inconvenient of her to die so early in your holiday, eh?"

He smiled, and Joe smiled too, guiltily. It was the kind of comment Nel would have appreciated. They fell into a silence again, until something occurred to Joe.

"I don't know what we need to do next."

"Next?"

"I don't know how it all works. The funeral. What happens to the house. Tante Truus. All of that. I don't even know how to set the alarm."

As he made the list, his panic grew. The funeral! Maybe he could ask Podge to fly out, but then he remembered Podge's dad's sixtieth birthday party was in the next few days – he couldn't make him miss that. Joe's mum would have been utterly useless. He didn't want to bother his dad and Pam. He was all alone. Who would help him? He was gazing at a glass bowl on Nel's table – empty and full of light. His eyes glazed over. The anxiety transmuted into something heavy, and he sank into utter hopelessness.

And then there was a voice. It was inside him, or outside him, but it definitely didn't come from what he usually understood as 'Joe'. It didn't use words, exactly. It was more like an understanding or a felt sense, but the message was clear: 'Everything will be okay'. Not just that, but: 'You will be okay – you'll find a way'. Everything will be okay. When he thought about it later, the sentence sounded like a cliché, but at the time it was the simple, luminous truth.

Joe still didn't have a clue about what he needed to do, but he felt sure the world would look after him somehow. By the time Joe looked back up at Willem, he felt quietly confident. It didn't stop him feeling scared, or sad, but he could bear it now – he could bear anything.

"I will help you Joe, I will be here all the way. Okay?"

"Okay." Joe looked into Willem's eyes, and he believed him.

Joe and Willem drew up a plan of action. Willem said his aunt had died last year – he had been responsible for arranging everything and so he was familiar with the procedure. Willem would get in touch with the undertakers first thing in the morning to arrange a date for the funeral. Funerals in Holland need to take place between thirty six hours and five days from the death, and they decided on three days time if it could be arranged. This would give Joe and Willem some time to write the cards to all the people they wanted to invite, and arrange some food so the funeral party could come back to Nel's house after the service. Willem said he could cancel his meetings for the next few days, and set up his office in Nel's house.

By the time Theo reappeared, they were almost finished. Willem hugged Joe again and promised to return the next morning.

After Willem and Theo had left, Joe thought he ought to try his parents again, but his dad's phone went straight to answer phone and his mum's just rang and rang. He'd failed to convince her to get an answer phone – maybe he could buy her one for Christmas and set it up before she had a chance to protest. After putting the phone down, he thought about food. He wanted something more substantial than the cereal and crisps he'd bought earlier, and so rummaged about in Nel's fridge. He felt guilty about helping himself without asking her, until remembering that the food would be no use to her. He heated up one of the posh ready meals in the microwave, and then he had another shower. It was stifling in the house – he still hadn't worked out how to turn on the air conditioning.

He added the question to the list of things to ask Claudia tomorrow – where the cat food was kept, how to work the washing machine... Willem had also suggested he should ask her whether she needed some time off. He said she'd worked for

Nel for three years, and she would probably be very upset – Nel had been good to her. Joe was hoping that she'd be happy to stay on in the short term while they sorted everything out, and tried not to think too hard about what he'd do if she said no. She had so much precious knowledge about how this house ran – he wouldn't be able to find it in a book from the library.

It was almost ten by the time he'd dried himself off and got into his pyjamas. It would be nearly nine in the UK. He called Podge's number, but he was out at the pub with his friend Nigel. Sarah was there. Joe broke the news to her, using the phrase he'd practiced with Willem, "I'm afraid I have some bad news – [pause] – Nel died unexpectedly earlier today." It felt much less blunt than, "Nel is dead", but Sarah still drew in her breath and went quiet. Then she quickly offered to come out to help him with the 'arrangements', insisting that they could find someone to look after the children and that it would be 'no trouble, really no trouble at all'. Joe was touched.

After speaking to Sarah, Joe was at a loss for what to do next. He didn't want to get started on any of the tasks Willem had left him, and he couldn't concentrate on the TV. Finally he had the idea of having a 'stiff drink'. Wasn't that what you were meant to do in times like this? It took him ages to find Nel's stash of alcohol – for a while he suspected she didn't have any in the house at all – but then he found it concealed in a cupboard in the living room which had fake drawers on the door. Most of the bottles had labels he recognised. He was tempted by the Baileys, but it didn't seem like a very manly thing to drink, even though there was no one there to see him. He unscrewed a few bottles and sniffed at the mouths before settling on Morgan's Spiced Rum.

Joe wasn't a big drinker. Podge would regularly go out with his friends on a Saturday and drink six or seven pints – if Joe drank that much in one go he'd have passed out. He splashed some into a glass and knocked it back in one. He poured out another three inches and took the glass up to his bedroom. From the chair in the bay he could see out onto the canal, where occasional passers-by walked their dogs, and a big Plane tree rustled in the glow of a street lamp. He felt more at home in this chair than he did anywhere else in the house, except maybe the equivalent chair in Nel's bedroom.

As he sipped at the rum, a warmth started in his centre and spread throughout his body. Just like Nel's cocoa. Is this what alcoholics felt? He thought of his grandfather, who died years ago of liver cancer (probably a result of alcohol-induced cirrhosis). What was it that made people turn to drink? Why did his grandfather need to look at life through an alcoholic fuzz – what was wrong with it as it was? Maybe it allowed him to look at himself through this screen too – so he didn't have a clear picture of the things about himself he didn't like. Joe could certainly understand that. He got up and fetched the untouched packets of anti-depressants from his wash bag. He slid the blister packs from the packet and popped each pill from its foil, gathering them on the table next to his drink.

He regarded the pile. They looked like sweeties. Was he serious about the thoughts he'd been having over the past few months? Did it make him happy, to see this opportunity in front of his eyes? It wouldn't take much. He could pop downstairs and bring up the contents of Nel's collection of pain-killers from the kitchen drawer. Swig them down with the rum in how many handfuls – ten? Twenty? Twenty swallows and it would all be over. He could just lie down on his bed, under his duvet, with Tante Truus for company.

Willem had said he knew what he was doing – he could arrange two funerals just as easily as one. He noticed how matter-of-factly he was thinking these thoughts. They had the same quality as, "I could have fried or scrambled egg," or, "What shall I wear to work today?" What he could wear to work led him to think about his new swimming shorts, which made him think of swimming, then bikinis, then Emmie wearing a bikini. There was a stirring of desire. He would masturbate instead, he thought. He would flush all his pills down the toilet, but first he would masturbate and try not to think about death.

Someone was knocking on the door, hard. It was pitch black in the room. Joe stumbled from bed, naked, and pulled on his jeans and his dressing gown. He felt his way downstairs in the dark, running his fingers through his hair and rubbing sleep from his eyes as he went. He opened the door to find Emmie on the doorstep. There was a taxi behind her on the street, the engine still running, and when she saw Joe she went over to pay the driver. Joe ran his hands through his hair again and wished that he'd brushed his teeth. The streets were empty, except for a man weaving his way home from a night out, concentrating hard on remaining upright.

The taxi drove off and Emmie moved towards him, her eyes fixed on him. He stepped aside, thinking she wanted to go inside, but instead she grabbed him by the lapels of his dressing gown and slid her hands around his waist. She tucked her head underneath his chin and laid her cheek against his chest, nestling in. She was freezing – he could feel the chill all down his front. Her blue hair was spiked up like a hedgehog, and he felt the hard tips of it pressing into the skin of his throat. He wrapped his arms around her, instinctively – she trembled a little as if she was a bird he'd saved from the cat. He stared over her shoulder at the drunk man, who'd leant himself up against a lamp post to take a breather before he set off again. He lifted his wrist behind Emmie's back, but he wasn't wearing his watch.

"What time is it?"

Emmie lifted her face up towards him in amusement. It was the way you'd fondly smile at a child if they'd got something wrong. She put her finger against his lips, took his hand and led him back into the house. He allowed himself to be led. She turned on the light in the hallway and he got a better look at her. She was wearing thick black eyeliner and bright orange lipstick, and was dressed in black – ripped fishnet tights, a tight leather skirt and a leather jacket. When they reached his bedroom, she zipped the jacket off and threw it onto the floor. Underneath she was wearing some kind of corset. Where had she been, dressed like this? The room was in semi-darkness – light spilled in from the hallway. Monochrome Emmie. She sat down on the edge of his bed and cocked her head on one side.

"So, do you want to fuck me or not, Joe?"

He thought about pinching himself to check that he wasn't dreaming. He opened his mouth, but nothing came out. He tried again.

"What time is it?"

"Does that make a difference?"

She looked petulant. He remembered her at thirteen, and their first kiss. He didn't feel turned on at all. What was wrong with him? He looked down at his hand and noticed it was shaking. Emmie followed his gaze, and he saw her face soften.

"It's okay, you idiot. Just come and sit down next to me."

He hovered at the edge of the room before saying, "Wait a minute," and going into the bathroom to brush his teeth. He didn't want to breathe stale coffee all over her. By the time he came back she was already in bed, the covers pulled up above her breasts. He could see the straps of her bra, beside the red marks where they'd dug into her shoulders. The strange corset thing and her skirt and tights had joined her jacket in a pile in the middle of his floor. He had the urge to fold them and drape them over the back of a chair. He went over to the bed and climbed in beside her, still wearing his dressing gown and jeans. He felt safer with his jeans on. He still felt nothing. She propped herself up in the bed a bit more, pulling the duvet with her so that it covered her bra. She opened out her arm and encouraged him to rest his head on her chest.

"I thought you might want some comfort. It doesn't have to be sex. But I've talked to Marika about it, and she said it's cool."

For a moment Joe confused the name Marika with Maartje, Emmie's mum, and wondered why Emmie would be talking to her about her sex life. He didn't say anything – as he leant in he'd been distracted by Emmie's smell. It was pungent – she smelled like she'd been dancing all night. He ought not to like it, but he did. It was animal, spicy. He could see the shape of her legs underneath the duvet. He started to imagine what knickers she might be wearing, and desire flooded into him.

"She asked if you might want her to come along as well, but I said I didn't think so, especially not tonight. That was right, wasn't it? I've wanted to have sex with you for a long time, Joe.

You know, just to see what it's like. And now I want to give something to you, like a present. After, well, you know."

She went on and on. Joe found it increasingly difficult to concentrate on what she was saying. His erection pushed against the stiff denim of his jeans. He wanted to undo the buttons of his flies, release himself, relieve the pressure. He was aware of the silkiness of her skin beneath his cheek now. He lifted his head, pulled the duvet down to reveal her bra, and lay his head down again. He could see black material, and felt smooth bare skin against his ear. This shut Emmie up for a moment, and then she said, "Ah, Joey." The 'ah' was long and drawn out, as if she was sinking into a hot bath.

Joe took this as encouragement – he brought his left hand up from underneath the duvet and found her right breast. He slipped his fingers inside the lacy material of her bra, and cupped it – it was chilled, cooled by recently evaporated sweat. He let out a breathy moan, and Emmie responded by turning and pushing her whole body against his, wrapping one thigh above his, pulling herself down in the bed to his level. They ended up facing each other, nose to nose in the semi-dark.

"Hallo, Emmie."

"Hallo, Joe."

He laughed. Here she was, right in front of him – the subject of endless masturbatory fantasies when he was a fourteen year old, back in Milton Keynes after his summer in Amsterdam. Here she was, right in front of his eyes. Within kissing distance. It was like he'd won the lottery. It felt completely natural to lean forward and kiss her on the tip of her nose, and then to close his eyes and kiss her on her bright orange lips.

It was only later, when they'd both taken off all their clothes, that he remembered that she expected him to have sex with her. It wasn't what would happen with his ex, Meg. Emmie wanted him inside her. He pulled back for a second, his eyes still shut, and started to say it.

"Emmie, I haven't…"

He didn't know how to get to the end of the sentence. He imagined Emmie saying, "WHAT?" and leaping out of bed, gathering up her things. She was in the middle of licking his nipple. She stopped and said, "What?"

He tried again.

"I haven't… it's the first time I've…"

"I thought you had a girlfriend?"

"She wasn't able to… she didn't…"

Joe was praying Emmie wasn't going to say, "Ah, Joey" again. That would have crushed him. Instead she said, "It's okay. You'll know what to do."

And with that she took his penis in her hand and manoeuvred Joe's hips closer to hers. They were still on their sides, facing each other. She pulled him down between her legs and he felt her pubic hair, coiled and thick, and then smooth, smooth skin – slippery and warm. She rubbed the head of his cock against herself and he thought he might come there and then. He let out a sharp grunt. She pulled him away from her again and said, "Just a second, Joey." Then she rolled onto her back and felt in her handbag for a condom. She held the foil with her teeth and ripped it, and slid it out, sheathing his penis in a single elegant movement. Joe wondered how much practice she'd had at that.

She guided Joe on top of her, still holding onto his cock. Joe decided she could lead him anywhere like that – around the house, or out into the dark street – he'd follow her willingly. And then she pushed herself up and forwards and all of a sudden he was inside her. He was inside her. His cock was enveloped by her, her flesh pressing at him from all sides. Was this what it was like to be inside your mother's womb? Held in place – an embrace so complete that he never wanted to come out. He never wanted to come. And yet it was too much for him, and after six or seven strokes, his buttocks clenching behind him, he unexpectedly climaxed, letting out a whimper and collapsing on top of her.

After a few seconds he felt one of Emmie's hands snaking down and the other clamping onto his bottom to keep him close. She rubbed herself with two fingers, and Joe put his hand on top of hers, wanting to know. She was hardly moving her hand at all, but started grunting rhythmically, it reminded Joe of the women's tennis at Wimbledon. After a minute or two she arched her back and he felt a strange sensation as her cunt contracted around his deflating cock in pulses. He fell asleep before he'd even withdrawn from her, holding one of her small hands in his.

When he woke, there was light at the windows. Emmie was wearing a fluffy pink robe and carrying a tray into the room. Her hair was wet and combed back flat – her face was naked. She looked so young. Joe caught site of the pile of her clothes in the middle of the floor. This was when he realised it must have been Nel's robe. Nel was dead. His body reacted to the realisation as it had yesterday, but not quite as violently.

The smell of toast and coffee wafted towards him. Emmie set the tray down on the bedside table and then straddled him where he lay, her dressing gown falling apart to reveal her small breasts and the slash of dark brown between her legs. Joe already had his usual morning erection, and he was ready for her when she pulled down the covers and sat astride him. Aaah, there it was again. He wondered if he'd ever tire of that first moment when he slipped inside her, further, further – all the way to his root. He lasted a bit longer this time – his hands tethered her at her waist and she bounced on top of him as if he were a Space Hopper. Her eyes were shut and she was smiling, and he smiled too, before the sensations overwhelmed him again and he was powerless to stop the sounds escaping, guttural sounds. She was silent this time, and as before she brought herself to climax with her fingers while he was still inside her, pressing herself against him as she squeezed him with her mysterious muscles.

Joe was starving – the hungriest he'd been for what felt like months. As he took a piece of toast, Joe asked Emmie who Marika was, and she explained that she was her girlfriend. Joe looked confused, so she told him that she 'liked girls and boys' as if she was explaining something to a child. He watched her as she ate, feeling melancholy. He realised that he could never have her. She would always be restless; she would always want something more. He had to give her back to Marika. It was a sad thought, but it also helped him appreciate every second of what he was receiving from her. She caught him looking at her, and stuck out her tongue. He stuck his tongue out back.

She disappeared as soon as they'd finished, and reappeared wearing a long baggy top over her short skirt.

"You don't mind, do you, Joe?" she asked, plucking at the top with one hand.

It hadn't occurred to Joe that it was his place to mind. The clothes didn't belong to anybody now. Although he supposed that wasn't strictly true. He considered the practical implications of Nel's death. Who did they belong to? Had Nel written a will? And if not, who would automatically inherit her estate? Joe guessed at his mum, which was a terrible thought. He might find out later today, when Willem came to help him look through Nel's papers. He shook his head at Emmie.

"Take whatever you want."

She nodded, and there was a silence as the cold fact of Nel's death hung between them. "Well. I'm going to love you and leave you now. That's what you say in England, isn't it? I'm meeting Marika for breakfast." As an afterthought she added, "Do you want to come?"

Joe loved the way that Emmie was making him feel like a normal person. Meet Marika half an hour after he'd fucked her girlfriend? He could think of people he'd rather have breakfast with.

He smiled politely. "No thank you. I'd like to meet her another time though." He didn't know why he said that, as it wasn't true.

Emmie shrugged and picked up her clothes, shoving them into a plastic bag. She slung her handbag over her shoulder and raised her eyebrows.

At the front door, Joe didn't know if she'd kiss him goodbye. She gave him a tight hug instead, which felt more appropriate.

"I'll bring her round tomorrow, then. See how you're getting on. You'll be here, won't you?"

Joe nodded. Emmie looked sad, and she took his face between her hands.

"You know it can only happen once? Those are the rules. I would like it to happen again, but we have to be friends again now."

Joe nodded again. Emmie tweaked him on the nose before turning and walking away.

As Joe moved back inside the house, he heard the phone ringing from the living room. He hoped somebody else might get it, but then he remembered he was the only one there. Maybe it was Willem, saying he couldn't come round after all. He broke into a trot, almost tripping over Tante Truus who was waiting impatiently for her breakfast. He remembered to answer the phone in Dutch. A man started speaking rapidly. He didn't recognise the man's voice, and he couldn't understand what he was saying. It sounded like it could be an emergency. The man didn't pause for breath, and eventually Joe interrupted him and asked him to slow down. He was selling windows. Joe was furious – he hung up while the man was still mid-sentence.

He picked up the receiver again almost immediately and dialled his dad's number.

"Hello, the Salt residence?"

"Hi, Dad."

"Oh, hello Joe. I got your message, I was going to…"

"Look Dad, I'm fine, but I've got some bad news." As he said this he felt an irrepressible urge to giggle. He pulled the phone away and put his hand over his mouth. The urge wouldn't die down, and so he forced it away by imagining Nel, lying alone in the morgue. Would she be covered up with a sheet? He hoped so, he wouldn't want her to be exposed. When he put the phone back to his ear, he heard his dad saying, "…Joe? Joe, are you there?"

He couldn't remember the phrase he'd practiced with Willem, and improvised. "It's Nel, Dad. She… she wasn't very well." Now he wasn't sure how to proceed.

"What's wrong with her, then?"

"She was… oh, shit. Dad, she died."

"Your language, Joe. You… What did you say?"

"She died, Dad!"

"Joe, she's… Are you sure? Where is she now?"

Was he sure? How old did his dad think he was – five? He had a memory of coming into Nel's old living room and seeing Jeroen on the floor. He didn't want to be having this conversation. He felt heavy and exhausted.

"Dad, she died suddenly – we don't know what it was. I suppose they'll do a post mortem... Her friends are helping me out with everything. It's all under control." As he said this he heard an authority in his voice. The weight eased. He had got it under control. His dad wasn't saying anything. Joe could hear voices in the background – it could have been Pam, but it was probably the radio – his dad listened to Radio 4 all day long. He tried to picture him, sitting in that familiar room. He knew it as well as he knew his own face. The nasty orange curtains, the walnut sideboard, and the blue cord bean bag which had been Joe's favourite place to sit for most of his childhood. He loved that bean bag. He remembered the polystyrene 'beans' escaping when the zip unzipped, and chasing them around the living room so he could feed them back inside. The bean bag beast: leaking strange white blood. He imagined his dad sitting in his usual chair with the phone on his lap. What did his face look like? Did he have his hand across his eyes?

"Dad, are you okay?"

"Oh, Boy. I should be asking you that question. And on top of everything else you're going through. You said there was someone helping you?"

Joe was touched by his dad's use of his old nickname. He hadn't called him that for years.

"Yes, her friend Willem is taking a couple of days off work. Nel must have talked about him when you…"

His dad interrupted. "Your mother."

"Yes?"

"Well…"

"You'll have to tell her, Dad."

"Do you think I have to? Wouldn't she be better off…"

"Of course you have to tell her. You always give her less credit than… She's not stupid, you know. Only mad."

"But they haven't talked for so long anyway. Do you think she'd ever find out? Maybe we should wait until your mother starts asking for her, or…"

Joe sighed. This was why he'd dreaded calling his father. Everything was so complicated. His mum lived a mostly independent life now – in supported housing in town. She'd visit the day centre, and had a modest social life with other people living with mental health problems. She wasn't the woman Joe knew as his mum, though. Something had been worn away. She was all blunt edges now, blurred. It was partly the drugs, he supposed. Although Joe wasn't convinced that she'd be better off without them – there used to be so much torment, so much chaos. At least she was easier to cope with this way.

"I suppose I could tell her. But you'd have to make sure someone was there with her when I called, she might be in a state afterwards. I'm such a long way away."

"Oh, no, Joe, I couldn't ask you to do that. You're right, she needs to be told. I suppose I could call her support worker, she usually goes round on Thursdays, that's the day after tomorrow…" He was talking to himself. "Don't worry, I'll sort that out. Do you want me to come out there right away, Joe? I could book a flight for later today?"

Joe was surprised by his offer. His dad hadn't left the country since he went to Belgium on business when Joe was a boy. He'd always preferred to holiday in the UK – the Lake District, the Welsh valleys.

"You don't have to rush, Dad. I'll let you know when the funeral is, okay? I'll talk to you soon – you've got our number here?"

"Yes, yes. If there's anything I can do, Boy…"

"Thanks, Dad."

They said their goodbyes and hung up. Joe felt relieved that his dad hadn't insisted on coming out straight away. Joe suspected he would have spent more time making sure that his dad was okay than being able to rely on him. Anyway, he felt he needed to do this on his own.

Willem arrived whilst Joe was finishing a second round of toast. He was finding his way around the kitchen, and had finally found the cat food in the cupboard under the sink. Willem was wearing a suit and carrying his briefcase – he said he'd had to pop into his office on the way and needed to go back later that afternoon, but that tomorrow he was completely free.

They decided to set up in Nel's office. Willem spent most of the morning making phone calls. He informed the tax office, and the notary, and at mid-morning the undertaker made a visit to the house to discuss the funeral arrangements. Willem also spoke to the media – the papers would be running their obituaries the next day. They decided on a venue for the funeral which would hold the big numbers Willem was expecting, and the date was set.

As the day progressed, Joe felt increasingly comfortable with Willem. They used a mixture of Dutch and English, and Joe acquainted himself with Willem's sense of humour. It was pretty dark, and he made a few jokes about Nel that Joe felt awkward laughing at. He treated Joe as an adult, and it made Joe think about how many people back in Reading talked down to him. His boss Herman would always take a certain tone with him – he didn't seem to do it with anyone else. It was as if Joe needed things explaining to him extra carefully.

When they stopped for lunch, Joe noticed that they were running low on butter. Stocking up on butter would be his job now. Claudia arrived as they were eating, and Joe took her into the living room to ask her his list of questions. She was keen to stay on until they knew what was going to happen next. She got upset again as they were talking, and Joe insisted she go home for the rest of the day.

They worked on through the afternoon, making a list of people to invite to the funeral and then writing the cards. There seemed to be hundreds of them. It was a satisfying job, and Joe felt as if he was finally productive again after all his recent failure. Every so often Joe would pause, and one of two sets of memories would float up. He might recall the sensation of his cheek on Emmie's bare breast, or he might see himself brushing out Nel's hair. Emmie's tongue in his mouth, or the colour of Nel's skin. Sex or death. Both sets of thoughts made him feel sad, and tender.

His love for Nel had intensified since yesterday. He'd never used that word to himself before – 'love' – but he did love her. Maybe even more than he loved his own mother. He felt a stab of guilt for having this thought, but tried to forgive himself – she hadn't been much of a mother for a long time. That wasn't her fault, but it was the truth. It wasn't surprising that he'd rather have had someone like Nel for a mother. Although would he really have been any better off with her, with people like Jeroen around? Always having to play second fiddle to her art?

They got to work looking through Nel's papers. Nel's solicitor had her will, and they had an appointment to visit him the next morning, but Willem said they needed to check that she hadn't made any amendments to her will or filed it with her general papers. Willem asked Joe to go through Nel's red filing cabinet, while he went through Nel's desk and then a drawer full of paperwork in her bedroom. This was the kind of meticulous job that Joe enjoyed, and he started to lose track of time. When Willem appeared at the door of the office, Joe was shocked to notice that it was nearly five. Joe was sitting cross-legged on the carpet in front of the open filing cabinet. He turned back to what he was doing and said a cheery, "Hallo."

Willem walked over and stood close to him. Joe pulled out another wedge of papers.

"I'm almost done with this drawer now, but…"

"Joe."

There was a gravity in Willem's voice that Joe hadn't heard before. He looked up and saw that his face was ashen. He put the papers down.

"Joe, I've found something. I don't think you know about it. I think we should…" He looked around the room. "Let's go through to the living room, eh?"

He held a hand out towards Joe, who took it and allowed himself to be half-pulled up from the floor. Willem held onto it as they walked from the room, and only let go when they reached the sofa and Joe sat down. There was a tension in Joe's chest. He swallowed as Willem sat across from him and leaned forwards on his knees. Willem sighed, rubbing his eyes with one hand, and then looked directly at Joe.

"I found some papers, Joe, hidden away at the back of Nel's desk. Nel never said anything to me, so I'm assuming she didn't tell you, or anyone else... She told me everything. Well, I thought she did. They were all in a big brown envelope. It was sealed and looked like it hadn't been opened for twenty years. I suppose it hasn't been... One of the documents was your birth certificate."

"My birth certificate? What was that doing..."

Willem held out his hand and gestured for Joe to wait.

"The name of the mother on your birth certificate was Petronella Taatje Reinke."

Joe tried to work out who Petronella Taatje Reinke might be. The surname Reinke – so it must have been a relation of his mother's. It hit him.

"Nel is on my birth certificate."

Willem nodded, waiting.

"Nel is... my mum?"

Willem nodded again. He looked so sad. Joe wondered why he was so sad. The words repeated themselves in his mind. Nel is my mum. The shadows of questions jostled in the background. He wasn't sure what any of the questions were – he was still in a blank place, pleasantly blank – calm, detached. He wondered if he ought to reassure Willem, he looked as if he might cry. He was aware of a burning sensation, and realised he needed to urinate. Badly. He got up abruptly and Willem lurched up after him, holding his arms out as if Joe was about to fall.

"I just need the toilet," Joe said as he was leaving the room.

"Are you okay?" Willem called out.

"Yup," Joe called back, already halfway up the stairs. He really was bursting. It was all the coffee, all the coffee that gets drunk in this country. He wasn't used to the caffeine again yet – it was keeping him up at night, making him feel jittery. He was aware of the fluttering in his stomach as he unzipped his flies. He listened to the first 'splash' as his urine started flowing, and watched it as it looped into the toilet bowl. He could smell the coffee in it – acrid. A dark yellow.

As he felt the relief in his bladder, he realised why Willem had looked sad. Nel was gone. It was too late for her to be his mother. And now the questions took shape, came flooding in. Why didn't she tell him? Did she give him up? Why? Why was he brought up by her sister? Was his mum even Nel's sister? How old was she when she had him? Who knew? Joe's mother – she must have known. Did Joe's dad know? His dad wasn't really his dad. Who was? Why didn't they say anything?

The questions started to overwhelm him. He concentrated on squeezing the last few drops from the tip of his penis, and then on washing his hands. He zipped up and went back down to the living room, where Willem was pacing, looking worried. They both sat back in their places again. Willem's forehead was scrunched up.

"You knew nothing?"

Joe shook his head. "Why didn't she... Why wasn't I here?"

"I don't know, Joe. She was very young. How old are you, twenty eight? She must have been, what, fourteen? Maybe she... Your parents have never said anything to you about being adopted?"

Joe thought back. He was trying to remember if anything had ever seemed odd. If anything had felt out of place.

237

It was always so difficult to look for a specific memory, like when somebody said, "Which was your favourite birthday?" When he thought about his parents, the memories started to flood in, but they were memories he was already familiar with and they gave him no further information. Here was the time he made a den with a sheet and cushions underneath the stairs, and stayed there for a whole day. Here he was being sick on his homework book. Here was his dad bringing his mum home from the hospital. Nothing. He looked over at Willem, who still looked concerned. He definitely didn't want to call his dad. Not his dad.

"He's not my father, then? Who is my father?"

"Oh Joe, Joe." Willem started to fiddle with his hands. He cupped his left hand with his right, and then swapped over, as if he was washing them under the tap. Joe was transfixed by them. He wondered if that was what they meant in books when they said 'wringing his hands'. Willem seemed more upset than Joe felt. Should he be feeling more upset? Did it even make any difference, that Nel was his mother? It would have made a lot of difference if she was still alive. It was too late now, too late for anything. He still missed her, but he missed her just the same degree as he had before.

"Do I have to tell my dad I know?"

As the questions occurred to him he said them out loud, not really expecting that Willem would have any answers for him. It was all too early. He knew it wasn't really the time for answers to questions like that. But what was it the right time for? What should he be doing in the meantime, while this new information sank in?

The door squeaked, and Tante Truus pushed her way into the room. She came straight over to Joe and wound her way around his legs. Joe felt flattered, before remembering that it was time for her dinner. He was just a walking food dispenser. He stroked her for a few minutes, before excusing himself and going into the kitchen to get the food ready.

While he was forking meat into the bowl, Willem appeared at the kitchen doorway.

"Shall I get you some coffee, Joe? Or something stronger?"

He'd had enough coffee to last him a lifetime. He was tempted by the thought of something stronger, but it didn't feel right.

"Oh, I'm okay thank you Willem. I feel okay, you know. I'll just need a chance to let it sink in." He looked at the clock on the wall. "Are we still going to go and meet the funeral director? Don't we need to get going now?"

"Would you like me to go on my own?"

"No, I want to come. It's even more important now."

Willem nodded his head vigorously. "Of course, of course. Let's get going. I'm parked just down the street."

After seeing the funeral director, the two of them shared a meal in an Italian restaurant. Joe returned to a dark house. Before he even took off his coat, he went through the ground floor and turned on every single light. He wasn't scared of burglars or ghosts. It was more that he needed to see the corners of the rooms. It helped him to feel less alone.

He was still hungry, and helped himself to another ready meal from Nel's fridge. He was starting to run out of milk and bread. He ought to go to the supermarket tomorrow. Was he brave enough to ride Nel's bike, the one she kept in a room off the hall where the washing machine lived? He needed to do some washing too. There was so much…

After eating, he called his dad to let him know about the funeral arrangements. His dad told Joe that his mother had decided not to come, which was a relief to both of them. His dad insisted he'd fly out for the week, or longer if Joe needed him to – and maybe Joe could fly home with him? Joe hadn't thought about going home. Who would look after Nel's house? And it was then that the idea occurred to him for the first time. Maybe he could stay. Maybe Amsterdam could be his home.

The next morning, Joe woke early. It was one of those rare mornings when his eyelids wanted to be open. His first thought was that his left thigh felt warm. He looked down and saw Tante Truus leaning against him. His second thought was that Nel's funeral was tomorrow. His third thought was that his dad would be arriving in (he looked at the clock) five hours time. His dad. It was only then that he remembered what Willem had told him yesterday.

He lay back and regarded the ceiling. It was painted a bleak white, unlike most of Nel's colourful house. What colours would he prefer to paint the walls? He noticed the proprietary nature of this thought and chastised himself. It wasn't his place. Even if he was Nel's son, who knows what would happen to her estate. It would be more likely to go to his mother, or maybe even Willem...

He tried to focus on what he needed to do before his dad's plane got in. He needed to decide what room he'd put his dad in, and speak to Claudia about getting the bed ready. He needed to find something to wear to the funeral – Willem had offered to lend him something, but he was twice Joe's weight (and Theo was two thirds his height). He thought about Claudia, and how she'd treated him yesterday as if he were 'the boss'. He wondered again why everyone was treating him as if he was in charge. The undertaker had been the same. Maybe it was because he was in a different country, and it was more difficult for people to pick up the signals that placed him low in the pecking order in the UK.

As he was brushing his teeth, the doorbell went. He found Emmie on the doorstep again, this time looking quite respectable in a long cotton skirt and an asymmetrical jacket. There was another girl with her – she was even slighter than Emmie, and was dressed all in black with long dark hair and dark plum lipstick. Neither of the girls was smiling. After a short silence, Emmie spoke.

"We thought you might want to come out for breakfast with us."

Joe looked at the girl in black, but she still didn't smile. It occurred to him that he wasn't smiling either. He held out his hand.

"I'm Joe."

The girl took his hand and did a strange little curtsey. Joe wasn't sure whether she was being sarcastic or not.

"Marika."

"Good to meet you, Marika," he said in Dutch. Marika giggled. Joe couldn't work her out. He turned back to Emmie.

"Give me a second, I'll just get my wallet."

Emmie took them to a place just around the corner. They chose a table near the window and waited for the waitress. The girls whispered to each other in Dutch, and Emmie started to rub her eyes. Was she crying again? It was still hard to imagine her showing any emotion apart from gruff annoyance. Although maybe she'd say the same about him. He concentrated on reading his menu. It was Marika who spoke next, in near-flawless English.

"She's sad because this is where she used to come with Nel."

Joe muttered, "Oh," and looked back down to his menu. He was being assaulted by mental images of Emmie's breasts, her waist, the shaved hair underneath her arms. He didn't know whether to feel turned on or guilty. He wondered if he ought to say thank you to Marika, for loaning her girlfriend to him. Was she feeling jealous? The whole set-up was a complete mystery to him.

He was saved from these thoughts when the waitress finally came over to take their order. He ordered rolls, cheese, ham and jam – he always ordered jam for breakfast in Amsterdam as it came with those sugary sprinkles. Marika told Joe she was impressed with his Dutch, which pleased him.

Emmie had taken a tissue out of her handbag and was blowing her nose. She didn't seem like the kind of girl to carry a packet of tissues around. Condoms, yes, but not tissues. Maybe he didn't know her as well as he thought he did. Maybe he'd invented a lot of what he knew about her, a by-product of her starring role in his sexual fantasies. This woman sitting in front of him looked so vulnerable.

He dropped his menu on the floor, and when he glanced under the table he saw that the women were holding hands. He would like someone to hold his hand. Maybe that affection stuff was more important than sex after all. Someone to hold his hand, and to whisper in his ear that everything was going to be all right. Then he had to stop thinking, because grief started to rise up in his throat.

As the waitress set down their drinks, Joe remembered what he had to tell Emmie. He thought he'd lighten the mood with a joke first.

"Where do you get chocolate mousse from?"

They both shrugged.

"Chocolate cows. Chocolate mousse – chocolate moos – do you get it?"

Marika sniggered, but Emmie wasn't even looking at him. Her face was deadpan. Joe sighed. He might as well get it over and done with.

"I had some bad news… No, not bad, good. Well. I found something out yesterday."

Emmie raised her eyes to him. Her lashes were clotted with black mascara.

"You know already?" she asked.

Emmie's face was guarded, and it created a mirrored sense of defensiveness in him.

"Know what?"

Emmie put her coffee cup down too abruptly, and spilt coffee onto the table without noticing. It was Marika who mopped it up with a paper napkin before the pool of hot liquid crept across the table and over the rim. She sighed and looked at Joe.

"Just spit it out, Joe."

"Nel is my mother." He watched her face intently, and thought he saw relief. "Fuck knows how. What were you going to say?"

She welled up again, and pursed her lips together. After a deep breath and a sip of her coffee, she looked up at him.

"I thought I had to tell you. I've been scared to. I should have told you that night…" she glanced over at Marika and trailed off. "I was going to tell you this morning. And you already knew? How long have you known?"

"Only since yesterday. Willem found some papers in Nel's desk."

At this Emmie humphed her breath out in annoyance. She brought her elbows up onto the table, taking her forehead into both hands and squeezing bunches of her hair between her fingers.

"Shit. So I was too late then. I was meant to tell you. I was meant to break it to you gently. Mother will be furious. You won't tell her, will you?"

"Maartje knows? How did she know? Why didn't you tell me before?" His voice rose in anger.

Emmie leaned forwards and touched Joe on the shoulder, her face pleading with him.

"I'm so sorry Joe, I really am. I just found out too. I wasn't meant to know, my mother wasn't even meant to know. Nel got really really drunk one night and spilled it all out, and when Mum talked about it the next day Nel couldn't even remember telling her. Nel went mad. She said she'd never told another soul, and made my mum swear that she'd never tell anyone. Mum said she'd never seen her like that before."

"Was she that ashamed of me?"

Emmie looked shocked.

"No, Joe, no! She was hysterical, she… Look, this is coming out wrong." She opened her handbag and started rustling around inside. "I wrote it down, everything Mum said. I didn't want to forget anything. She asked me if I wanted her to talk to you, but I said it would be better if… ah, here." She brought out a piece of paper and unfolded it.

"Okay. This is everything that Mum could remember. I asked her lots of questions, I thought you'd want to know everything. That's right, isn't it?"

Joe nodded, but he wasn't sure.

"It's very organised of her, isn't it?" said Marika, looking proud. Joe felt a flash of hate towards her, which disappeared as quickly as it had arrived. They were interrupted by the waitress who arrived with their food. Marika started tucking into hers. Emmie smoothed the paper flat onto the table. Her eyes flicked back and forth between the paper and Joe.

"So. Nel said when she got pregnant when she was fourteen, she never said how, I mean, who the father was, she said her parents were furious, but especially her mother. It wasn't the kind of thing that happened to the Reinkes. Her mum went crazy, was vicious, went on and on at her, saying Nel would go to hell and so would her baby, all kinds of terrible things. Nel thought about trying to get rid of the baby, I mean you, but by the time her parents found out it was too late. So her mother came up with a plan, to hide it from everyone – to make it seem more respectable.

"Ineke was born without a womb. They found out when she was a teenager. Did you know that?" Joe shook his head. "Your mother, I mean Ineke, had already organised going to the UK to go to design school or something, when Nel told her mum she was pregnant. Ineke was going to stay with a relative, an aunt or something. I guess she wanted to get as far away from your grandmother as she could. So your grandmother kept Nel in the house when she started showing, and then they took the baby over to Ineke in the UK as soon as she was born. This relative had never had children either, and liked the idea of helping Ineke look after it. Your grandmother thought it was the perfect solution. Your grandmother lied to her friends and said Ineke had married a man over there and that's why she was going to live over there. Something like that. Ridiculous, I can't imagine any of them believed it. Nel was emotionally blackmailed by her mum – and she couldn't bear her baby to be born into such a mess of a family, all that alcohol and repression. She thought you'd be better off in a different country with sensible Ineke. The worst bit for Nel was hurting her dad. He was so disappointed in her. She really loves her dad... I mean loved. God knows why.

"So she handed you over to Ineke. Like I said there was this relative, who agreed to take them both in, and then Ineke met your dad. She was probably desperate to meet anybody. He took the baby in as his own, promised never to tell you... Back in Amsterdam, Nel wasn't coping. She couldn't stop thinking about all the things her sister would be doing wrong. They were so different, I suppose... Nel said to my mum that the only thing that stopped her from going mad was to pretend you weren't really hers, that you really did belong to her sister. Whenever she started thinking about you as hers again, she said her head started spinning. She felt dizzy, sick... So as time went on she did it less and less."

Emmie looked intently at the paper for a while longer, turning it over and back again, and then looked up.

"I think that's it. Yes, that's everything that Mum said." She put her hand on Joe's. "She kept telling me what a state Nel was in, when it was all pouring out of her. It was like she was talking to a mad woman." Emmie glanced at her girlfriend, who was visibly enjoying her breakfast.

Joe looked at his own untouched breakfast and then back up at Emmie. She didn't seem to know where to put her eyes. There was a heavy silence, and Joe's mind went completely blank. He was staring at Emmie, but he was thinking of kestrels. He'd read in a book once that many species of bird, unlike humans, could see into the ultra-violet range of light. UV vision hadn't been found in all species of raptor, but as it existed in some, it was likely to occur in all species. One species of raptor known to use this light for hunting purposes was the Common Kestrel. Rodents don't have a bladder and so they leave a urine trail behind them in the grass. Their urine reflects UV light and a kestrel can then follow the trail to locate their prey. A hovering kestrel was actually looking for rodent urine. Rodent urine.

It was Marika who finally broke the spell. She waved her hand in front of Joe's eyes to bring him out of his trance. His attention returned to the café with a 'whoosh' – he became aware of the noises surrounding them again – the clinking cutlery, the whistling coffee machine in the background, the bell on the door as one of the customers left.

"Here we all are," he said.

That was how the world started up again.

The three of them managed to chat about everyday matters for the rest of their breakfast. Marika talked about her studies – she'd just started a part-time marine biology degree – and Emmie talked about her job selling cars. Joe couldn't imagine a job less suited to her, but Marika assured him that she was perfectly capable of turning on the charm when it suited her. Joe confided that he'd played with the idea of staying in Amsterdam, and they spent the rest of the time arguing the pros and cons. None of the things they talked about meant anything to Joe – the live music scene, the house prices – but he listened politely.

Even when the two girls were arguing, there was affection between them. Joe wondered how Marika could be happy, knowing that Emmie had... He didn't want to think about it. He made a decision to put that glorious night in a box in his brain, and padlock it. He'd look at Emmie as a friend from now on, and ban her from his sexual fantasies. Maybe he could get actual sex from somewhere else. Maybe Emmie could help him to find a girlfriend, a proper one, and teach him how to have a real relationship, like the one she had with Marika.

The time came for Joe to get going, and he was reluctant to leave the two of them. Emmie and Marika kissed him goodbye (three kisses each), and said they'd see him at the funeral. Willem was going to pick up Joe and his father from Nel's house, and Joe was grateful he wouldn't be going on his own. He didn't want the responsibility of finding the place, or of walking into the church on his own. He felt like Willem could play his father, somehow, leaving him to play the role of father to his own father. It was all very complicated. He glanced behind him when he was out on the street and he could see Marika stroking Emmie's hair.

Joe caught the tourist bus to the airport, and made his way to Arrivals. He recognised the information point and the phrase 'snacks and goodies' written on one of the shop windows. How many days ago was he here last? Was it even a whole week yet? Everything had changed since then. Not just a death, but a new mother. The loss of his new mother. He put it out of his mind, and what took its place was a mental image of Emmie's breasts. He was tempted to linger, but then Marika appeared next to Emmie, as if she was warning him. He pushed Emmie away too.

The third thought was of his workplace. It arrived all in a rush – a detailed visual image of his corridor with everyone in their offices. Eva with her solid hair (how much hairspray did she get through?), Gino with his pimply forehead and bad breath, and John with his habit of repeating back the second half of every sentence you said to him. Helle, and his manager Herman, and Thierry. A feeling started washing over him – a sludgy feeling, as if everything was pointless, as if he might as well hang himself right away. A familiar feeling. His death wouldn't make any difference to the world, not like Nel's.

His muddled emotions weren't going to be 'cured' by Nel's death. They were still lurking, back where they were before they burst out in the first place. Even if he did stay in Amsterdam, it wasn't realistic to imagine he could leave the whole mess behind in Reading. His demons would track him down. He thought of those programmes on daytime television, where whole families emigrated to Australia or Spain to get a 'new start' or a 'better quality of life'. He'd like to see what happened next. Sometimes the TV crews did go back, after six months or so – but he didn't think that was long enough. Give it five years, Joe thought. Give them five years in their new lives, and then show me where they are. Are their marriages in any better state? Do their children hold a new respect for them? Do they love everything about their new home?

He reached the Arrivals gate and glanced at his watch before turning on his heels and walking back the way he'd come. He had fifteen minutes before the plane was due. He thought more about the idea that we carry our problems around with us like a snail carries its home; that we recreate our problems wherever we are. It reminded him of a conversation he'd had with Nel, the night she died. Was anything really the fault of our environment, or the fault of anyone around us, for that matter? What if we can't blame anyone else for anything?

"It's all my fault."

The thought struck him with such strength, he said it out loud. He wasn't blaming or punishing himself, it was just a plain fact. Maybe responsibility was a better word than fault. Those colleagues down his corridor who drove him mad – they could only drive him mad with his permission. He had only grown so stressed about his project because of the pressure he'd put on himself. Nobody else had been telling him he was failing. Nobody else had expected him to work late night after night, or to wake at three in the morning and worry about his calculations.

He needed to do something about the situation he'd created... What could he do? He could leave, but was that the right solution? If he left, wouldn't he just end up recreating the same situation somewhere else? If he created his own feelings, his own depression, then what could he do about it? Was he doomed to repeat it, here in Amsterdam, with a different set of characters? Something had to change. He had to change, somehow. To start doing something differently. But what?

He looked at his watch. Time to walk back. On the way, he passed a bookshop and looked at the piles of books on display. All at once he missed books, as one might miss a lover. He glanced at his watch again, to see if he had time to pop into the shop and find something decent. There wasn't any time, he was already late, but feeling the desire to read again pleased him.

He felt lighter as he walked the final hundred yards to Arrivals. Even though he hadn't come up with any answers, his sequence of thoughts had caused some kind of shift. It was difficult to explain, but he felt more grown-up than when he'd walked into the airport half an hour before. He felt like he might be in his early twenties, rather than being stuck at fourteen. Just as well – he was about to see his father. He needed to muster all the maturity he could find.

And there his dad was, appearing from around the corner and dwarfed by his huge suitcase. He was just another little old man – scrawny and hunched – with thinning hair and a perplexed face. Was that really him? Where was the father of his childhood? Just before his dad spotted him, Joe was thinking about Nel's face, and of touching her hair. He felt motherly towards her, and then he felt motherly towards his father, who looked so relieved to see him. Tenderness rose in his chest, and blossomed into a burst of energy. It gave him strength.

"Hello, Papa."

"Ah – Boy. I'm so glad to…" He handed his suitcase over to Joe's open hand gratefully, and pushed his glasses back up his nose. Joe couldn't understand why he didn't buy himself a suitcase on wheels. He was the only person Joe knew who still lugged his old leather case around.

"I'm – phew, what a journey. The man next to me wouldn't stop sneezing. They shouldn't let people travel if they're ill like that, it's a menace to the rest of us. All the nasty germs that must be floating around on those aeroplanes… Germ soup…"

His dad went on. A little rant always seemed to do his father good. Joe could feel himself becoming a child again too, despite himself, internally sneering at his dad and wanting to tell him to shut up. Joe chided himself and put a hand on his dad's shoulder instead. This spontaneous gesture stopped his dad mid–sentence. He looked at Joe as if he was looking at him for the first time.

"My, haven't you grown? When did that happen?"

Joe smiled, and his dad patted him briskly on the back. That was the closest they'd get to a hug, but it was good enough for Joe.

"Come on, old man, I'll take you home."

On the bus journey back to Nel's they swapped easy news of the weather, his dad's work, Pam's back problems, and the state of the plastering in his dad's spare room. Joe showed his dad round Nel's house and they settled into silence as they sipped tea in the living room. Joe's dad seemed to remember something.

"How are you, son?" He looked down to his tea immediately, as if he didn't really want Joe to answer, especially with anything other than, "Fine thanks." That was fine with Joe – he didn't want to have a long discussion about his feelings either. Why break with tradition after all these years? But he couldn't put off telling him any longer.

"All right, Dad. But I do have some news for you, I don't know if you know it or not. If you don't know... well, it might be shocking."

"News? What do you mean?"

"It's Mum. Well... you met Mum after I was born, didn't you?"

"How did you?..."

"It's okay."

His dad sighed and put a hand on his forehead. "You were only a tiny thing. She'd only just had you, the poor thing. Chucked out of her home and sent to live with that awful old bat. No wonder she jumped at the chance of moving in with me. She insisted we never told you, Boy. Said it would be for the best. It never sat comfortably with me. I don't know if..."

Joe butted in, impatient. "I know, I know. I know all that. But Mum told you that I was... that I was her baby?"

"What do you mean, her baby? Of course you were her baby. Who else's baby would you be?"

"Nel's."

"What do you mean, Nel's?"

"I'm Nel's baby!" Joe caught the anger rising in him. He ran out of patience so quickly with his dad. He softened his voice again before he continued. "I was Nel's baby. Not Mum's. Mum couldn't have any children. Grandmother made her give me to Mum. Or I think that's what happened... There were papers, when we were sorting things out for the funeral. I talked to Willem about it, and..."

Joe stopped speaking when he noticed that his dad had changed colour. He swayed slightly on the sofa, and Joe clumsily got up out of his seat to go towards him. When his dad saw Joe looming towards him, he blinked his eyes hard, twice, and took a deep breath before holding his hand out towards Joe to keep him away.

"Just give me a minute, son."

His dad pinched the bridge of his nose between his finger and thumb. He looked pathetic, and Joe felt annoyance rising up again. He caught himself just before he said something angry. He waited for his dad to speak.

"I don't know what to say. Well. I must say, son..." His eyes were glazed over – Joe could almost see his brain whirring. "I must say. This does explain a thing or two. Not hers. How could she not have told me? It beggars belief. It beggars belief, it really does."

"What does it explain?"

His dad looked at him.

"What?"

"You said it explained some things. What does it explain?"

"Oh, just the way your mother was about you, I suppose. When you were still a babe-in-arms. So that's why she didn't want any more… you said she couldn't have them? Oh Joe, oh Boy!"

There was a genuine horror in his dad's voice, as if some of his father's actual feelings had leaked through the usual defences. Joe felt touched. He was also desperate to change the subject. He'd had enough of talking about things, especially as Nel's funeral was looming.

He didn't even have anything to wear yet. He shopped at Gap religiously, and his wardrobe was rather limited. For work it was black trousers and white collared tops, or white shirts with his blue tie if he needed to be smart. He wore dark navy jeans and t-shirts at the weekend (white, and occasionally navy blue). His mum kept buying him clothes in different colours for Christmas – he'd wear them on Boxing Day to keep her happy, and then they'd disappear into the bowels of his wardrobe, never to be seen again. The stress of finding a suitable funeral suit had begun to preoccupy him.

"I've got to go and get a suit."

"What?"

Joe remembered he'd just told his dad about Nel. "I need to get a suit for the funeral."

"Oh. Where will you get one?"

"I don't know – oh, I don't know."

His dad's question was enough to confirm what he'd already suspected. How could he have imagined that he'd survive out here in the Netherlands, on his own? Even buying himself a suit filled him with dread!

"I'll come with you, son. We'll find one together, shall we?"

Joe nodded and tried to smile. He felt grateful.

"I haven't been too good, you know. Mentally. I haven't really talked to you about it."

"I know, son, I know. It gets too much for all of us sometimes. You're not like your mother, though – you won't end up like her. I'll make sure of it."

How? Joe wondered. But he didn't say it out loud. His dad was trying his best. His father, who struggled to make him edible packed lunches when his mum went into hospital that first time. Who tried to help him with his maths homework. Who gave him an excruciatingly embarrassing (and unnecessary) lesson in 'the facts of life'. Often Joe was completely furious at him, for not being better at these things. And more rarely, like right now, he was just overwhelmed with love for him. His father, who really tried his best.

After a long afternoon shopping Joe's dad went up to bed early, and Joe stayed up late. He hadn't intended to, but he started looking through some of Nel's old photograph albums, and then he moved on to some old letters of hers, and before he knew it the clock had struck midnight, one o'clock, two o'clock. He forced himself to stop reading, but then on the way to his bedroom he was drawn to Nel's studio. He turned on the lamps that were scattered around the room. He wandered from painting to painting, gazing at them. He took in the shapes, the colours, the texture of the brushstrokes. He drank them in.

It reminded him of 'his bench' in a park near work where he often ate his lunch. As he ate his sandwiches he'd let his eyes rest on the scene in front of him. As he settled, the oak tree in the middle distance would claim his attention. Then he might trace the curving top line of the hedge, or hear children arguing in another part of the park. The details stepped forwards next – the glimpse of a wren in the interior of the hedge, or a shiny red sweet wrapper on the path. It was never the same from one day to the next. It was never the same from one moment to the next.

He'd cancelled his lunch hour when he'd started getting panicky about his project. Instead he'd hurriedly visit the canteen, feeling impatient with the queues, and shovel down his food, hardly tasting it. Maybe he hadn't realised how important his visits to the park had been to him. Maybe that hour of observation as he chewed his sandwiches had been keeping him sane.

When Joe's eyes started to droop, he picked up one of Nel's paintings on impulse and wandered into Nel's bedroom. He propped the painting against the wall and lay down on her bed. He could smell her in the room. It was a good smell – slightly musty, and there was sweetness, like coconut. Maybe she used coconut shampoo. Or was he conjuring it from thin air? Imagined or not, the smell made his eyes water. He missed her. Not just as Nel, but as Nel-his-mum. There were so many things he wanted to ask her. So many things he didn't know. Did she ever think of him as her son? Was she proud of him? Did she ever regret giving him up? Would she ever have told him? He shivered, and looked around her room for something to drape over himself. The thought of slipping between her sheets felt too morbid, even though Claudia had washed the bedding and remade the bed.

He saw a blue shape draped over one of her chairs. He dragged himself off the bed and fetched it back. It was a beautiful blanket – the blue of an evening Mediterranean sky, flecked with different coloured threads – pinks, purples. It was so soft – he wondered what kind of wool it was made from. There was a kind of rabbit, he knew they used their fur – were they called Alpacas? The blanket was large and thin – he wrapped himself in it like a mummy and lay back down on her bed. He held one of the corners of it against his cheek and brushed it back and forth. He remembered doing this as a child, with thistle heads in the autumn. He'd brush them gently all over his own face or, when he was lucky, on the cheeks of the girl from a few doors down. They were so soft, and such a beautiful grey. Like a squirrel's tail.

As the material kissed his skin, a knot of unsettled feelings crystallised into a realisation. Something was unfinished. There was something he regretted. He wanted to express his gratitude for the time Nel had spent with him, for all the letters she'd written to him over the years. He hadn't said thank you. How could he say it now?

He could wrap her up in this blanket. It would be like wrapping up a baby, the way they used to swaddle them when they'd just been born. Coddle them. He could tuck her in, and then she wouldn't get cold in the ground. She could feel the softness of this beautiful blanket against her cheek, and it would comfort her.

He knew that these thoughts were mad, but they also felt correct. Maybe this was what it was like for his mum. Maybe she knew that her thoughts were mad too, but she paid attention to them anyway, because they did make sense to her. More than rational thoughts possibly could. This was a completely new concept to Joe. He'd always put such stock in rationality. His whole life had been about facts. All that information sucked from books, all that sorting and ordering in his head. It was all he had, in a way – his intellect, his rationality. But it wasn't enough. Maybe it was a good thing that he'd gone a bit crazy at work. But his mother certainly wasn't crazy in a good way. How did you tell the difference?

He was tired of thinking. He lay there for a long time, brushing the corner of the blanket across his cheek. He was soaking it with his thanks. He poured his gratitude into it, and it streamed into the fabric, melding with it. It made him feel happy, that he could give this last gift to Nel. He didn't call himself mad or stupid. He just let the love stream out of him, and then when he got too tired, when his eyes started to close of their own accord, he left her room, shutting the door quietly behind him, and carried the blanket with him. He folded it carefully and placed it on a chair. He sank into bed and he dreamt of Emmie. In the dreams he felt safe, secure. In his dreams, she held him.

On the morning of the funeral, Joe felt too sick to eat any breakfast. He certainly couldn't face the coffee that Claudia had set in front of him. Instead he sat and sipped his strong, sweet tea and tried not to look at his dad, who was demolishing a full plate of bacon and eggs. Joe looked down at his suit. It had taken a long afternoon to find it. His shoulders must have been narrower than the rest of the male population. Most of the suits he tried on were far too broad at the shoulders. He'd looked like a child in his father's suit, or someone from the eighties. They'd found one eventually, a narrow fit, and his dad had encouraged him to buy a new tie too, and a new shirt. He looked pretty good, even if he did say so himself. His dad caught him looking at himself.

"Snazzy, eh?"

Joe grunted, internally rolling his eyes at his dad's use of the word 'snazzy'. He was tired after his late night. He'd woken up too early, and then couldn't get back to sleep because he'd started thinking about how he could get the blanket to the funeral. It was a personal thing between him and Nel, and he didn't want anyone else to know about it. But the blanket was too big to simply hide under his jacket. Eventually he'd decided to put it into a small rucksack, one he'd found with the coats downstairs. He hoped that no one would ask him about it. Hopefully they'd be preoccupied.

Joe was relieved when Willem and Theo arrived to take them to the church. As they walked towards the taxi, Willem hung back and had a quiet word with him.

"How are you, Joe?"

Joe thought for a moment, and stopped himself from saying an automatic, "Okay, thank you." He remembered his thoughts at the airport, and realized that this was an opportunity to do things differently. He could choose to speak the truth. What was the truth?

"I don't know, really."

This seemed to satisfy Willem, and he nodded empathetically.

"I will miss her, your mother."

It was difficult to hear Willem say 'your mother'. Willem saw this in Joe's face, and pulled Joe towards him, clasping him in a tight clinch. Joe wasn't sure if Willem was hanging on to him, or holding him. It felt like a bit of both. Willem was wearing the same woody aftershave as before, and Joe breathed it in.

Joe was overwhelmed by the number of people at the church. When Willem got out of the taxi he immediately started greeting people – shaking people's hands, nodding in recognition. Joe heard a cluster of people nearby use the word 'aneurysm'. He guessed people were still catching up on how Nel had died. Willem seemed to get a lot of attention, as if he was Nel's husband. Why was nobody looking at Joe? He realised that nobody knew who he was. It was a private matter, none of these people's business. But there was also a part of him that wanted everyone to know. He could stand on his tiptoes and yell it out in Dutch – "Nel is my mother." Or rather, Nel was my mother.

Joe felt a presence beside him and turned to see his dad, standing too close, as if he was trying to protect him. Or was he seeking protection from Joe? Everything was topsy-turvy. Joe scanned the crowd, and was glad to spot Emmie and Marika.

"Emmie!"

Emmie didn't hear him, but Marika did, and she pulled on her girlfriend's sleeve. She aimed a half-smile at Joe, then kissed Emmie and whispered something in her ear before disappearing off into the crowds. Emmie bounded over as if they were at a wedding, and gave Joe a bear hug. She quickly pulled away and appraised Joe's dad.

"Hallo."

Joe's dad stared blankly. Joe put his hand on his father's shoulder.

"This is my dad."

"Oh, hello Joe's dad," she said in English, before turning immediately back to Joe. "Don't you hate funerals?"

He nodded and grunted. Emmie slipped her arm through his and offered her other arm to Joe's dad. Joe wasn't sure what his dad would make of this, but he took her arm gladly, and they walked together into the church. Marika was sitting in one of the middle rows, and Emmie let go of Joe and pointed him towards the front. Theo spotted him and beckoned him over to the front row. Joe wondered who would be in the front row at his own funeral. Podge, of course, if he hadn't died first. Would there be a widow? Any children? It made him sad to think about it – he kept picturing an empty church. Nothing like this place, full to bursting with people who'd loved his aunt. His mother. Nel.

The funeral passed in a blur. Joe was mesmerised by the vicar's strong accent as he read the eulogy, and this distracted him from what he was actually saying. He heard him referring to Joe as Nel's nephew, and he imagined everyone in the rows behind him craning to have a look at him. He didn't understand much of the poem that Willem had chosen to read out, but it moved him more than anything else, because Willem's voice kept breaking as he read. When Willem sat back down next to Joe, his body shook. Heaving, as if he was being sick. Theo put his arm around him, and Joe let tears stream down his own cheeks. He didn't wipe them away. He didn't want to draw his father's attention, and he didn't want any pity. He let them stay there, until they felt cold. They tickled his cheeks. He hoped they'd dry out before anyone saw him.

After the service, everyone filed out into the sunshine. Joe spotted Emmie's blue hair amongst the crowds. He asked her if she'd look after his dad for a few minutes, as he needed to ask Willem something. He guiltily left the two of them alone together – when he looked back they seemed like the oddest pair he'd ever seen. They had nothing in common, really, except him. Did either of them really know him? He hoped they weren't going to swap notes.

He found Willem talking to an elderly couple. His eyes had red rims, as if drawn on with a red kohl pencil. Willem made his excuses to the couple and turned to Joe.

"I have something I want to ask, Willem. It's... it's awkward."

Willem raised his eyebrows a fraction and waited. Joe found himself mesmerised by them. They had lots of different coloured hairs in them, from white to pale red to dark grey, and they looked stiff, like bristles. They were so untidy – they didn't match Willem's neatly shaved head and smart suit. Maybe his chaos had all settled into his eyebrows. Joe remembered himself and went on.

"I wanted to see Nel one more time, on my own, before she gets buried. Is that possible, do you think? Where does she go now, straight to the cemetery?"

"You do know she's going to be cremated, Joe?" Willem frowned. "We went through this, when we discussed the arrangements? She's going to the crematorium next, and then she'll have a small plot in the family grave, with her parents."

Joe could remember Willem talking about plots, but he couldn't remember anything about a cremation. He felt as sick as he had at breakfast, and the ground shifted underneath him. He took a slow deep breath to try and keep the nausea at bay. Willem was looking at Joe's face with concern.

"Joe, is something wrong? What is it?"

Joe didn't say anything. His entire day had been anchored onto the fact that he'd be able to wrap Nel in her blue blanket. That he'd be able to show her how grateful he was. He'd touched his foot against his rucksack on the floor during the ceremony. He'd thought of the blanket when he watched Willem getting upset. How could he wrap it around a stupid pile of ashes? Pulses of anger rose up. Why hadn't Willem warned him? His own mother, and he hadn't got a chance to...

His fury swirled, looking for a target, but he could only find himself. He could remember Willem speaking to him about the crematorium now. How could he have been such an idiot? Once he'd turned the anger on himself, it metamorphosised into grief. Not a wishy-washy sadness, but grief of a strength equivalent to the pain of labour. Great crashing waves of contraction, enough to physically knock you off your feet.

He did wobble, and Willem's hand came out to steady him. Willem was looking at him with such concern. Joe couldn't bear it. He couldn't bear kindness, not now. He really would dissolve into nothing, and he'd never get himself back again. He stepped back from Willem, and once he'd made the initial movement it was easy to keep moving, walking backwards to start with, his eyes fixed on Willem, and then turning so he could see where he was going, dodging the other mourners, speeding up, and then as Willem shouted after him he broke into a run.

He didn't know how long he ran for. He slowed to a walk when he ran out of breath, then speeded up again as soon as he could. He counted as he ran, using his feet as they landed on the pavements – one two three four five six, one two three four five six. He passed through parts of Amsterdam he'd never seen before. He kept coming back to Rembrandt Square, passing through it three or four times, trying to get somewhere different but ending up there again. It was a mirror of what was happening in his head. However fast he ran, his feelings were faster.

He wanted to find a sanctuary, but there were too many people everywhere. All of the benches were already occupied. He found an empty one near a church, but he'd only been sitting down for a few minutes when an elderly lady sat down next to him, smiling kindly. He couldn't return her smile, and so he got up and walked off quickly. Maybe it was better to be on the move. Time seemed stuck. He felt thirsty, but it would have been impossible to go into a shop and buy a bottle of water. That was what an ordinary person would have done, and he wasn't ordinary at the moment. He would bend over a bird bath and sip water from the rim. Or maybe he'd find a can of coke on the ground and he could drain the dregs in one slurp.

He didn't think he was worthy of a drink, anyway. He deserved to be thirsty. He was a complete and utter waste of space. He couldn't even arrange to give Nel her blanket. He couldn't give his mother one thing. Not one single thing. He'd just cried on her, grizzled like a baby, and she'd had to put up with so much in her life. These thoughts eddied through him, leaves on the breeze. He couldn't put them out. He kept sweeping them away, outside, but they found a way back in. He kept thinking about his childhood rabbit, Albedo. He'd loved that rabbit. He thought about him, dead.

Once he found himself staring up at the sky, stock still, and he couldn't be sure how long he'd been standing there. Once he found himself sat on the pavement, rocking. "This is what it feels like to be Mum," he thought. He said it out loud. He saw people glancing at him, and they looked afraid.

Eventually, he found a quiet place to sit. He followed a dead-end path down the side of a small church. He crouched against the wall with his knees up and his bottom resting on the cold concrete. His legs ached. His whole body ached – right in the core of him, a kind of wrenching feeling. As soon as he sat down, his fingers started moving, tapping onto his leg. Thumb index middle, index middle fourth fifth. One two three, two three four five. Over and over, with a strong rhythm. He only noticed he was doing it after a few minutes, and then he couldn't drag his attention away from it. He tried to hold his hand still, but then his other hand started up. This frightened him and so he let his hand carry on. One two three, two three four five.

After a time his head started nodding forward a little after the fifth tap – a small jerk. It was like having a fit, he thought. Or an orgasm – when you reach that point when you can no longer control what your body does. That surrender, that moment of complete vulnerability. He sat on the path a long time, letting his body move, and looking at a patch of hedge.

That small patch of hedge, with the curves of leaves and the darkness of the interior – that was enough for him. There were so many different shapes, and a hundred variations of green. There was a whole universe in there. His legs started to complain more loudly, and so he lay himself down on his side, his head resting on a raised piece of concrete. His head kept bobbing forwards in time with his hands, but it was less pronounced now – maybe no one else would see it if they came across him lying there. One two three, two three four five (jerk). One two three, two three four five (jerk).

Eventually, he got tired. He didn't want to go to sleep on the ground, out here with all these people around him. He wanted to be in his own bed. He walked slowly back to Nel's place and let himself in. There was laughter coming from the living room. Laughter. He had to go through the living room to get upstairs. He wished he could make himself invisible. When he entered the living room, Willem was the first to see him, and the look on his face stopped the laughter in everyone else's mouth.

"Joe."

He sounded so serious. Joe had to suppress a burst of laughter. He watched Willem look at his dad, and his dad looked back – they had a secret between them, he could tell. Theo was there too, and another younger man, and an older woman with grey-blue eyes. They were kind eyes – she turned them on him and he felt them melting into him, entering him. He wanted to be melted, but also he didn't. He turned away from her but he didn't know where else to look, and so he looked above their faces, beyond them, to the stairs. His dad spoke.

"We've been worried sick about you, Boy. Where have you been? We were about to get the police involved."

"Just out."

He could hear the sulkiness in his voice, and he didn't care. Fuck his dad. Fuck them all. They didn't tell him it was a cremation. As he remembered this, he panicked momentarily, looking down into both of his hands. Where was the blanket? He felt behind him and realised that the rucksack was on his back. How could he get away from these people?

"I'm tired."

"Joe, is there anything you want to talk about? Would you like a cup of cocoa?"

This was the woman talking. 'Who the fuck are you?' he wanted to say, but he held his tongue. Instead he glanced at her, and then turned to Willem. He couldn't look at his father.

"I'm tired." He had a feeling he might have said this already, but he couldn't think of anything else to say. His tone was flat, dead.

"Okay Joe, do you just want to sit down for a minute?" Willem said, his intonation implying that this wasn't an invitation. Willem looked across at Joe's dad again, as if he wanted to reassure him. His dad nodded. What had they been saying, while he was out? He knows what. That he was mad too now, just like his mum. Not his real mum. It was so unfair. He didn't get the life he was meant to have. A life out here, with art, with love. That bitch grandmother. If she was still alive... And that drunkard grandfather too. He must have had something to do with it. Bastards, all of them.

He felt sick again. He hadn't eaten all day. He didn't know if he wanted to eat or throw up. If only they'd leave him alone, he could go and sleep. And then he realised, he didn't have to stay and listen to them. He wasn't a child anymore, he could do whatever he wanted. And with that he walked out, suddenly, without saying goodbye to any of them. He wished he'd been ruder to them, he wished he'd had the guts to tell them all what fuckers they were. That stupid woman, whoever she was. His cowardly dad. Willem's ridiculous boyfriend. He didn't want Emmie either. He didn't want Podge, or Sarah, or Meg. Everyone was completely useless to him. The one person he wanted to speak to was dead.

He was in her room and under her covers before he realised where he was heading. He didn't take off his clothes. His eyes didn't seem to want to shut, even though he was dog tired. He pressed his hands over them and they stayed closed. It was nice in the dark. Her curtains were still shut. He sniffed, trying to catch Nel's perfume, but the sheets smelt of fresh laundry. He'd forgotten that Claudia had washed them. The anger swept over him again, waking him up. How dare she wash them without him giving her permission? Did he have no say at all in his mother's affairs? All those people who've been pretending to help him – all the time they've been creeping around behind his back, doing things without asking him

Joe noticed his fingers moving again. They had taken on a new rhythm – he hadn't noticed when it had changed. This one went 'one two three four five two five'. It was a run of seven again, he noticed, but it felt much gentler than the last one. His fingers were less tight, and it was as if he was playing a quiet phrase on the piano with his fingertips. Like he was making music, to soothe himself. The anger faded slowly, and he realised that his eyes had sprung open again. He could see a patch of one of Nel's paintings from the corner of his eye. It was the one he'd brought in from her studio the other night. He couldn't see it properly from here but he knew it by heart. It was of a woman, lying back on a bed and propped up on her elbows. It wasn't finished. It would never be finished. The parts that Nel had already painted were mostly pale golds, the colours of a candle flame. He watched it as if were a candle, and let his eyelids droop slowly. The thoughts had all gone now. He felt almost blissful. He didn't have to go anywhere.

Joe didn't get out of bed for sixteen days.

The first fortnight passed in a blur. It was as if he'd been invited along to a film; 'Joe's life', but he didn't have any way of re-writing the plot or even the dialogue. Things just happened or didn't happen. He wasn't in control of himself. He forgot things that he said or did almost immediately, before turning over and going back to sleep. He slept as much as he could.

On the sixteenth day after first getting into Nel's bed, he woke up with a feeling in his belly. Hunger. He couldn't be sure that he'd eaten anything since he got into bed. It was only with effort that he remembered the bowls of soup a woman had brought in on a tray. Had she fed him? He had a fuzzy memory of clamping his mouth shut a couple of times, and of the cold spoon trying to force its way in. He lifted the covers and looked down at his body. His belly definitely seemed more concave, but he hadn't wasted away completely. He must have been eating something.

It alarmed him that he couldn't remember the details, and so he focussed again on his hunger. How could he get some food? He looked around his room. On his bedside table there was a large brass bell. How had that got there? He lifted it, and it made a soft dull clang. Had it been put there for him? Had he rung it before? He felt too embarrassed to ring it properly, as if he were the master ringing for his servants. A few minutes later there was a knock on the door. The woman walked in with a tray and left it on his bedside table with a smile. There was bread and ham and cheese. He tore at the bread with his teeth as if he was eating fresh meat. It was delicious.

After eating he thought of his dad. Was he still in Amsterdam? He vaguely remembered him saying something to Joe about 'sticking to his original ticket'. Joe couldn't remember feeling much at the time, except maybe a kind of relief. He can remember that he hadn't liked it when his dad had come to sit with him. He felt supersensitive to other people's atmospheres. His dad had brought a prickliness in with him, an awkwardness. Had he told his dad to go away, a couple of times? Yes, he thought he had. He hoped he hadn't been too mean.

There must have been a kind of rota. He could remember different people being in the room at different times. Emmie had been here. She came into Joe's room on her own but he could remember her kissing Marika goodbye at his open door, and Marika peeking in as if he was an exhibit at a gallery. Emmie had talked to him, or at him. He remembered some of the things she'd said and felt annoyed. She hadn't been very sympathetic. She'd said things like, "I see you are still being a drama queen," or "You are so boring, Joe, just lying there all day long." Willem came too, but Joe couldn't remember seeing him very often.

His favourite companion, surprisingly, had been Willem's partner, Theo. He remembered him being there a lot. When Theo came in, he'd first come over to the bed and check to see which way Joe was facing, and whether he was awake. Theo would move his chair so he was in Joe's line of vision, but not directly – just in the corner of his eye. He would say, "Hello Joe" in Dutch, and then he wouldn't say anything else – he'd just sit there, quietly. Sometimes he brought a book in with him, and sometimes he'd bring some knitting – Joe liked the click-clack of the needles, it comforted him.

After a few hours (it was impossible for Joe to know how long, he'd lost all sense of time) Theo would gather his things back up together, put the chair back where it was, and say, "Goodbye Joe," before leaving the room and shutting the door behind him. Joe always fell asleep after his visits, which was a blessed relief. Some days his whole body felt tight, and he couldn't find a way to relax. He was afraid of what might happen if he wasn't able to let go for a while. He'd always been glad to see Theo.

Joe put his empty plate back on the tray and slipped back into sleep. He woke again mid-afternoon. His bladder was bursting. He went into the en-suite bathroom, and as his piss splashed into the toilet bowl he remembered his previous visits here. The 'rule' (which came from nowhere) said he wasn't allowed out of bed, and so going to the toilet had presented a problem. He had to trick himself into doing it, by waiting until he knew he wasn't going to be disturbed, just after a visit from Willem or the woman who brought his food. The rules only allowed him to stay in the bathroom for the minimum time it took to use the toilet, and then wash his hands before hurrying back to bed. When he got back underneath the covers again, he felt as if he'd been holding his breath.

This time, something felt different. He wasn't as desperate to get back into bed, and instead he looked in the mirror. It was quite a shock. He had a beard, for one thing. Not just stubble – a full beard. His hair was tousled and there were great bags under his eyes, as if he hadn't been sleeping. As he looked at himself he became aware of something else. He sniffed under his arms. He stank. He remembered the woman coming in one day with a sloshing bowl of water and some soap, and trying to pull his covers back, but he fought her – why did he do that? He knocked the water onto the floor.

Would it be possible to have a shower? He felt a flash of panic, as if he were deep underwater and swimming further down. He sniffed his armpits again and was repelled – he'd have to make himself wash. His own smell wasn't usually offensive. His own farts, his own sweat – he knew the smells were unpleasant, but because they were his own smells they somehow didn't disgust him. But even he had to admit that this body odour had crossed some kind of line.

The hot water felt delicious against his skin. Nel's shower had amazing water pressure. He stood for whole minutes with his head tipped back, listening to the trickles and splashes. He was still counting in his head, one two three four two four five, but as the stream of water pummelled his back, there were brief pauses. As he was stepping out of the shower, he heard someone running into the room and calling out.

"Joe?"

It was Emmie. She banged on the shower room door as if the house were on fire.

"What?" Joe shouted through the closed door.

"Are you okay?"

"Why shouldn't I be okay?"

He heard her make a loud tutting noise and then she was quiet. He dried himself and wrapped himself in the robe he found hanging on the back of the door. He checked his face in the mirror. He still looked pretty awful, but the shower had helped a bit. And at least he smelt better.

When he walked back into the room he was hit by a warm, fusty smell. This room had been his nest, he supposed. Emmie was sitting in the armchair in the bay window, a mirror of the room he'd slept in before. Joe was torn between getting back into bed and joining her. He forced himself to sit in the adjacent chair without meeting Emmie's eyes. She was fiddling around with something in her pocket. Joe wondered if she was going to ask him if he minded if she rolled a cigarette. After a minute she took her tobacco pouch out and starting rolling one without his permission, then went to Nel's bedside table and opened the drawer to find an ashtray. He wished he smoked – it would have given him something to do with his hands. He knew that if he asked Emmie for one of hers he'd just cough and embarrass himself. Besides, he wasn't sure how long it was since he'd eaten properly – his stomach felt very odd.

"So, have you stopped being mad now?"

Joe snorted in reply, not knowing how else to respond. The word 'mad' echoed in his brain, and he thought of his mum, and winced. Then the word 'Mum' echoed, and he winced again.

"What day is it?" Emmie asked, looking at him interrogatively.

Joe shrugged in reply.

"And who is our Prime Minister?"

He shrugged again.

"Well, that's settled then. You're still mad."

He looked over and noticed a smirk at the corner of her mouth. He snorted again. She started to grin, and the situation struck them both as outrageously funny. It was as if they were fourteen again.

After laughing, Joe felt himself relax a notch, and let out a sigh. This changed the atmosphere again. Emmie sucked on her roll-up with commitment – hardly pausing to take a breath.

"So, what are we going to do with you?"

Joe shrugged again, and Emmie let out a sharp, frustrated sigh. She furiously stubbed out her cigarette in the ashtray and crossed her arms. Joe smiled. He liked how she got furious about things all at once. It was like the wind catching a sail and filling it to the brim – the next moment it could just as easily empty and sag. He looked out of the window, the smile still on his face. The expression made his skin feel odd. It reminded him of when he and Podge had stolen one of his mum's mud face masks and plastered it on each other's faces. As the gunk had set, it had shrunk into a hard rind. When Joe tried to open his mouth into an 'O', the mask held him back. Maybe it had been a long time since he'd smiled.

After a while, Emmie uncrossed her arms and looked over at him.

"And what are you smiling about, smiling boy?" He could hear amusement underneath her anger. "We've been worried to death about you. Well, I have been. Willem seemed to think that it was perfectly normal for you to get into bed and not get out for two whole weeks. He's been completely infuriating. And your father ran back to the UK at the first opportunity, the useless man. That doctor, I don't know where Willem found him, and worst of all, the person who I really want to talk to about all this has gone and died."

Her voice broke. She started furiously scrabbling about in her pockets for a tissue. When she couldn't find one, she disappeared into the bathroom. He heard her blowing her nose, noisily, not in a lady-like fashion at all. Had she really been worried about him? He wasn't feeling anything. Did that make him a bad person?

She didn't come out for a little while, and when she did he noticed that she'd re-done her eye make-up. The black around her eyes was even fiercer than before. If she cried again, it would drip all over her face. Maybe that was why she'd drawn the lines so thick – they were acting as a deterrent. She sat back down next to him and put a hand on his arm, speaking to him in Dutch.

"Are you going to get up now, Joe?"

Her voice was so soft. He did feel sad then, and stared out of the window. He was desperate to climb into her lap and sink into her. She looked so soft. Her breasts, her neck... the down on her cheeks... He conjured Marika, hoping it might help him to keep his mind off sex, but instead it made it even worse, as in his fantasy Marika just took off all her clothes and invited him to join them both... He moved his arm, brushing her hand off him, and then when he saw her face he felt guilty. What could he say to make it better?

"What would you like me to do?"

She brightened. "I'd like you to get dressed and come out with me. For a cup of coffee. Like a normal person. Anywhere you like. We don't even have to talk if you don't want to."

The thought of leaving the house terrified him, but he didn't want her to get upset again. He agreed to meet her downstairs in ten minutes.

Downstairs he found Emmie talking to the woman who'd brought him food. Joe assumed she was an assistant or a nurse. Maybe Willem had hired her. When Joe appeared, they both stopped talking and looked at him. He felt light-headed, but tried not to show it. It felt good to be downstairs. He looked around the house, and wondered what would happen to it. Who did it belong to now? It was too big for him to live in alone, wasn't it? Although Nel had lived here alone. Did she ever get lonely?

He greeted the woman in Dutch, and then stood there looking awkward. He wasn't sure what else to say. Was this the woman who'd attempted to give him a bed bath? He blushed scarlet. He had a strong urge to turn on his heels and go back to Nel's bedroom, but he knew he needed to go on to whatever was next. He bowed to the nurse, as if he had suddenly become a Japanese geisha, and then looked at Emmie expectantly. As they were leaving, the woman said something else to Emmie in Dutch that he didn't catch – her accent was strange. Emmie nodded, and Joe guessed they were saying something about how weak he was, how careful Emmie should be with him.

They went to the same café they went to last time, when Marika was with them. Just after they'd had sex. It seemed like a lifetime ago. Emmie went to grab a table, and left Joe in the queue to get the coffees. He could rely on Emmie not to give him any special treatment. While he was waiting to be served, his thoughts returned to the time he spent wandering the streets, the day of Nel's funeral. After Willem had told him that Nel was going to be cremated. Cremated was just a fancy word for burnt. Why didn't people just say that? It was like 'interred' instead of 'buried'. Why couldn't people be more straightforward? We're going to dig a deep hole in the ground and then cover her over with earth. Joe thought about Nel. He could only imagine her in the ground, whole. She wasn't there. She wasn't in one piece anymore. Her body was in thousands of pieces. Why was this so difficult to handle? Whenever he got close to the thought, it hurt. Why should it make any difference if she was in a hole in the ground instead?

He put the coffees down in front of Emmie, and a huge cinnamon pastry for himself – he was starving. He ate the whole thing in a quick succession of bites, and Emmie sipped her coffee, looking up at him occasionally. When he was finished he started on his coffee, which was still too hot – Emmie must have fire-proof lips. He said what was on his mind.

"I don't like the thought of her being burnt."

Emmie nodded. He liked the way that she accepted whatever he said. With most people, it was such an effort to be understood. Even Podge could be remarkably slow on the uptake sometimes. He wished Emmie could be his girlfriend. This led to more sexual thoughts, and he forced himself to swerve away. He'd felt really horny since he'd woken up that morning – how long has it been since he'd masturbated? More than two whole weeks? If so, then that would be a record. He considered excusing himself and going to the toilets in the café – the urge was so strong. He promised himself he'd take care of it later, but this thought didn't help either. He kept talking to distract himself.

"That's why I ran off. Willem said after the funeral about her being cremated. I'd wanted to…" He hesitated, not sure he wanted to tell her everything. But who else could he tell? "I wanted to wrap her in a blanket, one I found in her room. It's really soft. I thought it would feel nice against her skin. Not that she'd feel it, but… I wanted to wrap her in it, to say thank you for… all the stuff I never said thank you for. All the things she did that I never even noticed. It's too late now, though, isn't it? That she can't hear me say thank you – I just can't… It cuts me up. She never knew how much I… how much I…"

Emmie nodded. He waited for her to say something – he wanted to hear something comforting, something reassuring. Eventually she spoke.

"It sucks."

And with that she got out her tobacco and started to make a roll-up. That was it? 'It sucks'? That was the best she could do? Useless – just like everyone else. She could have said Nel knew Joe loved her, or something. But maybe Emmie didn't know that. She could have said… He searched, and came up with nothing. Fuck it. Fuck it.

"Fuck it."

The words felt good coming out of his mouth, and so he said them again, with more staccato, with more violence. He spat them out.

"Fuck it."

Emmie screwed her mouth up to the side and said the words to herself, mournfully.

"Fuck it."

He copied her, trying to mimic her accent. Then he said it again, but louder – almost a shout – and Emmie drew back, shocked. A few people in the café look over at them. Then she smiled, and shouted it back. This left a small pool of silence in the café, which slowly filled up again with the murmuring of voices as people realised the show was over. They sat across the table from each other and Joe said, "Will you let me fuck you? Just one more time?"

Emmie shrugged noncommittally, and took his hand over the table. And so they left the coffee shop, walked back to her flat, and fucked. The first time was quick, he couldn't stop himself, but after that he wanted to make her happy, he wanted to give her pleasure. He listened to her instructions. He said,

"Like this?" and "More?" He said, "Your body is beautiful." He said, "I don't ever want to do this with anyone else." And after her third orgasm, she asked him to lie back so she could rest her head on his chest. She curled up with her head on his heartbeat, and went to sleep like a cat, and he cried, silently. He cried softly, the tears streaming down his face, and it felt like there would never be an end to them. When the tears finally slowed down he looked down at her for a long time before allowing his eyes to close too. He didn't want it to be over. She was so beautiful, and she was here, asleep on his chest.

The next morning, Joe left Emmie's flat and returned to a welcoming Committee. They were all in the living room, probably discussing him again. Willem was there, and the woman, and Theo, and a man he didn't recognise with a sharp nose and a neat black beard. Even Maartje was there. He hadn't seen her since the funeral, and he acknowledged her awkwardly with an 'All right', feeling like he was fourteen years old again. They all looked up at him for a moment, and then most of them looked at Willem. Who'd put him in charge? Joe wondered. He was feeling furious about something – if only he could put his finger on what it was…

He saw a painting on the wall. He hadn't noticed it before. It looked like one of Nel's. Willem started saying something, and his words came to Joe through a fog of feelings – his voice was all muffled as if he was underwater. After a pause Joe realised that everyone was looking at him again and that he'd better say something.

"Pardon, Willem?"

Willem was getting up from his seat now, and so were the others. Maartje said goodbye to Joe and Theo and left, and the woman gathered coffee cups onto a tray and went into the kitchen. The bearded man hadn't moved. He looked strangely familiar to Joe, and as he lingered over his face he realised that he'd missed what Willem had said again.

"Sorry Willem, I'm not all there at the moment."

It was a relief to admit it. He snorted in amusement at himself, and Willem smiled too. Willem motioned to the sofa and Joe sat down. A smell of freshly brewed coffee had started to emanate from the kitchen next door, and he felt suddenly hungry again.

"Is there anything to eat?"

"Shall I ask Aneke to make you something? I think there is some pizza?"

"Mmm, pizza. Thank you."

He was getting the hang of talking again. His throat still felt tender, as if it had rusted up while he was in bed. He had a sudden image of Emmie's nipples, the ring of darker pink around the middle bit. What was it called again – the oriale? Auriole? He'd have to look it up later. The most beautiful word ever invented. It must have been a woman who invented it. A man wouldn't use a word like that. He'd make it something crude, like tits or cunt, or something clinical, like some of the other words for parts of women's bodies. Vagina. That was the worst of them. What a terrible word. He noticed that Willem had returned from the kitchen and was looking at him. He couldn't keep his mind on anything.

The man with the beard was opening his briefcase and getting out a folder. He placed it on the tinted glass table in front of him. What was this about? Willem noticed Joe looking at him.

"You remember Dr. Jansen?"

Joe shook his head. He was disconcerted. Only once in his life had he been drunk enough to forget what he'd done the night before. It had been a regular occurrence for Podge throughout their late adolescence – Joe would call Podge in the morning to tell him what he'd said and done the night before. Podge had always wanted to know everything, even the things that weren't interesting, and he said he could trust Joe to fill him in. Joe had a brilliant memory for things like that and he could almost tell Podge what he'd said verbatim. One night Joe went home early and left Podge alone, and Podge didn't speak to him for a week – he was furious that he'd abandoned him to his blackout. Joe tried to reassure Podge that he never did anything stupid anyway – but Podge made Joe swear he'd never leave him alone again. Joe suddenly understood how Podge had felt. He took a guess.

"Are you Nel's solicitor?"

The two men exchanged a glance. Joe wished people would stop doing that.

"No," said Willem, "He's a friend of mine – a psychiatrist. He came to speak to you at the beginning, and asked you lots of questions. You don't remember it?" He was watching Joe's blank look. "Do you have the papers?" he asked Dr. Jansen in Dutch. Dr. Jansen looked through the folder, and handed Joe a form. There were lots of questions in Dutch, and tick boxes. At the bottom he saw his own signature, and the date. He couldn't remember it at all. He nodded and gave the papers back to Dr. Jansen.

"As I said, Joe, Dr. Jansen is a just a friend of mine, he's not here officially. He's kindly come out to the house to... to help us think about what's best for you next. You've had a shock. First your problems at work, then Nel's death, and then finding out… And of course before that there were your own mother's… problems. It's really no surprise that you shut down."

Joe listened as if Willem was talking about someone else, but it did feel good to be hearing it. It had been a lot. Maybe he was entitled to be finding things so difficult.

Willem continued.

"Dr. Jansen did some tests, Joe, and he's also called your doctor back in the UK. You hadn't seen a psychiatrist there, had you?" Joe shrugged, he really didn't know. He wished he could clear his head. "The tests showed that you could do with some… support. You should keep taking your medication. But the support will only be good for you if you want it. Are you ready to get some help?" Willem didn't wait for an answer, and looked at Dr. Jansen as if for approval. Dr. Jansen nodded. "Is there anything you want to add to that, Pieter?" he asked.

Dr Jansen put his hands together in a prayer position and spoke for the first time. His voice was deeper than Joe expected it to be.

"Willem is right, Joe – it might be that you will get better in time and doing nothing. But there are other things we can do which will improve the diagnosis. Willem says you are thinking of staying in Holland?" Joe nodded. "We can arrange for you to come to a group, which is very effective in these cases. We can arrange for individual psychotherapy. You need to decide if it is important to you."

These words didn't mean much to Joe. Willem's question was still echoing though his head. "Are you ready to get some help?" Was he ready? Did he need help? Yes. There was no denying it. So what was so difficult about saying yes?

He had a flashback to when he was seven. He was stuck on his maths homework. He never usually struggled with school work, but he couldn't understand the instructions his teacher had given him, and the work was due in the next day. He'd left it late, which was unlike him. He was furious with himself. He could remember sitting there for hours, struggling with it, getting more and more angry. His dad was out, and he knew his mum was in a weird mood.

Finally, from desperation, he asked his mum whether she could help him. She went mad at him. He couldn't remember why. She actually took his book and threw it across the room. It wouldn't take a genius to make sense of that memory. He wanted to tell Willem about it, but not with the psychiatrist there. The words got stuck in his throat. He was tired again. Would he ever stop feeling tired?

"I'm tired," he said.

"I know," Willem said, smiling. This made Joe feel sad, and he wanted a hug. He hardly knew this man. He was so desperate to have a dad – a proper one. It wasn't fair. None of it was fair. He realised that it was the sadness, making him tired. It had coagulated, it was clogging up his veins. He wondered if he could shift it if he cried it all out, or if he'd be left instead with nothing inside him – a wrinkled skin. He turned to Dr. Jansen.

"I think I would like some help, please."

His voice was croaky. Dr. Jansen just nodded, in a doctor-like way. Willem crimped his mouth empathetically. Joe felt a little strength return to him, and he walked across the room to shake Dr Jansen's hand. "Thank you, Doctor," he said, and he turned to do the same for Willem but when he looked at him the tears sprung to his eyes. He nodded at him without making eye contact and left the room with his head bowed, saying "I'm just going for a lie down." He almost ran up to Nel's bedroom. There was the blue blanket. There was her wonderful bed. There was the duvet he could crawl under, into the wonderful warm dark quiet.

The next couple of weeks passed slowly for Joe. He was amazed by the bending of time – at how quickly the previous fortnight had passed, and how full and spacious his days were now. On several occasions he'd worried about not having enough time to get something done, and could hardly believe that it had only been twenty minutes since he last looked at the clock.

He started to get an idea of what his life would look like over the coming months. His dad had persuaded him not to cut all of his ties with the UK until he'd given Amsterdam a trial. He'd spoken to Herman, who'd said they were happy to hold his position open for another month before speaking to him again and seeing what the situation was. He thought he'd know more by then. He'd started looking into all the legal implications of staying, with Willem's help – Nel's copy of his birth certificate would make things much simpler. He'd even found a Dutch tutor, one of Emmie's acquaintances, and they'd already had their first lesson. She was an older woman, schoolmarm-ish but with a mischievous glint in her eye. Joe liked her a lot.

He also had an appointment for the following Tuesday to attend a therapy group, as advised by Dr. Jansen. He was terrified about going, and changed his mind several times a day about whether he was going to turn up or not. His brain came up with an endless list of reasons for not going; he felt better now anyway, he wouldn't understand what anyone was saying... but he was suspicious of himself. Somewhere underneath he had a quiet determination to just 'go and see what it was like', and he hoped that this part of him would win out on the day. The psychiatrist had reassured him that he didn't have to say anything at all if he didn't want to, not for a while at least.

He had slowly started reading again after his book drought, but he wasn't interested in his usual fare for some reason. Facts were leaving him cold – even his previous reliable obsessions – meteorology, ornithology. Instead he was devouring fiction.

His days were filled with people who wanted to see him. It made him feel important. There were documents to be signed, and decisions to be made. Legally, the house and Nel's assets were his but things were moving slowly. He didn't trust himself to make any decisions on his own, and so spoke to Willem at least once a day, either over the phone, or at Nel's house or Willem's office. The financial situation was gradually revealing itself. Nel had enough money coming in from her various investments to support her on a basic level, and to cover the running of the house including the wages for Claudia, but without a great deal to spare.

Joe was pleased about this – he didn't like the idea of knowing he'd never have to work again. This way there was a necessity for him to get a job, but not straight away – and Willem calculated that he could probably do something part time and still be comfortable. Joe had no idea what he wanted to do, and he put this aside to think about at a later date. As Dr. Jansen kept saying, "One day at a time".

Joe's dad had been in regular touch, which had surprised him. Willem told Joe that his dad had called every day during that first fortnight for an update. Since Joe had been up, his dad had called him every few days. They mostly spoke about practical issues, but he did manage to ask Joe how he was feeling. Joe mostly said, "Fine, fine," but he appreciated being asked. He'd book another trip in a month or so, maybe with Pam, when Joe knew more about what he'd be doing.

Socially, Joe continued to meet up with Emmie and Marika. He found a shared interest in etymology with Marika, and this had made their relationship much easier. The couple also introduced him to a male friend of theirs, another Jeroen. Joe tried to put Emmie off at first but she insisted, and eventually they all met for coffee. After a while the girls disappeared, and Jeroen showed Joe around the natural history museum. Joe had arranged to meet him again – half because he knew Emmie and Dr. Jansen would approve, and half because there was something about Jeroen that reminded him of Podge.

He missed Podge. They had talked on the phone a couple of times, but neither of them liked the phone very much and their conversations had been stilted and short. They'd been in touch mostly by text message. Joe had hidden the worst of his bedridden fortnight from his friend. He'd responded to Podge's increasingly frantic texts when he was up and about by saying he'd lost his phone. He hoped that Podge could come over and visit him someday – there was plenty of room in Nel's house for Sarah and the children.

Joe still had up and down days. Sometimes he felt almost normal again, but then he'd have to prise himself out of bed as if he'd fused with his mattress during the night. Even the worst days felt much better than the wasteland of his fortnight in bed. Sometimes, when he felt upset, his grief for Nel was mixed with a much broader grief, for all the things he'd missed out on. Maybe he could talk about it in the therapy group.

One rainy Friday, after lunch and a long chat with Claudia, Joe went up for a nap. He'd got into a habit of crawling into Nel's bed and falling asleep for an hour and a half in the afternoons. When he woke up he wondered how long it would be before he started calling it his bed rather than Nel's. Maybe it would always be hers. His favourite chair in the living room was his, but he'd sat on that when Nel was still alive. When would the front door keys feel like his, or the electricity bills? He still couldn't even operate half of the appliances in the kitchen, and was forever calling Claudia for help. He felt so clumsy all the time, as if he was learning everything again from the very beginning.

He stretched and fussed Tante Truus, who often accompanied him on his naps. He'd thought he might want to go out for a stroll when he woke up, but the rain kept him inside. Instead he fetched himself a cup of tea and got back into bed. He pulled the covers up to his neck and leaned back against the headboard. He gazed around the room with relaxed eyes.

Emmie had bought him one of those calendars where you tear off a page every day. It had cartoons with Dutch captions – none of the jokes were particularly funny. She'd bought it for him when he confided after his fortnight of sleep that it was difficult to keep track of what day it was anymore, without the structure of work and weekends. He liked to open his eyes and see clearly that yesterday was Tuesday, and rip it off to give him a new day. Today was the 3rd of September. The date rang a bell. He couldn't think why.

After reading for an hour, he got out of bed and started to mooch around the room. He was getting to know all its nooks and crannies. The rest of the house was so big, he hadn't wanted to overwhelm himself by acquainting himself with the whole place. One room at a time. One day at a time. All of Nel's personal stuff had been moved out of the bedroom now – some of it was stored in the other bedroom, ready for Joe to decide what he wanted to do with it. Some of it had already gone to Nel's friends, or to the charity shop. The blue blanket was draped across the chair that looks out onto the street below. The one he'd sat in next to Emmie, after his illness. His resurrection, as he wryly referred to it in his head. It was his favourite place to sit in the house. He often sat there before he went to bed, reading – he could see people moving about on the street below, walking their dogs or taking a letter to the post box, and it helped him to feel part of the rest of the world.

There was an old-fashioned chest of drawers on one side of the bed. It looked expensive. The rosy wood was polished to a sheen – he'd have to ask Willem what it was. Walnut? Willem seemed to know everything. Joe had emptied it of Nel's clothes, and it now held his own paltry collection of t-shirts and boxer shorts. He'd arranged to go clothes shopping with Emmie next week – she said she didn't trust him to choose anything by himself and had banned him from buying anything until it had her seal of approval.

He ran a fingertip over the smooth wood. The drawers slid smoothly on their runners, except the one second from the bottom which shuddered and caught. He pulled it out now, and pushed it back in. Sticky. It was as if it was pushing against something. He removed the drawer below and inserted his arm inside the chest, right to the back, and when he spidered his fingers upwards he touched something smooth and cool. He slid to the edges and identified it as Sellotape – what was it doing in there? He found the edge and put a finger nail under it, peeling it as he went, following its path. He was kneeling awkwardly with his arm swallowed up by the chest. The sellotape led him upwards, to something sharp. He ripped the tape away and took the sharp thing between his finger and thumb, pulling it out towards him.

It was an A5 brown manila envelope. It had something inside it. When he saw what was written on the front, his stomach lurched. It said, 'Joe'. It was Nel's handwriting, of course. Joe. He felt afraid to look inside. He got back into Nel's bed where he felt safer, and then got out again a few seconds later to wrap the blue blanket around his shoulders. Goose pimples blossomed on his arms. He huddled in the bed for a few moments, looking at his name, and then opened the envelope. There was a thick wodge of paper, folded over. He ruffled through the leaves quickly – the top pages looked brand new, but the paper got older and more yellowed towards the bottom of the pile. The letters were all in English. He started to read the most recent, which was dated 11th of July 2010.

Dear Joe,

Dear Joe. Dear Joe. You will never read this. I need to tell things to you – but you can never read them. You must never know these things. Nobody should know. But I need to tell someone or I'll burst. I'll go mad. I'm adding to this little bundle of paper again. I said I wouldn't, the last time. Just one more time, I promise myself. After I've finished I'll hide it all away again. Maybe someone will find it, years after we're both dead. Maybe it'll never be found.

You'll be arriving at my house in a week's time. My lovely big house, paid for by my paintings. How lucky I am. I keep thinking about the last time you stayed for the whole summer. How long ago was it? You were a teenager – so young, so muddled. It was so difficult to look at your muddle and not see it as my fault. But even back then, I knew you'd be all right. How can I describe it? You had a – well, fighting spirit isn't quite right... Maybe it was something about your independence. You reminded me of myself, I suppose. And I always knew that I was going to be all right, in the long run. I knew things would work themselves out. Not my relationships with men, not really – I never got that right. But the art was always there. I knew it would provide for me, financially. And I also knew underneath all of that – before I even started getting any real money – that it was all an illusion anyway. Nothing really stays for good. Even if you think it's going to stay – it'll leave eventually. Or you will.

But that's not what I wanted to write about. This is what I wanted to say. I've been doubting myself in these past months. I've been wondering if I've done the right thing, by holding my silence for all these years. This doubting voice is familiar – I've been listening to it ever since you were born. How could it be otherwise? But this time I can't make it shut up. I keep thinking, what if it's too late? What if I leave it until it's too late? But that shouldn't make any difference to anything. My reasons for not telling you don't depend on me being around –

they are about your welfare, not mine. So why won't the voice shut up? Why won't it leave me in peace?

I think I know why. I think I'm acknowledging that my reasons for staying silent weren't really completely selfless, after all. I told myself they were. I've told myself that for all these years. We all like to think that we're doing things for other people's benefit, don't we? We like to think we're straightforward, good hearted, uncomplicated. But I think I've had a selfish reason underneath all that, and it's been rotting away all this time. It's like when you're in a relationship with someone, and you think that you're choosing to be with each other because you like each other, you love each other, and then you discover that all the time it's only been your pathologies keeping you together. She stays with him because, secretly, she doesn't think she deserves any better. He sticks with her because he needs her to prop him up. Whatever it is – it works fine while both people want to play, but maybe when one person gets healthier, the whole thing starts to crumble. I think my reasons have worked for me while I pretended they were completely selfless. But I can't keep lying to myself. The truth is relentless.

It's so difficult to write this down, even though no one will ever read it. I'll know I've written it down. That's the hard bit. Acknowledging things about ourselves – awful things – it hardly matters if no one else sees. I'll know, from then on. It'll leak out of me, people will find out. Here is the truth. I didn't want to be a mother. And

I wouldn't have been any good at it. I would have been a terrible mother.

God, it's a relief to have said it. But how terrible, how terrible. How can I carry on looking at the job that Ineke did, and condemn her for it? To judge her for failing you, Joe. I've judged her so harshly. At least she was willing to try. At least she was brave enough to take you on – all the uncertainties, all the – what did she call it – grunt work. Even knowing what she knew about herself – as she must have known back then – that she had a weakness, that she was liable to break. When I was growing up, I always thought she was the stable one. But all those things that happened to me in the family – they happened to her too. Dad's drunkenness, Mum's crazy obsession with his drinking. Ineke must have done something different with all that shit – tucked it away inside herself somewhere, put it in a locked box. I didn't know it was going to come out like that, Joe. I really didn't know. I wouldn't have handed you over to her if I knew. But by then it was too late. And like I say, I didn't want to be a mother. Which would have been better? A bad mother who didn't want you? Or a mad mother who did?

Joe put the pages down for a minute and stared into space. He tried to choose. Which? Which would have been better? He thought about his mum, and his whole childhood ran through his mind. How badly did she mess it up, raising him? She did love him, didn't she? She still did. Had that been enough? He went back to the letter.

I don't know the answer to that. And it's too late anyway. The question is redundant. It's too late for you to have another mother. I wasn't there when you really needed one – when you needed the shit cleaned from your bottom, or when you got sick in the night. When you had nightmares. I wasn't there then – Ineke was, and your father was. They did all of that. They did it without complaining – to me, to you. They didn't have to. You weren't their child. Do you understand? They gave you that gift – they chose you. You'll never know that. It seems like such a shame, that they won't get the credit due to them.

If you found out, maybe it would help you see your father in a different way. Maybe things could get better between you. But I'm protecting myself. There, I've said it. If you found out, you could be angry. You'd probably be furious. And you'd have the perfect right to be. I would be if it was me. I wouldn't believe any of my reasons for giving you up. I wouldn't think they were good enough. You'd be right, to think me cowardly. I am.

But does any of this change anything? So my reasons weren't as pure as I thought. So I'm protecting myself. So what? What can I do for you – that is the most important question. How can I rearrange all of this and do what's best for you? I still don't know the answer to that. I don't think I'm much use to you, as I am. An eccentric aunt, in a different country. No – that's not fair. I do know that you care about me – I know that I'm important to you.

Joe's eyes filled with tears. He wiped them away and carried on reading.

And you know I care about you more than anything – I know that. But what else? Is it enough? What else?

There's no hurry – I don't have to decide right now. It's helped – writing it down. All I can do is meet you at the airport and bring you home. Maybe you'll want to stay here for longer than six weeks, maybe you will find a kind of sanctuary in this house, my beautiful house. I'd like to help you find your way, Joe. I can hardly bear to think about your suffering. Not just because I think I caused it all, but because I love you. Oh, I love you. Joey, my Joey.

This was where the section ended. Joe swiped viciously at the tears on his cheeks, and shuffled these pieces of paper to the back of the pile. The next letter was written in different ink, and dated the 1st of January 2004. It was only a single scrawled sentence.

Oh Joe, I miss you. I miss you I miss you I miss you. Lots of love, your mum.

Joe put this piece paper to the back. The next section was dated the 22nd of July 1994.

My dear Joe,

It's been nearly fourteen years since I wrote to you last. I hadn't planned to write to you again. I haven't even spoken to you in my head – for at least ten years now. It was too painful – it stirred up too much. I thought I might go mad. And now I think my sister is going to go mad instead. I'm so scared for you. I'm so scared that I've done something terrible, by handing you over to her.

I want to tell you why I did it. I'm telling myself, really – you'll never read this – but I'm also writing it down for you. Why else would I be writing in English?

Oh, my life is in a mess. I don't know how I'm going to carry on taking money from Henk. I want to be with Jeroen, really, but he's even more of a mess than I am. He can't help me or my art. And then there are my parents. I don't even want to start writing about that. All of this is their fault. Is that fair? I'm an adult now, I suppose, I can make my own decisions, my own choices. But I want to blame them for everything, and it's easy to – because in so many ways they are monsters. Mum is a monster. I don't like to think of dad as a monster, although he's the one everyone else sees as the bad one. The evil one. He can't help it, though. He wants to be good. He loves me. She was the one making the choice – to stay, to try and control him. I don't think I could even explain to you how awful she is. I don't think you'd believe me. But maybe you know how awful mothers can be, Joe?

I haven't told you, and I will never tell you, that I am your real mother. It would destroy you. This is my reason. If you knew that you were a mistake – that your real mother fucked a stranger at fourteen, and was then persuaded by her own mother to give you up – how would you live with that? What kind of mother would give up their son, because somebody told them to? Mother needed to hide the shame, to preserve 'the good name of the family'. She's had such a lot of practice at that, living with an alcoholic for all these years. It's her speciality. Just another problem to sweep under the carpet, just another inconvenience to take care of. Take the baby from the screwed-up daughter, who is too young, and too crazy. Hand her over to the sensible daughter, the one born with no ovaries or womb, the older one, who is going to another country anyway. Do it in secret. Don't tell the baby. Don't tell the relatives. There – everything better. Simple.

I hate her, for being right about this. You are better off without me, Joe. But I wanted to keep you, I wanted it so much. She forced me. She threatened me. She even slapped me once – a few weeks before you were born. Hard across the face. I stumbled backwards, almost fell. That could have been the end of you. Dad was in the other room, he could hear us shouting. I think he was in company – in the company of his bottle. He was more interested in what the bottle was saying, than in what I needed.

Oh Joe. You are spending a whole six weeks with me. Your mother tells me she's worried about you, but I'm more worried about her. I always knew you'd be okay. You have my genes. You'll muddle through. I hope I can help you, a little bit, but I'm in such a mess right now... Maybe we can muddle along together for a little while? You already have a mother. Maybe I could play the role of eccentric aunt. Maybe you'll be glad of my company.

The cutting ache in my chest – it isn't quite so sharp now. If your mother failed you in some important ways, it doesn't make any difference to my decision. My mother's decision. I gave up my right to you when I drank that bottle of whisky, to try and get rid of you. It was dad who found me. He probably smelt me out. He broke his way into the bathroom. I was so far gone, I didn't even care about him seeing me naked. He dragged me out of the bath. He took me to the doctor. We never told Mum. He made me promise that I wouldn't do it again. He'd always had a thing about abortions, maybe he was terrified that I'd go to hell or something. He promised me that my mum would sort things out for me, said she always sorted things out. He was more like my brother than my dad. He seemed so lost. I kept my promise to him. I told her I was pregnant myself – I knew it'd be too hard for him. She was so furious, but she didn't say anything, didn't let any of it out. Except that time she slapped me. Maybe I deserved it, that time. The things I'd said to her...

That's all in the past. I'm sorry, Joe, that I tried to make you invisible. I didn't know what else to do. I was a fucked up fourteen year old – I don't know if you can understand. I don't expect you to understand. I'm just so sorry, for that, and for all the rest. I don't think about you, it hurts too much – I couldn't get out of bed if I thought about you. I'd probably have to kill myself, and having an eccentric aunt who killed herself wouldn't be much help to you. I don't think about you, but I radiate love for you. It comes out of me all the time, as if I'm the sun. I know it reaches you, all the way across the water. It would reach you anywhere. You've been taking it in all your life.

This letter ended here. Joe cried again at the image of Nel as the sun. He cried because he knew the truth of it. He felt stupidly happy. He put this last sheet on the back of the pile, and saw that there was only one sheet of paper left. It was brittle and yellowing. There were only twelve words, he counted them before he paid any attention to their meaning, and a date – 22nd of July 1980 – the date of his birth.

Goodbye, Joe. You are the most beautiful thing I have ever made.

As Joe put this last letter down, it was already unfolding in him. It wasn't a conscious thought; it was just the next thing – the next right thing to do. He found a piece of paper in the bedside cabinet, and a pen. He wrote it down. Twelve words.

I forgive you. I love you. I'll be okay. Your son, Joe.

He put this piece of paper on top of all the others, carefully folded them back up, and slid them inside the envelope. He had to go to the kitchen to hunt around for some sellotape, and then he taped the envelope down. Then he went back to the chest of drawers, and taped the envelope back up – in the middle this time so it wouldn't catch on the drawer. He put the drawer back in. There. Now it was finished.

As he left the room, on his way out to meet Emmie and Marika, he noticed the date on the bedside table again. He remembered what it signified. It was the 3rd of September. Fifteen years to the day that he returned back to the UK, back to his mad mother. He wasn't going to go back this time. He needed to go forwards. He needed to make himself a good life, for Nel. He'd be all right, he knew that now. Her love was in his blood, it was in his bones.

Acknowledgements

Family gratitude to Duncan Hall for his extremely beady eye and to Wendy Hall and Harry Hall for proof reading.

Editing gratitude to Joanna Swainson, who is always spot on.

Gratitude to Graham Pilling and Alex Valy for design advice.

Dutch gratitude to Marleen Reinke for her careful reading and advice, and also to Linda Oppenmeer, Truus Posthumus, Judith Uyterlinde, Eric Cohen and Anne-Mieke Swart.

Meteorological gratitude to Manfred Kloeppel for his time and interest and help, and also to Martin Kidds and Althea Howard.

Having–faith–in–me and many cups of tea gratitude to my husband, Kaspa.

I am a foolish being. Any remaining errors or inaccuracies are mine and mine alone.

About the Author

Fiona Robyn was born in 1974 in Surrey and grew up in Sarawak. She runs Writing Our Way Home with her husband Kaspa. She lives in Malvern in the skirts of the hills with her three cats.

 ~Writing Our Way Home~

Most of us live crowded lives. We don't always remember to pay attention to what's around us – to pause and really listen to the blackbird's song, or to notice the bright poppies by the roadside.

But when we pay attention to other people & to the world, we start to see things more clearly. We become more intimate with them. We feel more loved and loving. We feel more at home in the world, with others, and in our own skin.

At Writing Our Way Home we pay attention by writing. We write short observational pieces called *small stones*, and we write in our journals. We want you to help you wake up to the beauty of the world through writing too.

At the heart of what we offer is a smorgasbord of e-courses personally tutored by Fiona or Kaspa. These month-long adventures are for people who are ready to clear space for writing, learning & growing.

We also have a free online community of people who support each other in paying more attention to the world.

Find out more and download your free ebook '*How To Write Your Way Home*' at: www.writingourwayhome.com.

towels and shirts and pillowcases show me the shapes of the breeze

*

tulips: upturned spanish skirts in poster-paint yellow, raspberry ripple, virgin white, purple-brown

*

He asks for the order seven times. Two small sausages, two fish and three chips. He's stopped from putting the plastic bag where it will melt. He smiles at his mistakes. He wants to get it right. People get impatient, despite themselves. 'He's a good kid really', the owner says to the customers, and we all feel better.

*

bluebells hover above ground, a mist of spring. dark greens, the snap of twigs. at the exit of the woods the fields drop away. in the bowl of the vista, neat rows of poplars blaze orange.

*

we sit outside in the first warm-enough sun of the year. we drink our tea. there is a small slug in the grass. kaspa pulls two white hairs from my head.

small stones by Fiona Robyn

Lightning Source UK Ltd.
Milton Keynes UK
UKOW030036141212

203648UK00015B/484/P